About the Author

From sedate banker to searching for oil around the world

To my family who are spread across the world in Norway, Scotland, England and America.

David York

THE BILLION POUND QUESTION

A CIP catalogue record for this title is available from the British Library.

ISBN 9781785545740 (Paperback)
ISBN 9781785545757 (Hardback)
ISBN 9781785545764 (eBook)

www.austinmacauley.com

First Published (2016)
Austin Macauley Publishers Ltd.
25 Canada Square
Canary Wharf
London
E14 5LQ

To Wikipedia, for making research so much easier

Part I: The Inheritance

Chapter One

December 2011 / January 2012 Picking Up the Pieces

Tony Latimer had been a very lucky banker, transforming an inheritance of only seven thousand pounds received just before his twenty-first birthday, into a fortune of over one billion pounds by the time of his accidental death just before his sixty-third birthday. He died when the private light aircraft that he was travelling in to Aberdeen to celebrate Hogmanay with his wife and Scottish friends, crashed into the Cairngorm Mountains sixty-five miles to the west of its destination. He had accepted a lift from a wealthy fellow horse owner whom he had met the previous day at the races. Tony did not know that his new friend had only just gained his pilot's licence as they had set off from Newcastle in perfect sunshine. Conversation was light hearted although one of the ladies expressed her fear of flying, which eased once take-off was successfully accomplished and the glorious views of the Northumberland coast with its many castles could be enjoyed. Tony spoke to his new friend and they discussed the chances of their stables' entries for the Cheltenham National Hunt Festival next March. Tony invited all the passengers to join him in Mary's house for lunch and drinks and to watch the race on television on the twenty-sixth of December. The pilot had a full load of passengers for the first time in his limited experience and the weather had deteriorated as they approached the highlands. He miscalculated the time needed to gain the elevation that was necessary to clear the Glenshee watershed, and found himself unable to see the ground through the clouds as he vainly tried to gain height on the approach up the glen. The crushing collision with the hillside came as a total shock to all but the pilot and death was thankfully instantaneous.

Tony had matured from being reclusive by nature into a family man with property and a place in society. His luck had come from his

1

decision to leave his supposedly good job for life as a bank clerk - a job that had changed over the years into an uncertain and reviled occupation - but also from his investments that turned him into a private fund manager. His first major investment had been based upon an entirely false CIA cover story meant to divert attention away from their operation to recover a sunken Russian submarine, by saying that it was a commercial venture to recover precious metal nodules from the beds of the world's major oceans. This story had caused Tony to put all his considerable savings into purchasing shares in the company hired by the CIA to do the job. This was the company that employed him, but he could not be accused of insider trading as he believed the false cover story which was available to all the public. He quadrupled his investment by sheer luck. This cautionary investment had provided him with the capital and the caution to investigate further, and not listen to gossip, before making any further investments. He had been successful, more than once predicting the rise in the price of gold, spotting trends in the fluctuating property and stock markets, and predicting the 2008 banking crisis. Settling down at fifty-three he had gone on to invest one tenth of his fortune in a luxury country club and farming estate. He lived with a widow whilst taking care of his four illegitimate children, none of whom would be eligible to inherit any of his one billion pound fortune as he had died without leaving a will.

Tony Latimer had not kept in touch with his family since his parents died in 1970 when he was twenty-one and he had gone to work overseas, but his death was going to correct his failure to communicate with them. Now that he was dead his billion pound fortune would be inherited by his relatives, the descendants of his father's and mother's brothers and sisters. As a teenager he had met some of his uncles, aunts and cousins but had no idea what had happened to them. Now the latest generation were in line for a multi-million pound surprise.

Ben Macdui lies on the north side of the Lairig Ghru, a mountain pass through the central Cairngorms connecting Braemar in Aberdeenshire and Aviemore in Inverness-shire. It used to be the only country ramble in the UK that could not be comfortably completed in one day, but that was before the walk was shortened by the post-Second World War roads into the Lairig Ghru from Braemar to Linn of Dee and from Aviemore to the new Ski Pistes to the West. It wasn't until 1847 that the National Ordinance Survey established that Ben Nevis was the highest mountain in the UK and that Ben Macdui was the second highest only about one hundred feet lower. When the light aircraft carrying Tony Latimer crashed into Ben Macdui, it was another two hours before the alarm was raised and the nearest Mountain Rescue team in Braemar were asked to search for the crash site.

Tony's partner Sarah, and Mary their hostess for the Hogmanay celebrations, were waiting at Aberdeen airport. Sarah had not been worried when Tony had phoned to tell her that he had accepted the offer of a lift in a private plane and giving her the estimated time of arrival, as she was aware that he had often used non-scheduled flights throughout his working life. When the light aircraft failed to arrive and Tony's mobile phone failed to respond, the two women managed to contact the Air Traffic Controllers who confirmed that they had lost contact with that aircraft, and that they were initiating a search after checking with several small landing strips in the area. Sarah and Mary were at the same time introduced to the friends of the pilot who were also awaiting the arrival of the same private light aircraft, and they confided that the pilot was not very experienced, so that they were all left in a great state of anxiety. Mary took a stoical Scottish attitude to the worry and did her best to calm her friend Sarah.

Darkness arrives early in winter in the Cairngorms, and the heavy clouds blown in from the east that had contributed to the crash, were now depositing snow on ground more than five hundred feet above sea level. The chance of there being survivors was remote; nevertheless the mountain rescue volunteers make every effort short of suicidal in their dedicated attempts to reach people in trouble on their mountains. The last reported position of the flight and reports of smoke, from mountaineers coming down off Ben Macdui and out of the Lairig Ghru, gave them a good idea of the crash location, and they reached the crash site on the steep mountain slope before midnight. By the light of their helmet lamps the rescue team quickly established that there were no survivors, and radioed the crash position and their immediate plans to their base. Satisfied that there was no further danger of fire in the mangled wreckage they retreated to a mountain hut that they had established for just such an occasion as this, and awaited the forecast better weather in the morning.

Sarah was told that there were no survivors by telephone during that dreadful night, and sat on her bed curled up in a tight ball leaning against the headboard. Mary too was devastated, remembering Tony as her lover when she was in her prime, and the strong man who helped her develop her own business, but she could not bring any comfort to Sarah. Sarah's whole life had been transformed by Tony, from a lonely sexually frustrated woman without any meaningful activity other than as a social necessity to her first husband, into a busy mother to Tony's extended family, and manager of his properties. Her whole being was suffused with love for him as an individual whom she longed for with every fibre of her body. Now both body and mind were frozen with grief. Any thoughts that escaped were only of the bleakness of the future, or how to eliminate the future all together. She had already suffered the agony of telephoning her home on The Fallowfield Estate and telling family and friends that Tony was missing. They couldn't help heaping their distress at the news on Sarah as she was the head of the mainly female family. They couldn't help but blurt out foolish assumptions, maybe they found a field to land in we mustn't give up hope! Now she had to call again with the awful truth. Mary was at least able to help by phoning some of their mutual friends and taking care of transport for Sarah whilst making sure that she was not left alone for any length of time.

The 28th of December dawned without any precipitation but the sky was covered by high cloud and the wind had dropped a little. At the crash site there had only been a small fire in the heather, fuelled by leaking oil in front of the hot engine, and driven down the hillside by the strong wind until the storm extinguished it. All the bodies were removed to the Aberdeen mortuary leaving the air crash investigators from the Department of Transport to discover the cause of the accident. As had happened before to light aircraft the pilot probably had lost sight of the ground in the clouds when he failed to climb high enough to get over the mountains. Maybe he had a glimpse of the Lairig Ghru pass through a gap in the clouds and hoping that it would lead to the flatter farmland to the north of

Aberdeen he had changed course. It might have been possible for a very experienced professional pilot in bright sunshine, but Tony's new friend in his new aircraft flying blind in the clouds had failed to see the bend in the pass and the looming Ben Macdui straight ahead.

The news of Tony's death rapidly spread around his extended family as Sarah returned home, unable to stay in Scotland whilst the whole country celebrated Hogmanay. Home was the five thousand acre Fallowfield Estate that Tony Latimer had bought from Sir John Wallden on the first January 1999, and had then developed it into a luxury country club and hotel with a successful horse racing stable and grain producing and marketing business. There was no end to Sarah's pain there and it was only her responsibilities to her young ward Becky that helped her to postpone the worst agonies until after dark. Fifteen year old Becky had already lost her mother when she was five years old. Now mature enough to want to reduce Sarah's suffering but at an age when she struggled with day to day emotions, she tried to be calm for Sarah's sake. It didn't work and the pair of distraught women found themselves in a tearful embrace in the middle of the night. Sarah's daughter Pamela with her partner Barbara took care of all domestic arrangements whilst Sarah received the condolences of the estate staff, professional acquaintances and the horse racing fraternity from all around the country.

In Norway Marit, recently divorced from her unfaithful husband, nearly gave up under this second blow. Tony had been her only true love forty years ago, which was the reason she had asked to bear his child when she realized that he would never marry her. Now alone she could only think of those idyllic days when she was young and truly happy, remembering the times that she and Tony spent weekends in the family cabin in the pine-covered forests. They walked and talked and she had tried in vain to improve Tony's command of the Norwegian language, for which he had no aptitude. She had grown bored with the property business that Tony had helped her build up, and having cashed in on their oil economy inflated property prices by selling all but her home, a flat in Oslo and one hideaway cottage on an island in Stavanger fjord, she had little to occupy her time. Her only comfort came from her and Tony's son Per and her daughter by her recently divorced husband, whose philandering was partly caused by the realization that his wife's true love was still Tony. Nevertheless Marit telephoned her condolences to Sarah at The Fallowfield Estate and pledged to attend Tony's funeral which would be delayed until after the Fatal Accident Inquiry released his body.

Per, who had grown closer to his birth father Tony since he himself had married, had his wife and son and daughter to comfort him, but felt angry that Tony had risked taking a lift in a light aircraft piloted by an inexperienced pilot. He remembered Tony as a mainly absent birth father who created great excitement by turning up for birthdays and Christmas celebrations with expensive presents, or at least sometimes sent them by mail. When Per was eleven Tony had taken him on a magical holiday to Disney World in Florida without his mother and answered all and any questions that he could think of. Now a well-established engineer in Norway he caught the first plane from Stavanger to London to offer his assistance and comfort to his half-sister Becky and his half-brother Harry, Barbara's son conceived with Tony's sperm in a fertilization clinic, who both lived on The Fallowfield Estate. Hiring a car for the short drive down the motorway to Cambridgeshire, he was as always struck by the closeness of Norway to England and yet they had such diverse landscapes. Norwegians consider the English to be slightly more emotional Norwegians and Per felt comfortable in England, especially in the company of Becky and Harry. They were fifteen and nine to Per's thirty seven, and considered him to be more of an uncle than a half-brother. He found both Becky and Harry subdued and by talking to them about his experiences with Tony he was able to coax their experiences and memories out of them. The first time they had ridden a bicycle and a horse and Tony had been there, memories like these brought both comfort but then sadness, as they realized that there would not be any more experiences with their beloved father.

In Milan Fabia wept loudly exclaiming the grief that she truly felt for the loss of the father of her only child Gina. Her whole life had involved the transfer of her emotional attachments from person to person and she had never married any of her many lovers, so she soon recovered her composure. Nearing fifty she had been a Member of the European Parliament on the Lega Nord list for three years now.

Still attractive, Fabia had entered politics ten years ago and used her many contacts to gain promotion within the party, before being selected to stand for election in the constituency of Milan where she had her Antique shop. Her illegitimate daughter Gina was much more upset at the loss of Tony her natural father. She was aware that her mother had asked Tony to conceive a child with her knowing that he was adamant that he would never marry. Although she would have liked more attention from him in her formative years she had never doubted his commitment to her and his love for her. Gina assuaged her grief with the memory of her wonderful eighteenth birthday celebration that Tony had arranged for her on The Fallowfield Estate. It was the first time that Tony had brought his four illegitimate children with their surviving mothers together, and Gina had finally felt that she had a big family after all. With a weeklong celebration made up of trips to Royal Ascot and London followed by an open air dinner in the summer sunshine with lots of presents, Gina had become complete, and happily went on to become a full time mother to a growing family. She and Fabia telephoned their tearful condolences to Sarah at The Fallowfield Estate, and when advised that the funeral would be delayed, Fabia's whole family arranged for and attended a Remembrance Mass at their regular Catholic Church in Milan.

Gina then decided that she should join her half-brothers and sister at The Fallowfield Estate in order to offer any comfort or assistance that she could. Fabia recognized Gina's symptom of distress that she had often expressed at the absence of a regular father in her home life when young and immature, and her resentment of her mother's many lovers, so she encouraged her to go and volunteered to make arrangements to take care of her grandchildren. Gina e-mailed Per and managed to arrange a flight to Heathrow that allowed her to share the hire car with Per to complete her journey to Cambridgeshire.

Back in Sandyhill the nearest town, and Westway, the nearest village to The Fallowfield Estate, the tragic news spread to general regret and sadness. Most residents had enjoyed some contact with Tony, and he was held in general respect because of the success that he had made of turning a rundown country estate into a going concern that generated lots of local employment.

A rough triangle of land had been retained for the family residences with a building in each corner, the refurbished and rebuilt gatehouse for visitors, a new luxury detached home that Tony had shared with Lady Sarah and Tony's natural daughter Becky, and the racing stables with an apartment occupied by Lady Sarah's daughter and Tony's racehorse trainer Pamela, her partner Barbara and their son Harry. Becky had been made Tony and Sarah's ward by the American court following her mother's death in New York's twin towers on nine eleven. At fifteen with both of her birth parents dead she was in effect an orphan, but she still had Sarah who had been taking care of her for ten years. Their loss was too great to be eased by words or even physical contact. Reminders of Tony's existence were everywhere in their home, his fastidiousness showed in the tidiness of his personal possessions, and photographs emphasised the lushness of his white hair which seemed to get thicker with each year that passed. Both women had been prone to hang on to a handful of his hair when they cuddled up to him on a sofa, seeming to gain strength and comfort from doing so. His personal characteristics, by their absence, created in the pit of the stomach an ache of longing, as they missed his bustling walk, the way he pushed his spectacles up his nose, and even the way he fastidiously moved the food about his plate with his utensils. Worst of all his favourite chair stood empty in front of the television.

Lady Sarah's daughter, with her deceased first husband Sir John, Pamela was Tony Latimer's race horse trainer and lived in one of the flats in the stables with her partner Barbara. Harry was nine and knew that Tony had been involved in his creation, although quite how was not clear to him. In fact the two women lovers had bonded for life and wanted a child using Pamela's egg, as Barbara was infertile, and Tony's sperm by In Vitro Fertilization. Harry was the result and had spent his entire life living at the stables. With younger children the hurt of a loss of a close relative can't be maintained all the time, but it is no less painful and stays buried deep inside them, often resurfacing in the dark of a bedroom. So it was with Harry when he went to collect Becky and take her to the Gatehouse to greet their arriving half-brother and sister, Per and Gina. Pamela and Barbara were upset by the news of Tony's death as he had made an incredible impact on their lives. Apart from helping to get them married and helping out with producing Harry, he had set a penniless Pamela up as a trainer and helped her develop one of the biggest and most successful racing stables in the country. Nevertheless there were worries caused by Tony's death as he owned all the horses and the stables. Pamela would have to wait and see what happened in the now uncertain future.

When Tony Latimer had bought the Norwood Estate and given up traveling the world as an investment fund manager, he had brought three Personal Assistants with him. They had been promoted to Managers by the time of Tony's death and his considerable effect on their lives now left them grieving as much as his family members. Indeed he had treated them as members of his unorthodox family. Fiona had been promoted first to Buildings Manager and then to CEO of Tony's one hundred million pound investment in the country club. Nicole had been promoted to Estate Land Manager and then to CEO of Tony's investment in the trading of grain. June had been promoted to Manager of Tony's Horse Racing Investment and lived in the other flat at the stables. Fiona and Nicole shared properties on the estate with their partners and all three managers were shaken by Tony's death. He had been their inspiration and guide and, despite the considerable confidence that they had developed thanks to their success in their jobs, they now felt uncertain and fearful to carry on without him. They did what they could to comfort the family members and give practical assistance wherever they could but the whole of The Fallowfield Estate was in mourning.

When Tony Latimer had first purchased the Norwood Estate from Sir John Wallden and re-named it The Fallowfield Estate, he had selected the Gatehouse to be rebuilt and refurbished as his bachelor pad. That was before he fell in love with Lady Sarah Wallden after the suicide of her husband, and she had moved into the Gatehouse and added her more feminine touches to it. Now it was full of the chatter of the two younger children as they greeted Per and Gina who had unpacked and were going to stay a couple of nights in its two bedrooms. Settling down in the open plan living/dining room they were surrounded by reminders of their birth father, and Gina needed her handkerchief to regain her composure, but she was the first to speak.

"I do wish that I had spent more time with Tony", they all called him Tony rather than father or dad, "and I did talk to him about that. He was always sympathetic, generous, and always said that if I needed him he would come running, but in fact I think that he needed to feel free and quite liked being alone by himself. Mama told me that he was emphatic that he had no interest in marriage, or of having children, and we all are the result of our mothers' decisions, not Tony's." This struck a chord in Becky whose experience of Tony was quite different from that of Gina.

"I suppose that I got the most of his time," replied Becky. "The American court made him and Sarah my guardians when I was only five. I can still remember my mother but Sarah of course has been a lovely replacement mother to me, but I agree that Tony was different, he had so many interests that consumed his entire attention and he loved detail more than most people, to the extent that he could be quite boring on the rare occasions that he opened up. By the time I came into his life it was twenty years after Per was born and ten years after Gina was born, and I think that it was falling in love with Sarah that changed him. Although they never married the responsibility of looking after me turned them into a proper couple, and by the time that Harry came along he had matured into a proper husband and Dad." Per had children of his own and was careful not to treat his half-siblings as children, but he was keen to emphasise the value of a regular family to them as he knew that the effects of Tony's lifestyle had not all been good.

"It is clear that Tony had a powerful effect on our mothers, and whilst my mother clings to the memory of what was the most exciting time in her life, it has left her unable to settle for the more mundane existence in a more normal relationship. It must have been different for your mother though Gina?" Indeed it was clear to Gina that each of Tony's four children and their mothers had experienced their own uniquely different relationship with Tony.

"Yes, I think that Fabia is very much like Tony, and that they recognised that similarity. I don't think that Mama ever wanted to marry Tony, or any other man, she just loves manipulating the people that she takes an interest in. She was still a great mother to me, but with parents like that it is surprising that I turned out to be an old-fashioned housewife." Harry knew some of what his siblings were talking about but with two mothers he had definitely relied on Tony for men's stuff.

"Well I am missing him already so maybe you Per could be the person that I turn to in future." Per was pleased to affirm that he would like that, and made sure that Harry had his mobile number.

Harry commented that his mother Pamela had said that Tony didn't know one end of a horse from the other end, and yet he loved to watch the racing, and often commented that it was a wonderful exciting spectacle, and that it must have been an incredible experience to ride such powerful animals, especially over fences. Becky had often watched the racing on TV with Tony and added,

"It was the complexity of the runners' form detail that attracted him and was another example of his need to concentrate and his ability to provide his own diversions.

"Well," said Per, "I think that it has been nice to have a good discussion about Tony's life and personality, and I hope that will ease the pain of his passing for us all. One thing is for certain we are all going to miss him, and the more we talk about him the more we will be able bear his absence."

Gina certainly felt a lot calmer and turned to smile at Lady Sarah when she joined them. Sarah had come to take them all to dinner in the Country Club hotel, and they all walked down the snow-covered drive together. They were joined by Pamela, Barbara, and the three managers Fiona, Nicole and June, who as Tony's personal assistants had all helped in the development of the one hundred million pound Country Club with its additional properties and sporting facilities. Over dinner Sarah told them all that Tony's funeral could not be held until after the accident enquiry was completed, and at that time they would all find out how Tony's fortune would be dealt with. She was sure that they would all be taken care of, because they were all beneficiaries of the trust that owned The Fallowfield Estate. She thanked Per and Gina for coming as it had done them all good to talk about Tony's extraordinary life.

Chapter Two

January 2012 Anthony Latimer Died Intestate

To one man in Sandyhill the news of Tony's death brought a worried frown to his brow. Mr Coldstone, the senior partner of solicitors Coldstone & Logie, was an old man on the verge of retirement. He had acted for The Fallowfield Estate since its formation when Tony Latimer had first arrived in Westhill, although he knew that he was merely the local representative for Tony's London firm of lawyers, who had recommended him in the first place. He had come to know Tony well and enjoyed social invitations to The Fallowfield Estate, issued by Lady Sarah his companion. He knew of the complexity of Tony's background and approved of the transformation that he had brought to the local community, especially of the transformation of Lady Sarah into a happy and involved member of that community. The full extent of Tony's international wealth was not known to him, and he had no inkling of the absence of any will and testament, but he knew enough to realize that it would involve a considerable amount of work.

The fees would be welcome, but he asked Mr Logie to step into his office to discuss the tragedy, and to prime him to tackle most of the work. The two men were at a distance from the full emotional impact of Tony's death, but both felt the normal need to shake their heads and mutter to each other about how sad it was for the family, and how great an effect it would have upon them and the local community. Mr Logie expressed the opinion that, as they had represented Mr Latimer in all his property and business deals since he had arrived in Sandyhill in 1998, they should have the inside track for processing his last will and testament. Mr Coldstone agreed but reminded Mr Logie that they would probably have to bring in Tony's London solicitors.

They agreed that, as Lady Sarah had been back at Fallowfield for a couple of days, and as the funeral would be delayed until the FIA released Tony's body, it would be appropriate for them to telephone their condolences and offer to visit Lady Sarah to discuss any practical assistance that they may be able to give her. Mr Coldstone spoke quietly into the telephone for a couple of minutes and after listening for a shorter period of time he replaced the receiver. Mr Logie looked at him expectantly until a thoughtful Mr Coldstone said,

"Yes, she will see us tomorrow. She sounded very subdued, not at all like the Lady Sarah that I have known for so long." Coldstone and Logie's most recent work for Tony Latimer had been advising and assisting in the setting up of a Trust Fund with The Fallowfield Estate as its one hundred million pound asset. Both partners now set about reviewing the trusts details as preparation for their meeting with Lady Sarah.

Soberly dressed as always they drove to The Fallowfield Estate in silence on a sunny January morning, with that clarity of light that only comes with a frost. Becky opened the door to them and quietly invited them in to the lounge where Lady Sarah accepted their condolences with a sad resignation. She had slept little and her natural attractiveness had been diminished as much by sadness as it had been increased by happiness in recent years. Her appearance was nevertheless of dignified neatness in a simple black dress with her hair tied back, emphasizing the paleness of her face where the only makeup was to reduce the redness around her eyes. After some more murmurs of comfort and regret, Mr Logie received the agreed signal from Mr Coldstone, and Fergus asked:

"Is there anything that we can be of practical help with Lady Sarah?" Of course during the past couple of days Sarah had had the occasional worried thought about what she would have to sort out, but had made no attempt to take those thoughts forward. With the funeral delayed however, she knew that events might overwhelm her, and she had gladly accepted Coldstone and Logies' offer to visit.

"Tony was completely in control of his assets, it was a game for him, he enjoyed accumulating rather than spending, and I am sure that he kept very good records as he was obliged to do in accord with his own nature, but he never explained or discussed anything with me, other than what affected the family on a day to day basis. I got the impression that I could buy anything, no matter how much it cost, just so long as I gave him a proper receipt." This was music to the ears of the two solicitors, an acceptance that she would need and expect help with Tony's affairs.

"Mr Latimer didn't raise the subject of a will with us," advised Fergus, "Do you know if he has a will here or with his London solicitors perhaps?" Sarah hadn't looked for a will and hadn't even thought about one, such was her trust and reliance upon Tony.

"No, he never mentioned a will to me, but I have the keys that he always carried with him, would you be so good as to have a look through his records in his study whilst you are here, and discuss the matter with his London solicitors, I will be happy to hear your advice on the outcome." Lady Sarah led them to Tony's study and indicated the keys that she had left on his desk.

"I will go and prepare some coffee and biscuits for when you have finished," She said, pleased to accept the help offered.

Mr Coldstone added that they wouldn't be long, as finding a will was the key to everything. They would just search for it in the files, as all future financial actions would be dependent on what was in the will. Messrs Coldstone & Logie were only in the study for half an hour. Lady Sarah was right; Tony had left very good records, including an index for his files. There was a grey four-drawer filing cabinet with Twinlock open top hanging files, more of the same in the desk's deep bottom drawers, a shelf full of Lever arch files, and a dozen drawers in the desk and a cabinet with a writing slope. The file index simplified their initial search, leading them to Twinlock files entitled documents, personal and official, medical, travel, and other, but no will. They persisted in going through the drawers and all the other files even though their titles were not relevant. Their eyes fell on spreadsheets printouts and bank statements studded with amounts that surprised them by being so large, but still no will. Leaving Fergus to make a thorough search of all the files, just in case the will was misfiled, Mr Coldstone reported back to Sarah.

Over coffee and biscuits they agreed that they would make enquiries with Tony's London firm of solicitors. He gave her a sealed envelope, that they had found in the personal documents file, that was addressed as: To be opened by Sarah in the event of my death, A.L. Coldstone & Logie had agreed that the contents were too thin to be a Last Will and Testament, and told Lady Sarah that she might wish to open it in private when they had gone. She agreed, and they said that they would be in touch by telephone tomorrow.

On the drive back to their office in Sandyhill they speculated about the total of Tony's fortune and the fees that would be normal for an administrator, although if the London firm of lawyers held his will, then they would undoubtedly get the largest share of the billings. Whilst driving Fergus mentioned that all the locals had speculated about Tony Latimer's total wealth ever since he arrived in the area, but that nobody had ever found out the truth. Now, will or no will, the total truth would come out.

The junior partner of Coldstone & Logie, Fergus Logie, had never set foot in Scotland. His grandfather had migrated from Aberdeenshire before the Second World War looking for work. The family had retained their fondness for Scottish names, but Fergus was determined that the practice would end with his children, as he was happily settled in Cambridgeshire with a degree in law. Summer holiday office work for Mr Coldstone in his home town of Sandyhill had at first hardened his resolve to go out into the wider world in search of a life as a great barrister specializing in criminal law! Not that Mr Coldstone was anything but encouraging and helpful, with a Pickwickian set of habits and gestures that suited his rotund frame and genial manner.

After graduation from London University's school of law with an upper second class degree, Fergus had obtained employment as a solicitor with a London firm. The city had its unique attractions for a young bachelor and Fergus had enjoyed the excitement of living in one of the world's greatest cities with its museums, theatres, pubs and clubs. London reserves its greatest pleasures for those with deep pockets, but Fergus found that playing rugby for a club better suited his pocket. The playing fields of London are mainly confined to an outer ring of less expensive land. Fergus would travel out to his team's club house, or that of their opponents on a Saturday lunch time, sometimes picking up team mates on the way. He joined a decent club after playing for his university's second team but only made the third team most of the time. A sturdy forward who was not fast enough to play wing forward or number eight as he wished to, he mainly played blind side prop and liked to look for the ball in the loose plays in the hope of getting to run with it in hand. He occasionally made a telling pass or beat an opposing forward to score a try, but the game was good for socializing. On Saturday evenings, following their plunge bath clean-up and a few encouraging beers, a romantic atmosphere could develop when wives and their unmarried friends arrived to distract the bachelors. Fergus enjoyed several affairs, some more intimate than others, but there was no chance of marriage on his salary with the capital's house prices well out of reach.

He could reach the office with one short underground trip from his only just habitable flat and didn't really need a car, but it was necessary for the ladies. Second hand was all he could afford and with a large deductible on his insurance, he managed to run it over the weekends. Driving to his flat alone after an unsuccessful date one evening, he was overtaken by a fast moving sports car which cut back in front of him too quickly. Catching Fergus's front offside bumper with his own nearside rear bumper, the driver a young man was immediately apologetic and unsettled. Fergus's analytical legal mind realized that the young man had not only been drinking, but that something else was troubling him. It turned out that he had taken his father's car without his permission and that an insurance claim was out of the question. Without any feeling of sympathy, Fergus accepted the young man's cheque for a thousand pounds and fixed the little damage to his own car, in the road outside his flat, with the aid of a spanner and a lump hammer. The road in which Fergus's flat was situated had two distinct sides. On the opposite side of the road from his flat, which was in one of the crumbling Victorian mansions that lined that side, were several detached post-war houses with nice big gardens. Unbelievably, on the morning after his brush with the sports car, Fergus stepped onto the pavement just as a lady from the house opposite reversed down her drive and failed to turn sufficiently to avoid colliding with Fergus's car's rear passenger door. The apologetic lady was intent on not letting her husband know about her latest mishap, and willingly handed over her cheque for two thousand pounds, a cheap price to pay for a new door, according to Fergus. Once again he managed to beat out most of the dent with his trusty lump hammer. Fergus could now afford to motor in London for a few months longer and was keeping his eye open for any chance of more profitable bumps. Unfortunately the next one cost him money. At a

16

rugby teammate's wedding he went for a rare parking space outside the reception restaurant, going in front end first he collided with another guest correctly reversing into the same space. As the other driver was the groom's father, Fergus decided to accept liability for repairs to both cars and even had to go and look for another parking space. The realization however, that life as a great criminal law barrister was the unlikely outcome of his best efforts, was not long in coming. During the course of his four years' working there, the ever-increasing cost of living in London reduced his lifestyle comforts, so that they compared unfavourably with his frequent visits to his family's home in Sandyhill. During these visits he maintained his contacts with Mr Coldstone, and was finally offered a junior partnership provided he gave up rugby. Fergus had not realized it at the time, but his employers in London had also employed a youthful Peter Coldstone, who had maintained his links with them after setting up on his own in Sandyhill, to their mutual satisfaction. The London law firm of Fortune and Fulbright had a name that appealed to Tony Latimer, and he had used them in his dealings with the bank whose Sandyhill branch had brought to his attention the fact that the Norwood Estate was for sale. When Anthony Latimer decided to buy The Norwood Estate, and before he renamed it The Fallowfield Estate, he had called his London law firm of Fortune and Fulbright, who were only too happy to recommend the local Sandyhill law firm of Coldstone & Logie to act as his local legal advisors. It was advisable to use a local firm as they would be aware of local land and building prices and any local practices or conflicts of interest.

When Peter and Fergus had returned from their visit to Lady Sarah, Peter Coldstone was happy to make it clear to his junior partner Fergus that he should take the lead in all matters relating to The Fallowfield Estate. Fergus at thirty-nine and married with two daughters aged nine and eleven, was happy to accept more responsibility. Since returning from London fourteen years ago he had gained plenty of experience and was now relieved to realize that Peter Coldstone was nearing retirement. Having married a pretty local nurse, whose knowledge and skill regarding raising children had been a great relief for him, he was now ready for a step up in work and more responsibility.

The next morning Fergus telephoned Fortune & Fulbright, and quickly established that Anthony Latimer had never discussed a will with them. They advised that the next step was to put an obituary in the Financial Times, the Wall Street Journal, the Aberdeen Press and Journal, the Houston Chronicle, and the Sandyhill Recorder. That covered the financial world, the oilfield world, and his only settled home world. They would also go ahead and widely advertise in the legal profession's publications and notice boards, that anyone with an interest in AL's estate should contact Fortune & Fulbright. Meanwhile Fergus should telephone Lady Sarah and discuss with her the contents of the obituary with regard to ensuring that it satisfied her wishes.

It sounded simple, but Sarah had never been made aware of any family on Tony's side, and whilst he had carefully introduced her to three illegitimate children and their mothers, she knew that his life before buying The Fallowfield Estate had been thirty years as a bachelor who travelled all over the world. After many long telephone conversations with Mary in Aberdeen, Marit in Stavanger, Fabia in Milan, and her own daughter Pamela at the estate stables, she and Fergus finally met to finalize the obituary. They settled on describing AL as:

'A financier who had predicted the increases in the price of gold and the 2008 world banks debt crisis, and had used his old-fashioned values to build an extended family supported by the successful modernization of The Fallowfield Estate.'

With the obituary published some people were puzzled by its lack of detail but on reflection decided that, yes that was Tony Latimer, a bit of a mystery. Fortune & Fulbright's enquiries throughout the legal profession drew a blank response, apart from one barely literate letter claiming that Tony Latimer owed ten million dollars to a family called King in Dallas. The briefest enquiry established that any Kings had long since left the address given and that most of them were in prison. It finally became certain that Anthony Latimer had died intestate.

Anthony Latimer's body was released for burial by the Department of Transport within one month of the crash, and the official cause of the accident was given as pilot error brought on by inexperience. His body was brought back to the rooms of the Sandyhill Funeral Parlour, where Sarah received the coffin and asked for a few minutes alone with it. The coffin was closed and Sarah let her upper body lean on the top of it as her legs felt too weak to bear her weight. The anguish of loss was too much for the mind and the tears flowed which helped alleviate the pit-of-the-stomach feeling of hopelessness. Recovery was forced upon her as she was awaiting the arrival of Becky after school, only to be plunged back to the depths of despair as she watched Becky suffer the same anguish. They supported one another and returned home to meet the local minister and discuss the funeral arrangements.

Tony had not attended his church, but had contributed handsomely to the church's roof repair fund. Sarah knew that Tony simply wanted to be cremated and have his ashes scattered on The Fallowfield Estate without any marker or headstone. The minister was happy to attend at the crematorium and speak about Tony's local achievements, but nobody could help him regarding Tony's friends and relations from his childhood. Invitations were sent out to America, Norway, Italy, Scotland, and locally, and there was no shortage of mourners. Accommodation and transport arrangements were made, and as is the way with funerals, most mourners cheered up at the reception after the service, as they renewed acquaintances that had lapsed in recent years.

The following day, after most guests had departed, the close family scattered Tony's ashes in Becky's hollow on The Fallowfield Estate. Becky's hollow was a quiet tree-filled spot between the Gatehouse and the Hall. It was away from the drives, paths, and estate tracks, and was a place where those who wished to remember Tony could lay some flowers without being disturbed. Becky extracted a promise from Sarah that, as she had lost her natural mother and father by the tender age of fifteen, Sarah would take care of her and live for a long time yet. Sarah tearfully agreed that she would do her best, at least until Becky had married and built a big family of her own by having lots of children, but in the meantime they still had Pamela, Barbara, and Harry, they were family too. Sarah had assembled several of Tony's personal items, watches, antiques, and souvenirs from his travels, and distributed them to close family members and his friends and employees.

Before departing for home, Tony's women found themselves all together in one room for the first time ever. Sarah the court-appointed guardian of his youngest daughter Becky, Marit the mother of Per his oldest son, Fabia the mother of Gina his oldest daughter, Pamela and Barbara parents to his In-vitro-fertilized youngest son Harry, and Mary his Aberdeen mistress on and off from 1975 to 1998. Marit broke the ice by congratulating Sarah on getting Tony to settle down and make a home together.

"Well the settling down came before we got together," Sarah said, " and I think that after living out of a suitcase for so long, he just made an impulsive decision when he saw the Estate and decided to buy it. Even then when we discovered that we were compatible he made it quite clear that marriage was not an option, just as I believe he did with you ladies." Sarah had no feelings other than affection for Tony's other women; after all, being his last lover gave her great satisfaction.

Fabia was quick to respond. "He suited me because I didn't want to be married either, although of all the men that I have known he was the one whom I enjoyed spending time with the most when we weren't having sex, and that's why I asked him for a child. I always wanted one child and by persuading Tony to be the father I could look forward to more of his company later in life, and that is why I am so distraught now." Fabia was unconcerned about Tony's other women, whether she liked them or not was a matter of how compatible they were to her rather than how compatible they were to Tony. In fact she preferred the company of men more than the company of women.

"Marriage never even came up as a subject for us," added Mary, "we were too busy making money, but I agree Tony's attraction was the attention that he paid to me; he obviously cared about me and my future, and he was deliberately romantic, if romance can be deliberate?" Mary had formed a strong friendship with Sarah during the time that they had overseen the refurbishment of the Gatehouse as Tony's bachelor home, and she had approved of their subsequent romance after she returned to Aberdeen. Marit and Fabia were a bit too foreign for her tastes, but as they had known Tony as she had, then she was happy to share reminiscences with them.

"Yes he tended to work to a set of rules, but managed to make me believe that it was all spontaneous." Marit was thinking back to their long summer nights together in the Norwegian fjords. "But his main focus was the accumulation of wealth, his game as he thought of it. At that stage of his life marriage or living with a woman and having responsibility for children would have distracted him from what he clearly enjoyed doing, and he was determined to avoid any distraction." Marit was almost as distressed as Sarah about Tony's death as he had been her only true love. She didn't feel comfortable with Fabia and Mary but couldn't help liking Lady Sarah who was so kind and considerate.

"I don't think that any of us really wanted to tame Tony" concluded Sarah. "When I first got together with him I knew that he had secrets from my talks with Mary, and he told me that he would tell me all but only a bit at a time as he thought that the whole story would be too much for me to accept at one go. His first revelation was Linda, Becky's mother in Houston. I only met her on our first evening there but she was quite friendly and seemed pleased that Tony had somebody to live with. She was quite willing for Tony and me to look after Becky for a couple of days whilst she went to New York on business. She was killed the next day in the twin towers when they collapsed on nine eleven in New York, and we have brought Becky up ever since. His next revelation was forced on him by Marit's invitation to Per's wedding in Stavanger, and then a year later he brought Fabia and Gina over to The Fallowfield Estate for Gina's eighteenth birthday. That left only poor Melba who was murdered in Dallas. Her death involved Tony in a money laundering trial in America, so he had to explain his connection to her as well, although she didn't have a child with Tony. We were all liberated by Tony's business acumen, and maybe that's what we all found so attractive in him, it wasn't just the physical love but the full time involvement in his active business interests that made us so excited by his very presence. He totally changed our lives for the better, but at the same time he did like to get away and be on his own quite a lot, but he made up for it by giving us his full attention when he was with us. He did need us all and now we can only keep his memory alive by cherishing our time with him and enjoying the maturing of the children that we asked him to father."

As they parted Sarah advised everyone that they had not yet discovered Tony's will, but that the lawyers were working on it, and they would all need to return soon to hear about the disposition of Tony's assets.

Fergus awoke early on the morning of his next meeting with Lady Sarah, which at her request would be held in his office in Sandyhill. He was excited at the prospect of being involved in such a large and lucrative legal case. Up before his thirty-five year old wife Helen, he prepared the breakfast table and fussed over his two daughters as they reluctantly got ready for school. Helen, sensing his excitement, gave him a full body hug as he departed and said, "Enjoy your work darling." As he drove to the office he reflected on his researches and how he wanted to put them to Lady Sarah. He knew that she was still emotionally devastated, but she was still on The Fallowfield Estate payroll as the general manager, and would need to resume her gentle guidance of the other senior managers, which would, he hoped, help her to recover a little. As he entered the offices of Coldstone and Logie he instructed the receptionist to alert his secretary as soon as Lady Sarah arrived. He briefed Mr Coldstone the senior partner and received his blessing to carry on alone. His secretary gave Fergus his opened mail as he passed into his office, where he made sure that two comfortable armchairs were positioned one on either side of the coffee table in front of his office window. The view from his office window was not spectacular so he tackled his mail whilst he waited.

Lady Sarah arrived at the agreed time, and seemed relaxed to Fergus as they exchanged pleasantries and settled into the armchairs. She refused coffee as it was too soon after breakfast, so Fergus plunged straight in and advised Lady Sarah that to the best of his knowledge, Anthony Latimer had died intestate. Sarah smiled and responded that she was sure that was the case after reading the letter that Tony had left for her, the one that Fergus had found amongst his documents at their last meeting.

"I won't tell you everything that was in the letter, but Tony spelt out in detail several actions that he had taken, of which I was only vaguely aware when he made the arrangements. The house that we live in was bought freehold in my name along with all its contents. He even paid the income tax that accrued to me for the receipt of a valuable gift from an unrelated friend. I knew that he had opened a bank account in my name, although I never bothered to access it before now. I followed Tony's instructions for internet access and found that it contains one million pounds plus some interest, again after payment of income tax due on a gift from an unrelated friend." As Sarah paused for breath, Fergus said,

"Well that is a relief then, he did provide for you for the foreseeable future."

"More than that," she replied, "he has done the same for Harry with the stables and horses under Pamela's guardianship, and Becky with the Gatehouse under my guardianship until they reach eighteen. So as a family we have the freehold for the whole triangle of land that we always considered our private little estate, and three million pounds in cash. He also reminded me that as Becky's surviving ward appointed by the Houston court, I was responsible for Becky's major shareholding in her mother's computer company, so she will come into several hundred million dollars when she reaches her majority." A relieved but surprised Fergus was quick to assure Lady Sarah that he was pleased to hear of these arrangements, but that Coldstone & Logie and Fortune & Fulbright had had no knowledge of them. Sarah continued,

"Tony was like that, he used lots of different banks and lawyers and only he knew the whole picture, but he kept good records and after reading his letter I am confident that I know where everything is, including his fortune of more than one billion pounds. It is with the disposal of this large sum that I am hoping Coldstone & Logie can help me." As with most country folk she was all for giving any business or work at her disposal to local firms. That was exactly what Fergus wanted to hear, and he outlined the following course of action as sensitively as he could.

"Intestacy requires the estate of the deceased to be administered under probate law. The Administrator is appointed by the local District Probate Registry (DPR), which will be Ipswich for you, and the DPR court does this by granting a letter of administration to the next of kin, who must hire a lawyer to get the process started."

Sarah interrupted to say that she would be happy to hire Coldstone & Logie for that very purpose, but the next of kin for Tony was a bit of a problem. Fergus didn't think so, as the Provision for

Family and Dependents Act 1975 allowed claims for sufficient provision for cohabitees and dependent or stepchildren without questioning a will.

"I think that the DPR court will appoint you as Administrator knowing that you were Mr Latimer's cohabitee and that you have hired ourselves."

"Well that's good news Mr Logie, please start that process and I will send over to you Tony's account files and computer spreadsheets. The billion pounds appears to be all in Bonds and tracker funds, but I don't understand the status of The Fallowfield Estate, perhaps you would investigate that."

"I will give it my immediate attention, and I have prepared the letter of appointment for you to sign appointing us as your legal representative in this matter. We will prepare a receipt for Mr Latimer's accounts that we will sign for you when we receive them, then the next step will be to search for beneficiaries. The UK Intestate Law from 1st February 2009 provides that without a spouse, civil partner, children, parents, brothers, sisters, or living grandparents, the estate is divided equally between whole blood aunts and uncles or, their descendants. Am I right in assuming that you and Tony didn't go through a ceremony to become civil partners?"

"You are correct, and Tony didn't legitimise any of his four illegitimate children by marrying any of their mothers." Fergus was a little surprised at the depth of Lady Sarah's knowledge, but assumed that she had been thinking about this matter and checking it out on the internet.

Sarah had been stumbling back into normal life, and Tony's letter had reassured her. The families' future was taken care of, so she was not surprised or upset by Fergus's reference to beneficiaries. In conclusion Fergus said that he had already contacted a genealogist, and would keep Lady Sarah well informed at every stage of his investigations, but that he believed that she, Becky, and Harry would still have a minor claim against the estate under the 1975 Act.

"Provision for cohabitees and dependents can be claimed in proportion to the style and level of living previously provided by the deceased, so your claims will be substantial, but small in proportion to the total value of the estate. Unfortunately the vast bulk of Tony's fortune will be going to strangers."

"That is almost a relief to me", confessed Sarah, "I have Becky's American fortune to look after, and I have already been in touch with Tony's Houston attorney who will advise the court and the computer company of the change in Becky's custody until she is eighteen." Fergus escorted Lady Sarah to the door after she had signed the letter of appointment, and returned to brief Mr Coldstone once again, who agreed that a celebration was in order with lunch at his favourite restaurant.

Fergus was right about the DPR court appointing Lady Sarah Walden as administrator under probate law, of the estate of Anthony Latimer who had died intestate in December 2011. They were satisfied that she was his cohabitee and that she had appointed Coldstone & Logie as her lawyers. Sarah was right when she said that a little more than one billion pounds was in Bonds and tracker funds in Europe and the United States. When Fergus received AL's accounts on a USB stick recording the computer spreadsheets from Lady Sarah, he found them to be detailed and fully documented which made his task much easier. Nevertheless he had to contact all the institutions concerned and advise them of Anthony Latimer's death, and start the process of turning them all into liquid assets in a probate account. He was ably assisted by the bank that the deceased had used in Sandyhill, but it was a considerable task and would take some time. He also had to consider the effect of inheritance tax, which was likely to consume some three or four hundred million pounds of the estate. Coldstone and Logie were not international tax specialists and they turned to Fortune and Fulbright for assistance in ensuring that the estate beneficiaries inherited as much cash as possible.

Finally the status of AL's one hundred million pound investment in The Fallowfield Estate was clearly recorded and documented in his accounts. Tony Latimer had created a trust to be administered by appointees made by his Sandyhill legal company, bank, and accountants. Current appointees were Mr Coldstone of the local firm of Coldstone and Logie lawyers, Frank Williams' manager of the local branch of the bank, and Mr Brand of Ferguson and Brand the local accounting firm. The trust directed the administrators to appoint professional managers to run the estate as a profitable commercial operation, with net annual profits paid, one third equally divided between Lady Sarah and his four children Per, Gina, Becky and Harry, one third between estate employees in proportion to their annual salaries, and one third to local good causes within a ten mile radius of Sandyhill with preference to outdoor activities for the young, the elderly and horse charities. This trust had only been created in 2011 to commence on the 1st April just eight months before Tony's accidental death, another example of him being a lucky banker. During its first year the Trust administrators had left the management of The Fallowfield Estate in the hands of Tony's appointees headed by Lady Sarah Wallden. The first year's profits to the 31st March 2012 would soon be ready for distribution by the end of June, providing further support for Tony's family and friends. Without a will, Tony Latimer had taken care of his loved ones without burdening or demotivating them with huge inheritances. It would take a few months for Fergus to complete the administrative tasks and for the genealogist to complete his research. At that point the beneficiaries would be invited to the office of Coldstone & Logie to be advised of their good luck.

Part II: The Inheritors

Chapter Three
September 2006 University Graduation

Inside the Great Hall of Manchester University on Oxford Road and only a short distance from the city centre, Frank Latimer (Tony's nephew) and his good friends Bo Sung and Emily Tang, awaited their turn to receive their first class honours degrees. Frank a BSc in Computer Science, Bo an MBA in Business Studies, and Emily a BA in Modern Languages and Business & Management (Chinese). It was early September 2006 and the three friends had shared a luxury apartment in the city centre for the past three years. The apartment had been funded by Bo's Chinese communist parents, and had contributed to their popularity with their fellow students and a full social life. They had played and worked hard and earned their coveted Firsts. The boys had played rugby and Emily had enjoyed some minor success at athletics and tennis, so that their over indulgences in partying and alcohol had always been balanced by training for and participating in sport. Computer laptops had played a big part in their studying and pastimes as gaming and social networking were developing and they really felt that they were well equipped to face a world that in fact they knew little about.

The three youngsters were not alone, Frank's widowed mother Margaret was there full of motherly pride and anxiety for her son's future, and Frank's uncle Thomas Latimer was there partly to support his brother's widow, but partly because he acted as Bo's guide and counsellor at the request of Bo's Chinese parents whilst Bo was in England. Emily was from Hong Kong and was supported by her widowed father Li Tang. The relatives had met before as the three students had been together at boarding school and university for the past ten years, but their meetings had been brief exchanges of pleasantries so their knowledge of one another was superficial. Margaret and Li had their own hopes for their offsprings' futures but Thomas was fulfilling a business arrangement, although he had developed an uncles' guiding spirit feeling for the students over the years that he had watched them develop.

Once the three graduates' eager anticipation had been satisfied by the presentation of their scrolled degree, the video of the ceremony had been collected and paid for, and their rented mortarboards had been thrown in the air, they were anxious to dispose of their relatives and commence the real celebration with other classmates on their final visit to each of their favourite Manchester pubs. They escorted their relatives to the nearby Midland Hotel, and promised to return for a final dinner with them by tomorrow afternoon, after which the older generation would escort them to their separate homes to plan their future.

For three years the class of zero six had grabbed their pleasures and discussed the world's problems in the pubs of Manchester, now it was time to say a fond farewell to them all. Fortunately cash restrictions and a growing knowledge that drugs harmed the brain, had kept most of the students sober on weekdays. Now too they shouted their farewells at favourite pubs in Fallowfield and Withington from the top of the bus taking them as far out as Didsbury where they alighted at Ye Olde Cock Inn. Not a word was spoken about the future, nostalgia for the past three years was all they cared about. Some had played in the rugby seven-a-side competitions on the banks of the River Mersey just behind the Old Cock, and couldn't resist a stumble around the scene of their past triumphs. Finally they had to part and go their separate ways, believing that they would be best mates for ever, but in fact hardly ever seeing most of them for the rest of their lives.

When the three friends returned to their apartment in the early hours of the next morning, whilst they couldn't be described as sober, they surprised themselves by not being as foolishly drunk as had happened after previous celebrations. With a couple of exceptions the whole class had been very talkative and a little bit restrained by the fact that they were facing uncertain futures. Their lives to this point had been well organized by the parents, teachers and the institutions they had attended, but now that was all over and the future was theirs to decide. The next day by lunchtime the trio were up and packed and ready to walk round to the Midland Hotel. Whilst waiting for the landlord to check for damages and relieve them of their keys, they settled around the kitchen table with a last cup of coffee and Frank started reminiscing.

"It has been a whole ten years since our first meeting when we started at boarding school, when Bo and I were directed to the same dormitory and he smiled at me because my mother was saying exactly the same thing to me as Frank was saying to him, rubbish about washing behind our ears and that sort of thing." In fact Frank's first reaction to Bo's Chinese features had been one of revulsion, but his relative maturity and friendly attitude had quickly won Frank over when the reality of loneliness set in with his mother's departure.

"That's right," agreed Bo, who had thought that Frank looked a bit of a softy once his mother had left, "and I had already spoken to Emily, who started on the same day, but only because I heard her speaking Mandarin to her father. I was a bit disappointed when they put her in a girl only house as I wanted her in my dormitory because my English wasn't so good then." Bo had taken a fancy to Emily from that first day, although even after ten years the two boys still treated her as a mate despite her ever increasing female attractiveness.

"Well I didn't want to share a bedroom even with girls," said Emily, "I had my own bedroom back in Hong Kong, but I was pleased that there was another Chinese kid in the same year, and from then on we became firm friends." Emily was totally at ease with being a mate to these two boys even though it conveyed both protection and the risk of rumours about her.

"I don't mind admitting that I was a bit tearful that first night in the dorm," said Frank, "and Bo chatting away in his Pidgin English was a comfort."

"You Europeans, you are all soft, Bo and I were more afraid of letting our parents down than worrying about being lonely," interrupted Emily. The two boys didn't know how miserable Emily had been in the girls' dormitory on her first few nights, but she had quickly become as popular with the girls as she was with the boys.

"Yeh, but as soon as I got my laptop out and discovered that Frank was a computer geek like myself I knew that we would both follow the same path and become good mates," said Bo, who had realized early in their relationship that hard work was going to be the cement that bound them together. As the only son of highly placed Chinese communist officials he knew that they were expecting a lot of him.

"Once we settled down we didn't want to leave and Bo and I loved sport, and that's where Emily came in, she always had incredible stamina."

"Yes I enjoyed running, tennis, swimming, and especially the school trips to hike in the hills, and if I made you boys mad you generally couldn't catch me."

Emily was dark-haired and petite and for the latter part of their ten years together she had developed into a very attractive young woman with shapely legs and an athletic body. Her Eurasian face turned many heads, but there was nothing of the voluptuous seductress about her. She was in fact Frank's second cousin, a fact that they didn't become aware of until they went to university in Manchester. She knew that her grandmother had gone from Manchester to be a Methodist missionary in China, and with the aid of her two computer-literate friends had constructed a family tree. She had discovered the three lines of descendants from Horace Latimer's three sons. One led to Frank who had been taken to Spain by his mother Margaret as a newborn baby, the second led to Thomas who had brought Bo into her life, and the third had led to Anthony Latimer, whose mother was Emily's grandmother's sister. She and her husband had died in a car crash when their son Tony was only twenty-one. No trace of Tony Latimer either marrying or dying could be found in the records available online. Frank's mother Margaret Latimer had married Thomas Latimer's thirty-two year old cousin William in 1978 when Thomas was only seventeen and they were aware of each other's existence, but they had never met until that first day at boarding school when they delivered their charges. In fact it took a few meetings at the school before they worked out their exact relationship after noticing that they both had the Latimer surname. Frank was tall, muscular and handsome with fair hair cut short, the opposite of Bo whose Asian features and slim runner's body were exotically attractive to European women.

"None of us have any brothers or sisters, Emily and I have only one parent, and Bo's parents rarely make it to England and send my

Uncle Thomas instead, so you could almost call us family," remarked Frank.

"Yeh, that was some coincidence, my parents wanted an English mentor to make sure I was OK when they were busy back home, and totally unknown to Frank's mum, they chose her deceased husband's cousin. He has ferried me back and forth from school to home when I was younger, and taken care of my every need since then."

"How come, how did he know your parents?" Emily wanted to know, "didn't you ever ask him?"

"Of course I did, but all he ever said was that he had business interests in China and had met my father, so when father mentioned that he was looking for somebody in England to look after me, he jumped at the chance hoping for a business advantage. My father is a communist party official so that makes sense, but I don't know exactly what he does as I have been here in England since I was eleven, apart from school holidays, and he hasn't seen fit to enlighten me other than by saying that I should learn to understand the Occidentals' business and computers."

"My mother said the same about Uncle Thomas and confirmed that his work with Bo was a surprise to her up until the first time that he turned up at school. Thomas is fifteen years younger than his cousin my dad, and moved in a different social circle and age group, so Mum was never close to him and didn't know all that much about him. So are we ready to go and have dinner with them? I don't suppose they will enlighten us any more tonight, but we three must keep in touch, right?" "Right" said Bo and Emily, and after a group hug they handed over their apartment keys and walked round to the Midland Hotel.

The dinner that evening was dominated by the older generation; having longer histories they were more inclined to tell their life stories to anyone who would listen, and the younger generation were a captive audience. Margaret Latimer had clearly been a beauty in her prime and it still showed in her symmetrical features and the stylish way she dressed, using every artifice to cover a body that had only slightly thickened as it must with age. She did not want to say much that evening as she knew that Frank had questions that she could only answer in private. Thomas Latimer at the age of forty-five was a Liberal Party Member of the European Parliament with a seat on its International Trade Committee. Having worked for a merchant bank facilitating loans and overseas trade, he considered his political activities as an extension of his business activities. It was whilst visiting China as an MEP that he had met Bo's father and recognized the business possibilities of acting as a mentor for the only son of a top communist official. He was intrigued by Emily's father Li Tang who was a Hong Kong Chinese. Prime Minister Thatcher had negotiated the return of Hong Kong to China upon the completion of its lease in 1997. The agreement was that the principle of one country, two systems would apply for another fifty years. Thomas by a series of questions established that Li was not an enthusiastic communist but would not say anything overly critical of Beijing. Li Tang's wife had died from an infectious disease when Emily was eleven. At the time he was busy as a civil servant working on the return of Hong Kong to Chinese rule, and had followed his wife's wishes for Emily to be educated in England. The youngsters mainly listened to the older generation at the start of the dinner, when nothing was said about the future, and little revealed about the past. To fill the growing void they took over the conversation after a while with the only subjects that they ever discussed, Politics, Culture, Sport, Sex, and Religion, what else do intelligent youngsters discuss?

The next morning, Frank accompanied his mother to her home in Spain. On the journey Frank questioned his mother Margaret about his family history and speculated regarding his future. Before he started at public school, he had suspected that his father had been involved in criminal activities, but he had never discussed it with his mother. He didn't doubt her mother's love for him as she was always supportive and had faithfully travelled to collect him for all school breaks. She was always there for school sports days, school plays, and parent/teacher meetings, but if it hadn't been for Bo and Emily he would have felt lonely in his first year at school. His mother deflected his questions once again, saying only that Keith, her business partner was coming from Manchester to join them at home in Spain tomorrow, and they would all discuss his future together.

Emily and Li Tang travelled to their home in Hong Kong overnight, and her future had already been planned between them.

Emily wanted to follow her mother's footsteps and become a journalist in Hong Kong, and Li had already made enquiries on her behalf. With her language skills and Li's connections Emily would not have much trouble getting the job that she wanted. Despite all the time that father and daughter had spent apart they felt close to one another and enjoyed an easy relationship. Li was looking forward to retirement and held the simple hope that Emily would get married and provide him with a couple of grandchildren.

Thomas Latimer's job as mentor to Bo Sung was over when he delivered Bo to Heathrow airport to catch his flight to Beijing. They had never acquired any special rapport between themselves, nor any animosities. Bo like most Chinese children had been taught to obey his parents so as not to dishonour the family, and as his father had appointed Thomas as his mentor, then so be it. They were grown men and with a handshake and a smile they managed to part company without any unnecessary fuss.

Sant Carles de la Rapita sits on the coast of Spain between Barcelona and Valencia, a fishing port known for its production of rice and salt. Frank Latimer's mother Margaret had bought a small ranch in the hills behind the town in 1986, complete with a hacienda and miniature bullring. With her husband William recently murdered and a young son Frank to look after, Margaret had turned to William's partner Keith to run the business whilst she retreated to a quiet out of the way sanctuary. The town had had one moment of notoriety in 1978 when a passing tanker truck loaded with propylene gas crashed and exploded just as it was passing a camp site. Many of the campers were wearing only swimwear and the fireball that rolled across the site killed and injured many of them. One hundred and fifty-seven campers died following a delayed emergency response, many from shock when subjected to long journeys to hospital after suffering extensive burns without any treatment before they arrived. No sign of the accident remained, apart from some gruesome photographs on the wall of a local hotel, when Margaret arrived. She retained a minority interest in the Manchester business and offered sanctuary in her hacienda to Keith and the other gang members when it was needed. The introduction of young cows to the bullring created many afternoons of hilarity. Although without horns and fairly light animals, the young cows would lower their heads and charge at any human who entered the ring, and with only a few bruises to show for their bravery, gang members could practise wielding the bull fighter's cape.

Now in September 2006 with Keith, Margaret, and Frank settled with drinks on the patio, Keith started the conversation by asking, "What are your plans now Frank?" Margaret quickly interrupted, "You don't need to become involved with us Frank, you have a good degree and can build a career for yourself in virtually any industry." Frank had anticipated his mother's position but had already made up his mind to follow in his father's footsteps. This was his childlike feeling that he ought to do or find out something that would mark his father's passing, at least in his own mind.

"I have guessed the basics of your business Keith, and I propose that you enlighten me regarding the detail. I will try and keep my participation at arm's length to satisfy mother's obvious concerns, but I will be glad to offer my opinion on any problems that you may encounter, should you think that I can help. I imagine that you have a money laundering problem, and I suggest that I help with that by starting a legitimate computer business for you to invest in. That business will have two separate divisions, one legitimate to give me a good recorded presence with the authorities, and the other which will assimilate your profits until they can be distributed as dividends. What do you think Keith?"

Keith hadn't expected such a purposeful answer from the young graduate but was pleased that Frank had already anticipated one of his problems. "That will be fine with me, but your share of the existing business will come out of Margaret's minority cut, and as the current business's profits will be funding your legitimate computer business, its ownership will be split fifty percent for you, as you supply the ideas and management, and fifty percent for the existing business which will supply the capital."

"I need sixty percent so that I have control and can reward employees with a share incentive scheme," replied Frank, and Keith nodded his acceptance.

Keith and Margaret exchanged glances, they were both surprised at Frank's decision and seeming confidence, which implied that he fully understood the nature of his father's enterprise. They were both pleased that embarrassing explanations had been avoided. Frank however was far from the confident decisive young man that his mother thought that she could see. He was in fact being guided by the compulsive emotions that the lack of a father when he was very young had generated in him. Now it was almost as though he was trying to recreate the sense of having a father that made him seek to have the same experiences that his father had. He didn't care that dealing in drugs was risky, although he intended to be extremely careful, he was just following an emotional need to fill the aching void that his father's absence had created.

Later that evening Frank did ask his mother for more details regarding his family's history and how she and Keith had arrived at this juncture in their lives. Margaret agreed but said that it was a very long story.

Chapter Four

1897 to 1960 Horace Latimer

Fergus Logie's genealogist had little difficulty in his search for beneficiaries. The estate would be divided equally between the living descendants of Anthony Latimer's whole blood aunts and uncles. Fergus had advised him of the Manchester childhood with father Warren Latimer, born in October 1918 and died an accidental death in October 1969, and mother Anne Latimer (nee Richards), born in August 1922 and died an accidental death in October 1969. Paternal grandfather Horace was born 1897 in Ancoats, an area of terraced houses surrounding the mill in which his parents laboured for long hours each week. Manchester city centre was only half a mile away, but may as well have been on the moon as far as young Horace was concerned. His childhood world was confined to the narrow streets and back alleys of Ancoats with the occasional corner pub or shop relieving the monotony of the rows of drab houses with outside toilets. The main attraction though for his gang of urchins was the canals. The Rochdale and the Ashton canals terminated just across Great Ancoats Street, the boundary of Horace's world, and despite parental warnings of a dreadful death by drowning, the youngsters could not resist playing between the canal banks. But childhood didn't last long around the turn of the nineteenth and twentieth centuries, and Horace was soon sent foraging for anything that could be traded in for cash with the local cotton waste dealers and scrap merchants. The Education Act of 1902 provided for government funds to be used to support and expand church schools as well as establishing secular secondary schools. Horace didn't much like attending school, but he received sufficient education to make him literate, and to his surprise, he found that he was numerate as well. What he and his mates called foraging could well be called stealing by the owners of the cotton waste and scrap, and he now used his newly learnt numeracy skills to add another illegal activity as a bookie's runner, to his list of nefarious jobs. It was not long before Horace came to the notice of the police and he was finally cornered with stolen property in his possession. It happened after he delayed to try and rescue a drowning cat from the Rochdale canal, and his distraction enabled the policeman's hand to get a firm grip on his collar. From that moment both his and the cat's fates were sealed. Cats were more popular than policemen in Ancoats, and the local bobby suffered a certain amount of abuse when the story was retold by Horace's mates. It was only the 1908 Children Act that prevented Horace from going to prison. Instead a spell in a Juvenile Remand Home from when he was twelve years old, toughened his outlook on life considerably, without reducing his fondness for cats. Good mousers, his parents had told him, cats helped reduce the number of vermin in the factory and the home. His parents were too busy to show much concern over Horace's incarceration in the remand home and in fact were more concerned by the loss of income from his illegal activities. Anyway, he would probably be better fed and hopefully trained for some useful occupation. Horace himself didn't expect much in the way of an emotional farewell but surprised and pleased his mother by embracing her.

The Remand Home instructors maintained discipline as they themselves had experienced it in the Army, some more harshly than others, some with sexual tensions to release, and some interested only in staying in employment. The boys responded to what they were experiencing, some more successfully than others. As a twelve year old Horace quickly worked out that he needed friends amongst the older boys aged up to fifteen. He had travelled a long way to south of the river Thames, and had been fascinated by the green countryside that he travelled through, but when Bert in the next bed greeted him he barely understood his cockney accent. After surrendering his clothes and suffering a shower and brusque medical examination, Horace was allocated a corner bed in the dormitory for twelve year olds. Bert was part of the same intake and was from London, or the smoke as he referred to it, and they quickly established that they had experienced similar lives until misfortune had brought them together. They stuck together so that any older boy who wished to exploit them was always confronted by two boys obviously willing to back each other up. That didn't save them from all the initiation ceremonies that the older boys inflicted on them because they too had been initiated themselves. One of the most painful had its origins in Sparta without them knowing about it. Running the gauntlet of knotted towels as they exited the showers was unavoidable, and reporting their suffering to the instructors would have brought more retribution down upon them. The weaker boys were subjected to sexual interference from older boys and occasionally a frustrated instructor, but Horace and Bert were able to avoid interference whilst experimenting on themselves in the same way that most youths discover the joys of masturbation, privately and occasionally mutually. Football was another saviour of Horace and Bert, as they both discovered that they had a natural affinity for the game, and selection for the under thirteens' team brought them status with their fellow inmates. Horace would rather not have been there but he was amassing life surviving abilities that his parents lacked. He was literate and numerate which allied with his natural wit allowed him to demonstrate intelligence sufficient for advancement in life, and his physical dexterity brought useful popularity.

The remand homes were established to train these anti-social youngsters for trades that would help them support themselves when they were released, and Horace was directed to attend the cooks' course, whilst Bert was directed to the comparatively new trade of mechanic. By happy chance both boys showed an aptitude for their trade, which was in fact to prove useful in later life. It proved possible for Horace to pocket the occasional piece of cake or biscuit baked as part of his training, and he was careful to share some of his bounty with the fifteen year olds' dormitory. He and Burt were still willing to take risks however, and they devised a plan to drop the older boys in trouble with the instructors. Having carefully reconnoitred a clandestine route out of their dormitory and into the kitchen, via a toilet window deliberately left open by Horace after his latest cooking class, he and Bert stole a whole iced fruit cake. They took it to the fifteen year olds' dormitory and enjoyed a late night feast with them to much acclaim. The authorities took the theft as a serious breach of discipline, and quickly discovered the crumbs of cake scattered around the older boys' dormitory, but no trace of crumbs around Horace's bed. The older boys took their punishment without ever suspecting that Horace and Bert had planned that they should. By the time that Horace moved into the fifteen year olds' dormitory Bert was his dedicated disciple and the pair had several other close mates. He was smart enough not to challenge the instructors directly but he and his gang exploited the younger boys as they themselves had been exploited. They could however exploit some of the more liberal minded instructors by bartering good behaviour and feigned interest in their lessons, for trips, treats or comics and magazines. Unfortunately there were no girls or women in the entire institution as they were the subject of the boys growing sexual interest and fantasies, which could only be satisfied by hand, as the strength of Horace's gang kept the paedophiles at bay.

By the time of his release Horace was a proficient cook but a Borstal Boy through and through. It was a term that had meaning, and those that survived and prospered on remand were considered hard men in the making and not to be messed with. Horace would accept the deferential looks when other boys were informed that he was a Borstal Boy, but he had no intention of becoming a hard man, he was too smart for that, instead he used his notoriety to attract girls so that his fantasies could at last become reality, or at least a practical exploration.

Back in his parents' rented terraced house Horace managed to hold on to an unskilled job in the mill alongside his parents, and from this position of comparative stability he was just starting to show a preference for one local girl when war was declared in 1914. Horace was one of the few who did not rush to volunteer to do his patriotic duty, but by the time that he was eighteen in May 1915 he was fed up with his job and the pressure to volunteer was building as the casualties mounted. Brenda swore to remain faithful and wait for her hero to return, but that is a lot to ask of a healthy young woman at the most exciting time in her life. Horace had finally made some of his fantasies come true with Brenda and they had been lucky to avoid a pregnancy. Most young couples find their first intimacies less than the perfection of their fantasies but Horace had made an effort to gather together some information from older men regarding human sexual responses, and after only a couple of practice runs he began to give, as well as take pleasure with Brenda. She gathered sufficient information from older women to understand that a man like Horace was worth waiting for.

Horace felt no need to rush straight into the firing line, and using his Borstal training as a cook he managed to get into the Catering Corps. The Catering Corps' job was to prepare and deliver food for all army units, including the men in the front line. Corporal Latimer was eventually injured by shell fragments and had then caught an infection in the field hospital. These powerful personal experiences and the sights and sounds of those whose sufferings were greater than his, were the unexpressed reason for the change that Brenda noticed in him upon his return on sick leave in the autumn of 1917.

The man that returned was not the fit young footballer she and his parents had sent off to war. Like all of humanity Horace's early life experiences were his primary influences, and had made him more cautious. He was blessed with native wit and retained considerable self-confidence, sufficient attributes to maintain ambition whilst dampening any tendency to take risks. With Brenda's encouragement Horace recovered sufficiently to return to the war and he was posted to a UK transit barracks on the south coast to help feed the constant flow of troops to and from France. At Christmas 1917 Brenda declared that she was pregnant with Horace's child, and as Horace's Father had died of TB the year before, Brenda was able to move into the rented terraced house with Horace's mother.

By the spring of 1918 sufficient savings had been accumulated for a modest wedding, and their son was born in August and named Warren. Horace decided to stay in the Army after the war ended in November as he had been promoted to Sergeant, and earned enough to support a wife and child. After a difficult birth with Warren, Brenda was thought to be infertile, but in 1928 she gave birth to their second son David. Horace was now based with the Manchester regiment in the barracks at Ashton, which was only a stone's throw from the family terraced home in Ancoats. A third son Brian was born in 1929 but it was too much for Brenda who died in childbirth. Horace was distraught, the marriage had been a good one despite, or because of, the frequent separations caused by his army postings. Brenda had rubbed along well with Horace's mother who now comforted her son and took over the care of his children. In-depth analysis of emotional strains was not in the family's nature, but the introduction of a kitten into the household did a lot to help them all.

By 1933 Horace had eighteen years' service with the army, and with the Manchester Regiment about to be posted to the West Indies, he was discharged with a small pension. He was to support his family through the Second World War with a succession of jobs as a cook. The proximity of Ancoats to the centre of Manchester proved to be invaluable regarding work, as Horace could walk across Great Ancoats Street into the heart of the financial district with its many restaurants and cafes for the managerial and clerical classes of the Banking, Insurance, and Trading industries. Horace's good army record and experience of mass catering saw him never short of employment. The Second World War found him feeding the dock workers of the Manchester Ship Canal, which provided reserved occupation status for all its employees, and saved him from a return to the army. A disadvantage of living close to the city centre was that it attracted the attention of the German bombers. Horace's terraced house survived despite not receiving an Anderson Shelter and he was in fact in greater danger at work as the docks were a prime target. Reconstruction after the war was slow in coming, and although Manchester was not the worst hit city in Britain, its citizens got used to navigating around by references to the bomb sites. Full employment for the next fifteen years kept Horace busy and his sons thriving.

Finally reconstruction included the destruction of the old terraced houses of Ancoats in the slum clearance program of the nineteen fifties and sixties. Horace would have been happy to stay where he was but his sons were eager for change. They watched the growing desert of brick dust spread around them until it was their turn for the family to be moved to corporation houses in the outlying Manchester suburb of Wythenshawe in 1960.

Following Brenda's death and until he was discharged from the army, Horace spent little time with his children. Warren was fifteen by the time his father was discharged and beyond being influenced by Horace. In fact Horace found his oldest son strangely bookish and undemonstrative, which pleased him in that his educational success relieved his father of much responsibility, but sadly deprived him of friendship with his son. At this time his younger sons were only four and five years old, and Horace was pleased to try and teach them the lessons that he had learnt during his life. The two boys were naturally competitive and Horace was happy to encourage this competition as he knew that it would prepare them for the struggles to come. David was handsome and sociable whilst Brian was moody but clever. Horace's father, dulled by a lifetime of hard work had little time or money for anything worse than disturbing the peace when under the influence of alcohol, but had encouraged Horace to take an advantage whenever he came across one, whether it was legal or not. Horace now taught his two youngest boys that, if they saw any advantage that they could gain from, then to refuse to take it would be stupid. In his own life he had successfully balanced the advantages that he had taken against the penalties to be faced if they were illegal. His judgement had been honed by the early experiences of his time as a Borstal Boy in the remand home, and his time at the front in the First World War. Having passed on the first part of his philosophy, Horace found it difficult to get his boys to understand the second part regarding the dangers inherent in the first part, and how to build up judgement based on experience to minimise those dangers. He watched helplessly as David and Brian grew independent and beyond his influence so that all he could do was love and support them as best he could whenever they got into trouble.

Chapter Five

1918 to 1969 Warren Latimer

Horace Latimer's first son Warren was born on the 15th August 1918 and spent his early years mainly with his mother in his grandmother's rented terraced house in Ancoats. They benefited from Horace's regular employment as a cook, at first during a long career in the army and then with various cafes and restaurants in central Manchester. Warren discovered at school that he was as numerate as his father was, but instead of becoming a bookie's runner like his father, he became articled at a company of Chartered Accountants when he passed the School Certificate at the age of sixteen. During his years of articled servitude, whilst gaining practical experience and passing examinations, he was partnered with qualified accountants and did all the boring checking of entries in the books of the companies being audited. Occasional relief came in the form of humour when miscreant clients tried to explain their misdemeanours.

Finally Warren's salary was increased a little and he began to enjoy the facilities of the Manchester YMCA on lower Mosley Street, with its sports facilities. The building included a swimming pool, gymnasium, and indoor running track, and he began to improve his now mature physical ability. He played for the YMCA football team and joined their rambling club which took advantage of the extensive railway network to access the Peak and Lake Districts. This broadened his social circle considerably as he was meeting other more ambitious lower middle class young men, and this caused Warren to raise his sights and aim higher in life.

Walking to the YMCA one dark autumn evening Warren noticed a young woman coming out of the Methodist church on Oldham Street. There was nobody about and she seemed nervous of his footsteps behind her.

"I'm sorry if I have alarmed you, perhaps you would feel safer if you let me accompany you," he said as he caught her up. She hadn't actually been alarmed, just curious.

"That's kind of you, I am going to Piccadilly to catch a bus home is that on your way?"

"Yes, I'm going to the YMCA on Mosley Street."

"Oh you're a young Christian?"

"Well, only a sporting one, my parents only used the church for Births, Marriages and Deaths, but I have been getting more interested since I joined the YMCA." This was in fact true as YMCA leaders had approached Warren and prayers were said in the club lounge each evening.

"If you are interested my Methodist Church at Birchfields would welcome any newcomer, and I could meet you and introduce you next Sunday if you would like to try it?" Warren was trying to get a look at this confident young woman as they walked along but it was difficult to assess her attractiveness in the poorly lit street, so he decided to take a chance.

"My name is Warren and I would like that, what time is the Sunday morning service?"

"I'm Anne, if you take a bus to the corner of Oxford Road and Dickenson Road by around ten o'clock I will wait there for half an hour until twenty past, and if you turn up I will show you the way to the church." They were now in the better lit and more crowded Piccadilly and Warren said that he would be there on Sunday and saw her onto a number forty-one bus.

"Will you be alright to get home now?" he asked, "Oh yes thank you, the conductors are very good they don't allow any trouble on the buses, and I hope to see you on Sunday." Warren wandered on down Portland Street thinking that the young lady had a cultured voice, and that women were one missing factor in his life. The office was all male and his mother had discouraged him from dating the mill girls who lived in Ancoats, even though she had been one herself. Of course he knew girls from school but studying had left him little time to mix with them. Maybe it was time for him to study religion and girls!

They met as arranged and Warren found that church attendance was relaxing, mainly because he did not listen to the sermons. Anne was neat and attractive and introduced Warren to her parents and some of her friends. He was invited to Sunday lunch with Anne's family next Sunday, which saved him from making the decision of whether or not to continue with his religious activities. The Methodists did mixed-sex rambling, an improvement on the all-male YMCA rambling, so Warren was able to continue seeing Anne every weekend throughout that summer. Their friendship changed to courtship when they realized that they had similar ambitions for home ownership and a family of two children. Anne, who worked as a secretary, realized that Warren had earned a professional qualification, and was likely to earn a steady salary. There was however a cloud on the horizon in the form of war. The situation was similar to Horace's at the start of the First World War and Warren spoke to his father.

"Just don't get her pregnant until you are married," was his advice, but Warren knew that Anne was not going to allow that to happen. He knew that Anne's religious belief was profound, as was the case for her whole family, and he was now quite happy to commit to full church membership himself, which involved baptism and confirmation in quick succession.

Warren's brothers David and Brian, born in 1928 and 1929 were ten years younger than himself, and Warren had little contact with them now that he was working. They were unlikely to be affected by the war and were uninterested in his activities. They had barely been polite on Anne's one visit to the family home in Ancoats. Horace however could see Anne's quality and lower middle class status and was delighted at the prospect of her being his daughter-in-law one day. Warren left for the Second World War as an engaged man with a clear understanding that he and Anne would marry as soon as they could save enough for the deposit on a house in the expanding suburbs of Manchester. The Pay Corps beckoned and despite being an athletic twenty-one year old, Warren survived the Second World War with nothing worse than a little discomfort.

After returning to the firm of Chartered Accountants that he had worked for before the war and saving hard for a deposit, Warren bought a semi-detached house on a mortgage in Fallowfield. He married Anne Richards in June 1947 at the Birchfields Methodist church. This move out of Ancoats into a relatively new suburb four miles south of the centre of Manchester, further isolated Warren from Horace and his two teenage brothers, which was what Anne wanted. Their only son Anthony was born on the 5th January 1949 and visits to his father were reduced to Birthdays and the occasional Bank Holiday. With the death of Anne's parents, father in 1947 and mother 1957, family connections were beginning to thin out. Even Anne's seven year older sister Joan had disappeared overseas. A Methodist missionary, Joan had been sent to China in 1936 and had been interned in 1941 by the Japanese when they invaded China. Anne had resumed communication with her by letter sometime after her release after the war but Joan indicated that she was not in good enough health to journey home for some time.

Warren was well thought of by his employers and decided to start his own firm of Chartered Accountants in 1960. He and Anne moved to a detached house in Didsbury and bought a new Morris Oxford series V saloon. Their status as middle class professionals was now rock solid, and son Anthony had passed his eleven plus and was attending Burnage High School. They continued their rambling in the Peak and Lake Districts and in North Wales, but as a family unit rather than with a club. The car, and its regular three year replacements, freed them from the railways which were in decline anyway. A tax deductible expense required for his business which was expanding into Cheshire, the car expanded their horizons but restricted their social contacts which were mainly with the congregation of their local Methodist church. This was contributing to Anthony's reserved nature as he was already questioning his parents' religious beliefs. He continued to do well in school, having inherited his father's and grandfather's numeracy skills, and eventually passed his School Certificate well enough to gain employment as a bank clerk. This gave his parents great satisfaction as they considered it a job for life. Little did they know that banking in Britain in the late fifties and early sixties was a comfortable cartel in which banks did not compete for customers or employees and all followed the same salary scale and employment conditions with women required to resign as soon as they decided to get married. Tony Latimer accepted all this as natural when he joined the bank at sixteen, but as he matured he came to question the values that the bank stood for and became convinced that more competition in industry was important for a democracy. As Warren had not been influenced very much by his father Horace, who had been mainly absent until he was fifteen, he thought it natural and right not to interfere in Tony's life more than was necessary. This friendly but detached relationship contributed to Tony's natural tendency to independence. Warren and Anne could not have imagined that their son was eventually to make a billion pound fortune, and in fact they did not live to see him leave the bank and take a job overseas with a US company, as they both died in a car accident in October 1969.

Chapter Six

1928 to 1996 David and Brian Latimer

Horace's two younger children David and Brian had no memory of their mother who had died as she gave birth to Brian when David was only one year old. Brought up in Ancoats by their grandmother and their father they were not much concerned with their elder brother Warren who disappeared into the army at the start of the Second World War when they were only ten and eleven years old. They were competitive siblings but completely different individuals, always fighting one another when young and arguing when older. Brian seemed to have the edge at school and was quick tempered and moody. David was more physical and more sociable, being handsome with fair wavy hair and blue eyes. Their father Horace was quite strict with them, feeling that he had not been at home enough to influence their older brother Warren, and having suffered military discipline himself, he let the two boys know that misdemeanours would be punished. Subsequent events could be construed as an example of how a parent's good intentions can have little effect on their offspring.

Like all boys they liked a challenge and as they made their way home one dark evening they had to cross a railway line by a road bridge. Beside the railway line just before it passed underneath the road, stood a railway signal tower. Atop the metal tower that rose above the level of the road bridge wall, a signal arm was electronically moved from a position pointing towards the ground, to a position parallel to the ground when a train was required to halt. Brian dared David to climb the metal steps attached to the tower until he stood on the highest metal platform besides the signal arm. Always up for a challenge, David climbed over the wooden fence separating the pavement from the railway embankment and slid down the grass slope to the foot of the signal tower. It was an easy climb up the tower, and a sense of disappointment that the task was so easy was setting in, when the stern voice of the local bicycle-mounted bobby said,

"Come down from there lad."

Brian had noticed the policeman's approach before he wickedly issued the challenge to David. Fortunately in those days beat policemen considered themselves part social worker and part law enforcer, and he simply admonished David. The policeman knew that these lads lived nearby and that their greatest fear was of being taken home by the law, which would embarrass their father and make him angry with them. Instead the policeman extracted a promise that they would never again trespass on railway property, or he would tell their father. It was a lesson for David and sharpened his rivalry with Brian, as he could not be sure whether or not Brian had known of the policeman's approach before issuing his challenge. He therefore delivered several blows on Brian as they completed their journey home. The incident did not increase their respect for the law, it only reinforced their respect for their father's temper. Unlike their brother Warren the two youngsters spent their early years exploring the canals of Ancoats just as their father had, but without indulging in his petty theft of cotton and metal waste, which was no longer so readily available.

David was good at football like his father and was soon attracting the attention of the young women of Ancoats, but it was an older nurse who seduced him and, like so many in those unenlightened days, marriage was the only option when she declared herself to be pregnant. He had been unable to resist intercourse with an attractive and willing woman in the comfort of her rented flat where they were free of the fear of discovery. They married in the summer of 1946 and their son William was born in November. Older brother Warren was already boarding with his future in-laws in order to save for a deposit on a house purchase in the suburbs, so David and Jill had moved in with Horace and Brian. After leaving school at fifteen David had worked as a casual labourer on the building sites, and now with his wife and child crowding the rented accommodation, he wished that he had taken his father's advice and joined the army once the war ended and the fighting was over. His pleasure was playing football for a good amateur club with expenses paid, and then retiring to the pub to drink plenty of beer. Marriage was a total shock and he started staying longer in the pub after matches and on the way home from work, to the distress of his wife Jill.

He was rescued by National Service which he became eligible for when he became eighteen years old in 1946. Horace was in favour of some military discipline for his son and realized that he and the house would get more attention from his daughter-in-law when David was away serving his country. David's reputation as a footballer meant that several military units were happy to have him in their team, and he ended up in an infantry unit stationed in Lancashire during three months of basic training. Despite his large consumption of beer, his youth and the outdoor physical activities on the building sites and football fields postponed the inevitable deterioration of his health until later in life. Basic training was not a physical problem for David, but the lectures were. Lectures were held to explain the workings of the weapons, the organization of the army, the dangers of venereal disease, and the facts of Military Law, under which any activity of the lower ranks not approved of by the officers could lead to a charge under section nineteen. Section nineteen stated that, 'Any conduct prejudice to the good order of military discipline is an offence.' On the occasion of David's first lecture he attended optimistically looking forward to a pleasant rest, but found like all the recruits, that after all day in the open air with plenty of exercise, he could not keep his eyes open. The first recruit to be caught asleep by the instructor was put on a charge under section nineteen. After that the struggle to stay awake was torture to them all, and lectures became periods to dread. The pay for National Servicemen was considerably less than for regulars who signed on for a three or twenty-two year contract. This was because, with the de-mobilization of so many servicemen conscripted for the duration of the Second World War, the services still required many recruits to help re-build and police The Empire and Germany. David resisted the temptation to sign on for the extra pay as he was still getting perks for playing for the battalion headquarters football team.

Brian was due to take his School Certificate in the summer of 1945, and Warren suggested to Horace that he should enter him for the Town Hall administration examination. As a chartered accountant Warren was aware that the bright but not brilliant could earn a good steady living as a town hall administrator, and Horace agreed. Brian passed both examinations and was able to walk from Ancoats to his new job in the Manchester Town Hall each day. To his great relief he failed his medical for National Service, his different-sized feet making it difficult to find a pair of boots that would fit both of his feet. With David away doing his national service Brian could relax and concentrate on his new job where he had to start at the bottom.

David arrived in a devastated West Germany in January 1947, having surviving basic training with an infantry regiment. He jokingly described himself as a trained killer, because if he wasn't, the King was wasting the seven shillings a day that he was paying him. Of that seven shillings a day, three went straight to his wife despatched directly by the Pay Corps, leaving David with little for his beer and fags. He was surprised by the extent of the damage to the German cities as he passed through Dortmund on his way to his barracks in Sauerland. With their heaps of broken masonry that still clogged the sides of the streets he reflected that Manchester had suffered some air raids, but nothing like the devastation in Dortmund. He quickly gained selection to the battalion football team, and the training offset most of the effect of his growing dependence upon alcohol, but he needed another source of income. The German people had suffered during and after the war, and for a while cigarettes had been a currency tradable for food and sex and other goods and services. The British soldiers could buy cartons of two hundred cigarettes each month at a subsidized price from the NAAFI (NavyArmyAirForceInstitute), and this gave them considerable purchasing power with a mark-up of three hundred percent when sold on the open German market. Of course it was illegal to sell the NAAFI cigarettes to the Germans, but that did not deter David Latimer. Playing for the Battalion football team against local amateur teams gave him contact with Germans and David was able to smuggle cigarette cartons out of the barracks in his football kit, but the number of cartons of cigarettes each British soldier was allowed to buy was limited, and the battalion police would probably remember to search the team's kit at some time soon. He used some of his small profit as bribes, and his general popularity as a star footballer to get himself the job of storekeeper in the HQ company stores. Now with a place to stash cigarettes he began to buy them from the other privates at only one hundred and fifty percent mark-up, which was sufficient for them as it was a transaction without risk. David could then take a one hundred and fifty percent mark-up on his investment on many more cartons than he was allowed to buy himself. Two problems remained, getting his stash out of barracks undetected, and selling them to a regular and safe German contact. Wilhelm was the goalkeeper for a local team and spoke enough English for them to arrange a meeting in a local bar, where David paid for the beer. David probed to get some background on Wilhelm and was pleased to find that he did not hold back on personal information, and invited David round to his nearby home where they could settle matters without being overheard. Wilhelm was an enterprising young man who had learnt to survive towards the end of the war and the difficult peace since then. He had a motor scooter and was familiar with the layout of David's barracks. David had to deliver stores to the Officers Mess which was a separate building outside the barracks, and they agreed a once a week meeting on the road between the barracks and Officers Mess for the handover of a minimum of ten cartons a week. This gave David a ten pound a week profit, which he decided to share with the Quartermaster Sergeant who was in overall charge of supplying the Officers Mess - a necessary insurance - and by increasing the supply they eventually settled into a steady eight pounds a week each which was more than the average weekly wage back in Britain. David was able to send extra money home to support his wife and child and Horace, but it also enabled him to drink more beer. There are weak beers and strong beers and Germany had a history of multiple small local breweries, which were able to resume production quickly once the war ended. Distribution was a problem for large breweries in the first few years after 1945, but the smaller breweries had small local markets that were easy to service. David quickly became a beer connoisseur after several times becoming a victim of the stronger brews.

Post war West Germany was a dangerous place, as the population struggled to feed and house themselves. In the British sector army law applied for the British soldiers as it would until May 1955, when sovereignty was returned to the German people on the tenth anniversary of their unconditional surrender. In the meantime the Germans struggled to establish their own law and order, as the allies assisted them in establishing a democratic government in the city of Bonn on the river Rhine. Despite the authorities' attempt to collect all weapons, there were still plenty in circulation. German soldiers who had been recently demobilised and had managed to keep their weapons, were only too willing to sell them to those who had a use for them. David was well aware of the dangers even before Wilhelm advised him to be careful. He was meeting customers outside the safety of the barracks and had either cigarettes or cash in his possession. He and the Quartermaster Sergeant varied the customer meeting places and the routes that they took there and back. They also invested in a pistol as they hated the idea of being deprived of their profits without a fight. When they were finally confronted by a young German, he too had invested in a gun and like the British soldiers was trained to use it. His mistake was to think that he would not have to use it, that the threat would be enough to relieve the British soldiers of their wealth. David had the weapon that they had purchased, and his skill as a football striker was based on his ability to remain calm and react whilst the other team's defenders were whirling and lunging all around him. Not sure how many attackers he now faced he reacted instantly the moment he saw the German's gun. He let his gun slide down his sleeve from where it was concealed into his hand, which allowed him to release the safety catch with a quick push with his thumb, and in one single motion he fired a single round into the German's chest. The Quartermaster Sergeant, despite or maybe because of his long service during the war, was stunned into inaction, allowing David to circle behind him whilst he established that there were no other accomplices. The German gunman expired silently, his body hidden by the vegetation that he fell into. He would not be seen until a passer-by got close to him. There was no need to touch him and there were no other accomplices or witnesses to the incident which took place near a cemetery. David ushered his shocked partner back to their barracks. On the way he disposed of the gun by pressing it into the soft earth in the corner of some waste land well away from the incident, after carefully cleaning it. David reassured the Sergeant that, 'So long as they kept silent nobody could connect them to the dead German, who by morning would probably be one of several bodies discovered by the local population, as was quite common in those immediate post war days.' David found that he was exhilarated by the excitement of that night's events, just as he felt whenever he scored a goal. He had shown nerve and bravery in the face of danger and felt empowered to greater things.

In the following weeks they heard nothing about any of the many deaths in Dortmund, although the battalion was paraded several times whilst female German citizen rape victims tried to identify their attackers. David and the Quartermaster Sergeant continued their trade until the end of 1948. Like all members of BOAR (British Army On the Rhine) David was allowed regular leave to visit his family in Ancoats, where his growing capital was much appreciated by his wife, child, and father, with anything left over banked with the branch of Martin's Bank on Great Ancoats Street. With large numbers of conscripts who had served during WW2 being released after the end of hostilities, David had been recruited under the same 1939 Act as those being released, and was uncertain regarding his length of service. He was saved by the Parliamentary extension of the National Service Act in 1948, which when effective from the first of January 1949, reduced eligibility to seventeen years of age and the maximum term of service to eighteen months, making him due for demobilization as soon as possible in 1949.

Brian was not afraid of hard work and applied himself to his job in the housing department of the Town Hall, passing the progressive civil service examinations to improve his grade. As he worked his way up the administrative ladder, introducing new tenants to their new home and making evictions of those who fell behind on their rent payments, he despaired at the misuse that some tenants made of their council house accommodation. Council housing had been introduced at the end of the nineteenth century but really took off between the first and second world wars. Intended for the lower ranks of society who would never be able to purchase a property, most of the first council estates were taken over by the more prosperous council workers, policemen, firemen, and teachers, who were quick to spot the advantage of living in rent controlled homes maintained by the council. The Town Hall housing department was happy with this arrangement as it resulted in quiet estates with well-maintained gardens and well behaved tenants. Now, in Brian's post-second world war period, the well behaved tenants were prospering and moving on to become house owners, and the lower ranks of society were taking their place as had been the intention in the first place. Dealing with the many unemployed and even criminal tenants made Brian's job more difficult and unpleasant until by the end of the nineteen fifties he was promoted to assistant manager in the city's housing department.

Brian had lived with Horace, Jill and William, whilst David was doing his National Service, and spent as little time at home as he could. At work Brian came into contact with businessmen in his position as assistant manager and envied their lifestyle. He learnt to control his temper and joined a tennis and snooker club to channel his competitive nature. Money had always been tight before his promotion despite his bachelor status, and he listened enviously to the business success stories of other club members. He was intent on finding a way to gain some capital advantage for himself and thereby improve his bragging rights against David who seemed to be doing well for himself. Although more cautious than David, Brian still remembered Horace's philosophy, that anyone who could see an advantage was a fool if he did not take the advantage whether it was legal or not.

On his return to the UK in May 1949 David had a three hundred pound balance in his bank account and fifty pounds in cash. At a time when a labourer was only paid about twelve pounds a week he had no desire to work for a living. Back in the local football team he knew everyone in Ancoats and attached himself to the local criminal element by offering to supply smuggled cut price cigarettes for their local street market sales teams. David was still in contact with Wilhelm who continued to supply him with NAAFI cigarettes via returning National Servicemen. At the same time he began to build up his own group of like-minded friends in order to market the smuggled cigarettes that he purchased in bulk on trips to France, paying truck drivers to take the risk of passing through customs with the contraband hidden in the goods that they were transporting. With his mates selling cartons of cigarettes to regular clients on the fringes of local markets David was able to concentrate on supply and storage problems. Cooperating with other criminals his group took part in lorry hijackings, to improve their supply and raise their standing in relation to other gangs and to reduce the risk of friction between them. David's personality and reputation along with his organizational skills, were a major factor in propelling him into leadership. He supported any of his gang who were nicked for their illegal activities, and despite occasional confiscations and greasing costs, David prospered. The 1950s was the last decade of rationing and full recovery from the ravages of war. Prime Minister Harold Macmillan declared that the citizens of Great Britain had "Never had it so good" and ushered in the colourful era of the Beatles, Miniskirts, Mini Cars, Free Love, and Credit via Hire Purchase to boost retail shopping. David was not going to change but he would adjust as he sought to take advantage of any changes in society.

Towards the end of the 1950s Brian was at the heart of the Manchester Corporation's policy of slum clearance which included most of Ancoats. Some of the cotton mills would survive although some of them only to house other activities. All the early nineteenth century terraced houses were to be reduced to rubble by the wrecking ball, including the home that the Latimer family had rented for almost a hundred years. New council housing was being built in Wythenshawe a suburb about eight miles south of the city centre, and those displaced by the slum clearance were being given priority to occupy them. Brian was very busy at work but was by this time a frustrated man. Clearly losing the battle with David for capital wealth, and by the lack of it, failing to improve his status at the tennis and snooker club enough to attract a wife. Corruption is a nasty word but Brian was desperate. The Housing Department Manager was not a well man and whilst hanging on for retirement he relied on Brian to implement the new policy of slum clearance. The department's female secretary was friendly and a willing worker, not just a coffee maker and typist, but keeping neat and accessible records that enabled her to prompt Brian regarding his decision making and meetings schedule. Jennifer was not unattractive and in her mid-twenties but Brian had not made any move to attract her. She was a member of the tennis club and quite a good player, selected for the club's team more often than not, but she too had made no attempt to attract Brian. What brought them together was their mutual desire for a higher standard of living.

It was Jennifer's job to open the mail and she took time to note the company name, managing director's name, and the main terms of each bid for the slum clearance contracts. She also answered the telephone and kept Brian informed of attempts to draw him into discussions regarding the possible suitability of a bid standing the maximum chance when presented to the Town Councillors. They both came to realized that they were both amenable to influencing decisions in the matter of the slum clearance in Ancoats and the new builds in Wythenshawe, and that they could trust each other to keep quiet about it. Brian was still very cautious, there would be no expensive meals or gifts from those seeking his help. Instead he was thorough. He carefully assessed which bids were most likely to be supported by the most councillors, and then worked out by how much a bid needed to be adjusted to ensure acceptance if it also carried his bosses' recommendation. The sickening Departmental Manager would certainly accept Brian's recommendations, but it was the price that would be the clinching factor.

Jennifer was entrusted with the task of telephoning from home to make appointments with the selected Managing Directors of the bidding companies at an address rented by Brian especially for this purpose. Those selected had already tried to establish contact with Brian at his club or through Jennifer on the office telephone, and were considered ready to pay cash for the information required. Before the meetings Brian made sure that the bids were realistic ones and the companies involved were capable of delivering on the contracts. Indeed that was part of his normal job, and the advice that he delivered at the meetings was by how much the bids needed to be reduced to ensure acceptance. These contractors all knew that these reductions could be recovered by subsequent requests for increases based on variations in the council's instructions regarding manpower or design changes. There were several contracts inviting bids, and with each one Brian demanded the same reward. Cash now to cover the risk of discovery and consequent loss of employment. If a bid was successful then the company concerned would sell him one property a year over the period of the contract at a knockdown price and supply tradesmen to refurbish them with only a small below-market cost. He would then be able to start his own property business. Brian made five such agreements and four were successful with their bids.

The cash bribes gave Brian a sense of achievement and allowed him to buy a modest motor car. He moved into the accommodation that he had rented, with only Jennifer at work aware of these changes. His excitement began to rise as he contemplated and prepared for starting his own property business. Unfortunately he could not boast of his achievements to David as they were illegal. He suspected that David's money came from illegal activities rather than football, but Brian resisted the temptation to boast to David or to anyone else, he was far too cautious and sensible to take that risk.

Clearly Jennifer had to share in the illegal profits and Brian gave her one third of the five cash payments that he had received from the five contractors. At the same time he started courting her and whilst neither of them were particularly romantic, they did fit together quite well, both being numerate, bookish, interested in their own social improvement, and quite good at tennis. To their own surprise they found that they were sexually compatible at their very first attempt. Probably because they were both well read on the subject and took care to prepare thoroughly for whatever task they faced. That was enough for Jennifer. She had taken the least risk, and Brian's clever method of payment for his corrupt help to contract bidders, in the form of property complete with added value, should see their financial and social status rising in the future. Brian was quite happy to settle for one woman, especially as she was providing one hundred percent sexual satisfaction for him. He had never relished the hunt for a wife and would be happy when that period of his life was over. In 1960 at the age of thirty-one Brian married Jennifer thereby solving the question as to how they would share the profits from the property business, and ensuring her loyalty regarding his secret corruption.

It also allowed Jennifer to leave her employment at the Manchester Town Hall to set up their new home without arousing any suspicions. Brian was promoted to Departmental Manager and recruited a new secretary, and one of his staff was promoted to his prior position of Assistant Manager of the Housing Department. With his former boss now retired Brian greatly reduced his workload and relied on his staff to run the department, whilst he attended all necessary meetings and signing off on his staff's recommendations. Brian needed more spare time as he was busy building up his property business in partnership with Jennifer, except for a short period of her pregnancy from just before until just after she gave birth to their son Thomas in 1961.

Brian and Jennifer had assisted four contractors with their building and demolition contract bids, contracts that lasted over an average period of four years each. They turned over sixteen houses in that period, receiving four a year. Brian paid the contractors half the market price for each property giving him legal title to them. The contractors supplied tradesmen to do up the run-down properties, charging their time to the contracts that Brian had helped them win. In his position as Housing Manager for Manchester City Council, Brian had no difficulty arranging mortgages for these purchases and had plenty of cash for deposits. The tradesmen supplied by the contractors quickly turned the run-down properties into habitable homes with added value. With Jennifer choosing the decor and the bathroom and kitchen suites, all purchased at trade prices and paid for by themselves, they could then work out whether it was best to sell on or rent out each property. The first two houses were quickly sold at a good profit as Brian needed the cash to maintain the mortgage payments and pay for the refurbishment costs of the subsequent properties. By the end of four years they had retained four rented-out properties, and by ploughing all profits back into mortgage payments, they had not yet incurred any capital gains tax. Now that the business was well established, Brian resigned from his position with the Manchester City Corporation, so that he could concentrate on purchasing more properties at auctions. With his good contacts in the building industry he could organize the tradesmen required for improvements, but now he had to pay them himself. Jennifer still enjoyed the creative business of selecting wallpapers, paints, bathroom and kitchen suites, and was very capable at project-managing the tradesmen. Brian took care of buying the properties at auction and the administration and tax returns for their business. Soon they opened an office and employed an accounts assistant/secretary and Brian began to believe that he was doing as well as, if not better than David. At last he could boast about his legitimate property business, but had to settle for Horace's expressing his satisfaction as David did not cross Brian's path very often these days.

The Latimer family had all been relocated to two council houses in Wythenshawe in the early 60's, Brian and his family in one and David's family and Horace into the other one next door. As they had been living in rented accommodation in Ancoats, which was demolished because of the council's slum clearance policy, they were top of the list for council house accommodation. Neither David nor Brian wished to advertise their growing wealth, and after furnishing the insides of their new council homes to their taste they were quite happy to occasionally sleep there and use the addresses for all official mail. They both had other luxurious private properties that their families lived in, and city centre offices to go to, so overcrowding was not a problem. Horace considered a council house a step up anyway and although suspicious of his boys' sources of income, he regretfully remembered that he had advised them to take any opportunity that they saw, whether it was legal or not. Anyway, if he said anything to them they would only tease him about being a Borstal Boy.

Horace with his cat looked after the two council houses on his own most of the time. David and Brian stayed the night occasionally and visited sometimes with their families. David's wife Jill was back working in the local hospital and Horace would sometimes look after his grandchildren, who were a great pleasure to him. David's son William was soon to leave school and looked like a professional footballer in the making. Thomas, Brian's son, was still a child and Horace sometimes had to collect him from the nursery that Brian paid for so that Jennifer could keep on working. David and Jill's marriage had survived his absences and drinking mainly because Jill liked to shop and David was a good provider. Jill chose to ignore David's young mistresses and David made sure that they never met. Horace, in his sixties now, liked a little exercise and enjoyed picking up Thomas and watching William play football in the local Wythenshawe Park. To all outward appearances the Latimer family looked like a working class family that had improved its fortunes since the end of the war. Only Warren, Horace's oldest son had made it into the lower middle class, and he invited Horace around for Sunday lunch only a couple of times each year. David and Brian took little interest in Warren and only saw him on rare family occasions.

David's son William knew that his father was making plenty of money, but he was kept happy with a steady supply of consumer goodies and his own car when he passed his driving test. Bolton to the north of Manchester was not all that far away from home, but he used his football apprenticeship there as an excuse to leave his family behind him and start looking for a life in the fast lane as a bachelor with his own flat. Only his mother stood in his way as she made a habit of turning up at his flat early on a weekday morning with her vacuum cleaner, determined to make sure that the flat and William were kept clean and tidy no matter how much it embarrassed him.

David had seen the growing potential of the outer suburbs of Manchester with their more prosperous residents and had gradually expanded his illegal activities to include the supply of drugs. His patch for the supply of illegal cigarettes was the South Western suburbs and Cheshire next door was the playground of the increasingly wealthy professional footballers. David made Cheshire part of his patch by a combination of inclusion and shows of strength. His reputation went before him, but he was careful not to have it tested. Negotiation followed by inclusion in his organization of some of the opposition, was usually sufficient to incorporate new territory under his control. It was apparent that seemingly reckless criminals responded well to organization and security of supply. With his addiction to alcohol David had now grown too old and unfit to play football, but for a while at least he resisted the use of recreational drugs. His son William had developed a real talent for football and was signed as an apprentice by Bolton Wanderers FC. He and Horace were vaguely aware of David's illegal activities but they were not at risk as David never kept contraband in their Wythenshawe council house, or in his home.

As he had done with his cigarettes business, David worked hard to establish his sources of supply on the continent of Europe, paying for each consignment to be delivered at an agreed place and time on an agreed date. To reduce his criminal risk, David used his two

Captains to alternate in taking delivery of each consignment on the continent and then arrange for mules to deliver the drugs to Manchester. David continuously arranged and paid for an ever changing series of storage places, one for each drug consignment purchased. His Captain's moment of greatest risk came when a mule delivered a consignment to him in Manchester. The possibility of a mule having been detected and turned informer by the authorities, could lead to the Captain's arrest. This would be the end of that consignment with the consequent loss of the investment. Further expense would then be incurred in order to support the arrested man and his family, which was David's policy. David's point of greatest risk came when taking delivery of a consignment from his Captains, and he took great care to control the location of the handover. He would choose a point where he could view the handover location from a safe distance. The Captain would have been instructed to leave the package in a receptacle and depart. David would only collect the package once he was satisfied that his Captain had not been followed. He trained his Captains to use the same methods for receiving consignments from his mules. Once the consignment was safely stored, its location would then be revealed to one of their many Lieutenants, who would then be responsible for distributing it amongst his street pushers in their area, for sale at the going retail price.

The pushers took the greatest risks and individually kept the largest percentage of sales, but only of their small portion of the total consignment's value. The Lieutenants took a smaller percentage of sales from the pushers but with several pushers each it was a greater portion of the total consignment's value. David received a larger percentage of each consignment's retail value from the Lieutenants, but he had to pay his Captains, the wholesale costs of the original purchase of the consignment, the occasional cost of the loss of a consignment, and other delivery, storage and administrative costs. He did however take the least risk. Word had got around that he had executed a German who had tried to rob him when he was doing his National Service, and his reputation helped him maintain discipline within his gang.

Brian and Jennifer's life was disrupted in the mid-1960s with the arrival of a blackmail demand. The blackmailer had gone to the trouble of cutting out the required letters from newspapers to compose the demand, but had addressed the envelope in his own hand. Jennifer recognized the writing as belonging to a former work colleague in the Housing Department, and because of another mistake by the blackmailer, Brian knew that he did not have much to worry about. The demand note correctly identified the four contractors who had benefited from Brian's information but also included the one contractor who had won a contract without Brian's assistance. This told Brian that the blackmailer was working on a general assumption and that he did not have any specific evidence. Brian had been very careful in his dealings with the contractors and was sure that the cash rewards that he had received were untraceable. The undervaluing of the properties that he had purchased from the contractors would not look very good in court, but was defendable as a rundown property's price was a matter of opinion.

Nevertheless Brian did not want the stench of corruption sticking to him if it could be avoided, and knowing of his brother's reputation as a killer, he decided to swallow his pride and consult David. David suggested that he kidnap the blackmailer's wife as a frightener, with her return unharmed being conditional on the blackmailer leaving the Greater Manchester area with all his family. Brian was afraid that some men might not value their wives' life that highly, but when David said, 'OK his kid then'. Brian protested that he would not like any kids on his conscience. They finally decided that a couple of David's Lieutenants would take the blackmailer to a quiet spot and convince him to abandon his plan whilst stuffing his demand note down his throat. David insisted that Brian reimburse his Lieutenants handsomely, once their work was effective, which in fact it was. The whole episode was a reminder that once you are committed to the wrong path in life, you can't turn back.

Strangely enough this incident brought the two brothers closer together. David had seen Brian move from a good job for life to a successful property business, and had wondered whether or not it had been a matter of just hard work and intelligent planning. He knew that his brother was more academically intelligent than himself and capable of devious competitive actions, but it was only when Brian

63

brought his blackmail problem to him that he knew for certain that Brian had chosen the illegal fork in the road. David was much further down that same road and the fact that Brian was following in his footsteps gave him a warm glow of companionship. Now they were in something together and that gave them both the confidence that they would back one another up in future. Brian felt that there was no longer the same need to compete with David, they were both doing well, and had passed the point where the question of who was doing the best mattered.

The oldest of the three Latimer brothers, Warren, died alongside his wife, when their car was involved in an accident on the M6 motorway in October 1969. Warren the accountant died with an unblemished record having served his country during the Second World War, having paid all his taxes due, and never having broken the law. He had kept his younger brothers at arm's length, partly because of his commitment to the Methodist faith and partly because he instinctively suspected that they were up to no good. He didn't know that they had taken the illegal path with their businesses but his life had been lived in a different location and on a different social level. The three brother's paths simply hadn't crossed or met in recent years.

Warren's father Horace, his two brothers and their families, all attended the funeral, but his wife Anne's parents and sister were all already dead and only a couple of cousins turned up. They were well outnumbered by Warren and Anne's church and work friends. At the reception after the service the Latimers found it difficult to find much to say to each other about Warren. They had sympathised with Warren's only son Anthony as soon as he telephoned the news of the crash and again when they arrived at the chapel attached to the crematorium. They didn't know any of the other mourners who were all from Warren's social circle and his Methodist Church, but they dutifully circulated, explaining their relationship to Warren when asked. Horace was in fact very distressed at the loss of his eldest child, although he had been mainly absent in the army during Warren's early years. He was not able to express his sorrow in public and restrained himself by muttering that, "He was a lovely lad," or, "They were a lovely couple," to anyone who accosted him or pressed food and drink upon him. He did observe that Tony was very composed and seemed to have everything under control. All offers of help were brushed away by Tony saying that he was sure that he could manage, and everyone assumed that he would continue in his job for life with the bank that employed him. Most women present advised him to find a good woman and get married, advice he was about to ignore. The funeral reception was the last time that the Latimer family ever saw their nephew Anthony, who quit the bank and went to work overseas in January 1970, before himself dying in a flying accident in December 2011.

David Latimer's luck ran out in the mid-seventies. He had not become careless and he had maintained his usual hard work ethic. Some weekday mornings, leaving father Horace to look after his rented council house, he drove away in his unostentatious family car, thereby maintaining the fiction that he was an employed clerical worker with his home address in Wythenshawe. His first stop was at his luxury detached home in Bramhall for breakfast with his wife. Jill had resumed her nursing career when the family had moved to Wythenshawe and now that their son William had moved out to follow his football career, she had started a Private Health Club/Spa as a way of laundering David's surplus earnings. They had long since settled into an open but understanding marriage, held together by shared secrets. With a full English breakfast inside him David took his Toyota Prius with tinted windows and went on his ceaseless round of business contacts to ensure the regular supply of raw material and its safe, to him, storage and distribution. By early afternoon David would call in at his gym club for a workout and shower, before going on to whichever one of his apartments his current favourite mistress was installed in. He always called ahead to indicate whether he required feeding or fucking, or both. Over the years he had had a variety of mistresses but they all had the same desire to find out more about him, and tried all sorts of questions disguised as conversation to extract details of his activities. He knew why of course; if they could find out details of his operations that could be a form of insurance for them once they fell out of favour. Consequently David was very careful not to take any documents with him and responded to inquisitive questions with banal replies. So long as he escorted them to a few nights out at clubs, the dog racing, or theatre shows, they were usually satisfied with their time in the sun living in a luxury apartment. Alternatively he would play golf and drink with friends who were unaware of his true occupation, before returning for a nightcap with Horace. This idyll came to a close when one of David's Lieutenants was caught by detectives in possession of a consignment of prohibited drugs that he had just collected from one of David's storage places. His capture was not a matter of luck, as the drug squad had had him in their sights for the past year. They had compiled a dossier of facts about his activities without arresting him until now, when he was subjected to a long grilling about his activities. They had cornered, surprised and confused him, with their detailed knowledge of him breaking the law on many occasions.

David guaranteed support for all his lieutenants if they were arrested, and this insurance extended to paying for legal representation to try and avoid conviction; financial support for their families if they were remanded or convicted; and financial support and re-employment if they wished it for themselves when they were released. Unfortunately the drugs squad already had David's name and knew that he was the main supplier of illegal drugs in the area. The police convinced the arrested lieutenant that he was going down for a long stretch based on their knowledge of his multiple dealings. Not only that, but they claimed that they would soon be able to arrest David, and thereby deprive him of any insurance offered by his boss. Faced with this onslaught the Lieutenant agreed to help with a sting operation against David and thereby gain leniency from the judge for himself. The police then allowed the Lieutenant to sell his consignment and collect the money from the pushers. They then invisibly marked the money and waited until it was passed on to David Latimer. They arrested David in possession of the marked money and he was sentenced to five years, but as a first time offender he could be out in three.

David's son William took over the running of his operation whilst David was in prison but the police had removed the traitorous Lieutenant and his family, so that retribution could not be inflicted upon them. David had time to think in prison and reached the conclusion that, now that he had previous form another arrest would incur a much longer sentence. He still controlled the gang's operating capital and instructed Jill to release it as and when the Captains required it; the profit from the last consignment being deposited to one of David's many accounts before the cost of the next purchase was released. Of course the police were going to make life more difficult for them now that David was a known convicted criminal, and he began to overhaul his security routines in his mind. One thing he decided on was to let William take his place except for the control of the money. William would do the purchasing on the continent and arrange each new storage for each new consignment. That would provide one more cut out between himself the Captains and the Lieutenants. David would then simply control the turnover of capital, and transfer that activity and his residence out of Manchester to another city where he was not so well known.

With David in prison Horace felt a little lonely and sometimes wondered what had become of his grandson Anthony. David's wife Jill was happy to invite him for Sunday dinner every now and then, partly in order to lure her son William back to the family home in Bramhall. William was coming to the end of his time as a professional footballer, and with his father in prison he was trying to gain some control of his father's business, and take care of his mother until David was released. Horace had always enjoyed his food but fortunately had never shirked his daily exercise. Once retired and relocated to Wythenshawe he had made a habit of visiting the large local park and some days enjoying its pitch and putt short golf course. On the way home he would sometimes pop into the betting shop and limit his losses by backing first or second favourites, as it gave him the chance of a good natter with the other pensioners. Once safely home he would cook something nice and easy, with enough for any visitor who might turn up. Money wasn't a problem as David paid for the house and old people find that they don't spend much money anyway. Without suffering any debilitating illness or anything worse than the occasional shortage of breath, Horace died of a heart attack at the age of seventy-nine in 1976. It's not possible to know if Horace suffered as he died when he was alone, but his grandson William found him the next day and saw nothing but contentment on his face with his cat watching over him.

Chapter Seven
1964 to 1996 William Latimer

David's son William was fifteen when his cousin Thomas was born in 1961 just after their families moved to Wythenshawe. By the time Thomas was fifteen his father Brian was a successful property developer and had moved his family several times into newly refurbished accommodations until finally settling in a detached house with grounds in Altrincham. William at thirty had enjoyed a good career as a professional footballer but with teams just below the top level. The two cousins attended grandfather Horace's funeral in 1976, as did his eldest living son David accompanied by a prison officer. Brian had a few words of sympathy and encouragement for his brother, but privately he felt a moment of triumph, of which he was a little ashamed. The brotherly competition had finished with Brian better off than David, and he decided that the funeral of their father should be the start of a process to distance his family from David's. They would occupy totally different positions in society from now on. Thomas was studying for his O-levels and whilst a little envious of William's success as a professional footballer, the fifteen year old could find little to say to the thirty year old. The brothers' wives Jill and Jennifer were both used to and capable of hard work, and would normally have had plenty to chat about, but David's situation made it awkward. The two families were to drift apart after the funeral and the baton was being passed to the next generation.

When he first left home and moved to Bolton in 1964 aged eighteen, William had his own bachelor pad, and he began to work his way into the first team squad. At first he was just on the bench but then he began to get his chances as a substitute and to impress the manager and the fans. His apprenticeship was over and the club gave him his first two year contract. The maximum wage for footballers had been cancelled in January 1961, and William was earning much more than the national average weekly wage. Like all young men with freedom and a good income he was intent on having a good time. Football managers and the fans would have liked their sporting heroes to be fit and free of booze and drugs, but with youth on their side and rigorous training programs to follow, professional footballers with spare cash in their pockets could get away with plenty of partying in those pre-premiership days. In a town like Bolton everyone knew the stars of the Wanderers team and sought their company, including lots of attractive young women. William favoured his father and was handsome and aggressive, ready to take chances both on and off the football pitch. He was a quite mature individual for his age, after being a popular leader of the pack at school due to being captain of the football team. At the training ground and in the dressing room he did not kowtow to the senior players, but he did listen to advice, especially from the manager. Whatever the pleasures of the flesh were that these young men enjoyed, nothing came close to the ecstasy of winning a match or scoring a goal.

Once freed from training for the day, William led the younger players to their favourite places of entertainment in the pubs, clubs, or restaurants, or to the racetracks, cinemas, or house parties. He controlled himself better than most of his companions, no drugs, not too much alcohol, and he was careful with the girls who flocked around the team. He gained sexual relief from hand or blow jobs from the young women who got their satisfaction from boasting to their friends about their close encounters with local footballers. Of course the club constantly warned of the dangers of unprotected sex, and William didn't want to get stuck with a promiscuous young woman intent on claiming intercourse with celebrities. No young man's first full sexual experience goes entirely smoothly, but William was lucky to meet an older unmarried woman teacher, when he and two other Bolton players visited her school to encourage young schoolboy footballers. Helen was an attractive and a confident professional woman of the kind who would make a strong head teacher in time. From the very first meeting they bounced laughter and chatter off each other and after a couple of dates Helen accepted William's invitation to his flat. She sensed his virginity and using considerable tact Helen allowed William to climax, and then set about teaching him how to satisfy her. For a few months satisfaction was mutual but neither of them was interested in marriage, and their work and social lives were incompatible.

They drifted apart, and William was finally struck by the sheer beauty of a successful fashion model. He was a regular choice in the first team by 1966 and on an impulse he proposed, and they were married that summer. Seemingly they were compatible, both earning plenty thanks to their natural talents, and both were required to travel a lot to various work locations, Unfortunately she did not have such a vigorous training programme to follow as William did, and his wife soon succumbed to the use of heroin. The pressure to remain slender and yet be sociable made it difficult for her to eat properly whilst William needed plenty of calories to keep him running. Her only answer was to use drugs to keep up with work and husband. William recognised his wife's problem and tried to be sympathetic, but the discovery that she was unfaithful whilst he was resisting temptations put before him when she was away, was too much for him. Childless, they were divorced in 1970 just as William's contract at Bolton was about to run out. Bolton Wanderers managed to transfer him to Stoke City FC where he was able to start afresh when he was only twenty-four.

William's transfer was from the second to the first division of the Football League and perked him up after his divorce. In the first division competition was even fiercer and tackles just that bit harder. Just as his career was picking up, a series of leg injuries resulted in his enforced retirement by 1973. It was hard for a fit young man to undergo operations and sit still whilst waiting for the wound to heal sufficiently to resume training. Once light training was resumed it was insufficient activity to satisfactorily replace the surge of adrenaline that came with competitive action. Twice he worked his way back into the team only to suffer further breakdowns each time. His demoralization was complete when he reluctantly returned to the family home in Bramhall.

With some savings and some insurance payments for his injury, William's enforced early retirement resulted in depression which inclined him to be idle. His mother was anxious for him to find respectable employment as a salesman or in the hospitality industry, but his father David came to his rescue with the offer of one of his flats for William to live in so that he could keep his cherished independence. The father recognized his son's nature as being similar to his own, and began to draw him into his illegal substances dealings. For someone with a good social position and regular income, it would seem extraordinarily foolish for a father to deliberately perpetuate his own moral turpitude by introducing his son to his own criminal activities. David however never even hesitated. He did not have his father's trade to fall back on, he did not have his older brother's religious belief, and he did not have his younger brother's social ambitions. What he did have was a determination to take advantage of any opportunity that presented itself to him, so that he could take what he believed to be his share. That is to have as much wealth as the wealthy and not have to work to make somebody else wealthy. So he went ahead, teaching William all that he knew to avoid arrest and handle conflict with competitors. William was a willing participant and fancied that he was more ambitious and aggressive than his father, although he was careful not to express these thoughts to his father. At the same time he was aware of the dangers and confident that the more cut outs there were between the pushers and the leader, the safer his position would be. This confidence was dented in 1975 when his father was convicted of supplying Class A drugs and sentenced to five years imprisonment.

William did not attend the trial, as agreed with his father, because the police were not yet aware of his involvement with David, and it was best to keep a low profile for as long as possible. David might not spend more than three years in prison as it was his first conviction. Whilst his father was in prison pondering the changes needed for his organization in order to make his position safer from prosecution, William was busy filling that new position between the Captains and David. He took control of the supply and storage prior to the distribution of the drugs to the Lieutenants. With his mother controlling the supply of capital and collecting the profits the Latimer family was still in charge.

David was released from prison in 1978 just in time to attend his son's second wedding. With his confidence restored William was ripe to try marriage once more and hopefully start a family. His second wife Margaret was a childless divorcee and still beautiful, but not in the same delicate way that his model first wife had been. Her pretty face was full of character and readily lit by an easy smile, beautiful enough for men to notice even before their eye was drawn to her attractive figure. She preferred to dress casually and she had the confidence to enjoy any company. William had not lost his good looks and they made a very attractive couple, well able to take their place in the Cheshire set. Margaret's parents had died recently and she did not have any siblings, so with no invitation sent to David's brother Brian and his family, the wedding was a quiet registry office affair. Margaret's family had been market traders and she was not averse to making a profit irrespective of the rules and regulations. She knew that William was complicit in the risky world of dealing in dangerous substances, and she was willing to support him in any way that she could, as her parents had taught her to support them. From an early age she had decided that she would be an entrepreneur in order to be financially independent, and planned to continue trading after she married William.

William had decided to leave his expansion ambitions until his father was released, and spent the three years that David was in prison running a steady operation. He did however take on board David's new security measures, and started to use a cut out between himself and his Captains. To avoid the risk of following his father into prison should the police turn one of his lieutenants against him, he recruited a Manager for purchasing and to control the storing of consignments of illicit goods. The Manager was chosen with care from outside the ranks of his gang and was an old football team-mate. Keith, whose football career had been less successful than William's, became in effect the gang's second-in-command, and used his considerable physique and a certain amount of guile, to keep David's business going as profitably as before. Father David was more than pleased with William's stewardship of the business whilst he was in prison, and as soon as he was released on probation, he kept his distance by settling in Chester with Jill. He happily recognized Margaret's suitability as a strong wife to support William, as Jill had supported him. Having enjoyed the wedding he did all that he could to see William and Margaret settled in a detached luxury home near Macclesfield. Satisfied with his new security measure, decided upon in prison, that the family should remove itself from Manchester, he took a back seat in the family business, advising and occasionally helping out and hoping for grandchildren.

William and Margaret wanted a family but it wasn't until 1985 that they were blessed with the birth of a son, whom they called Frank. In the meantime William had plenty of contacts in Cheshire where the ever wealthier professional footballers from the clubs in industrial Lancashire were settling. With his Wythenshawe patch well established, with Keith managing operations there under David's watchful eye, Cheshire was being supplied with drugs by several smaller gangs operating from the scattered townships in the area. Even though fit young footballers only occasionally indulged in social drug use, their hangers-on were much more frequent users. Careful as always William slowly built up his supplies and concealed storage facilities, sometimes incorporating smaller operations into his gang with their leaders as lieutenants. Sometimes he met with resistance and had to use his greater muscle to oppose intimidation. William preferred to use more capital to support a price war, rather than muscle, in order to displace the existing suppliers but retain their pushers. His main advantage though was his personal contacts with professional footballers and through them the wealthy Cheshire Set, with whom he established a personalized, and for them a virtually risk free delivery system. William took personally collected payments, either pre- or post-delivery, and sent a pusher to make a delivery as and when the client requested a supply. Only the pusher took the risk of being caught in possession, and these wealthy clients paid top price for this executive service, which provided the cream of William's profits. He continued to follow his father's practice of supporting his Lieutenants and their families and pushers whenever they were arrested. He and Keith were however much more in-your-face aggressive than David had been, but only when it was necessary. Keith wasn't married and enjoyed a good social life in Cheshire with its idle and bored trophy wives living in large mansions. He frequently offered to fix William up with an exciting sexual encounter, but William knew the value of his wife Margaret and was quite happy to turn Keith down and return home.

In the summer of 1985 David's family celebrated the birth of William's son Frank whilst discussing a growing problem. A young girl had been found dead from an overdose of heroin in an apartment

73

in the centre of Chester, and her body showed signs of physical abuse. She was the daughter of a Liverpool crime family whose patriarch despised those who earned their living by the criminal supply of drugs. Against his wishes some of his sons were involved in the supply and use of drugs. Distraught with grief at the death of the patriarch's granddaughter, the family set about looking for the pusher who had supplied her with the fatal overdose, and their task was made easier because she had become involved with the handsome Pakistani pusher who supplied her. He had grown up in a family with little respect for women and he had thought nothing of using physical violence on her whenever she irritated him. They had been seen out together in the clubs and those who knew them were intimidated into revealing all they knew about the couple. Unfortunately the Pakistani pusher was not a pusher, he was one of William's lieutenants. Such distinctions did not bother the Liverpool crime family and they were not inclined to leave punishment to the legal system, after all murder was not suspected, just the illegal supply of drugs leading to an accidental overdose. The patriarch himself attended the abduction, torture, and murder of the Pakistani lad in a quiet glade of Delamere forest, but they did not know that their victim was carrying a miniature tracking device. He had already expressed to William his fears that his girlfriend's family blamed him for her death and that they were intent on revenge. William had suggested the tracking device and his lieutenant had managed to switch it on as soon as the abduction commenced. William had immediately called Keith to drive him whilst he tracked his lieutenant's device with his mobile phone. They were both armed and when they realized that the transponder was stationary in the forest, they parked on the road and continued on foot.

They arrived too late and were unwelcome witnesses to murder. The Pakistani was already dead and lying on the ground. Surprised by the sudden appearance of two armed men the Liverpool family raised their weapons. What happened next was entirely instinctive, William fired first and did not hit any human being, but was himself hit by two bullets fired by the Liverpool gang. Keith was behind William when he went down and managed to take cover behind the nearest tree, whilst discharging several shots of his hand gun, which resulted in a leg injury to one of his opponents. He could see William only a few feet away where he expired quickly, and Keith could have avenged him by putting another bullet into the patriarch, who had not taken cover, but he knew that he was out-gunned. The patriarch of the Liverpool family kept cool and called out,

"Hold your fire. We know who you are and there should be no further unnecessary killing. The Pakistani got what he deserved, and one of my men is hit and one of you is dead. We will pay compensation to the family of your man as we started this business, and we will respect your right to continue your business operations in Cheshire and Manchester. If you leave now we will put your man's body to be found in Wythenshawe Park in a way that leaves no clues for the police. We will make the Pakistani's body disappear; I assume that it contains a tracking device that we will dispose of. If you agree withdraw through the trees now and drive home."

Keith did just that, there was no way he could help William any more. William's body was discovered the next day in a stolen car parked by Wythenshawe Park and the police made little progress with their investigation without the gun or even the bullet that had killed him. Part of the compensation for William's death was given to the Pakistani's widow, despite his unacceptable treatment of his girlfriend having disqualified him from the gang's normal support for a lieutenant in trouble. Keith felt that his punishment was excessive and his widow would be more inclined to keep quiet if she received some compensation. As de facto leader of the gang Keith explained to her that her husband was dead because of his involvement with another woman, and his body would not be found. The widow had also suffered from her husband's contempt for women, and fortunately realized that any complaints would place her in danger. She retired to Pakistan where her compensation would go so much further. Keith was a big, bluff, but pleasantly cheerful man who was at ease with women. Some women were attracted by his willingness to take risks but surprisingly trusted him. The shock of the gun battle however, gave him pause for reflection that William's life had been snuffed out so easily and quickly. Imperceptibly his experiences and the passage of time caused him to look what was on the other side of the fence before he jumped over it.

Margaret was left a widow in 1985 with a young son to take care of and, with her father-in-law dying in the same year, she was distraught and afraid. William's father David was only fifty-seven when he died of a massive heart attack following William's murder. It was more the result of his lifestyle than the shock of what had happened to William that caused his death. Without ever becoming an addict he had never stinted on alcohol and cigarettes, and unlike Grandfather Horace he was not one for exercise outside the bedrooms of his mistresses once his football career was over. Of course the nature of his business contributed constant stress and he was unfortunate to be alone when the heart attack struck. In these circumstances it was only natural that Margaret began to lean on Keith's broad shoulders.

Keith stepped up to the mark and showed real leadership qualities in taking over and reorganizing the gang. He organized the funerals which were sparsely attended, as no contact was made with Brian's family, and then he helped Margaret to retreat to Spain with her baby son Frank and mother-in-law Jill. The idea was David's last one, and was that Margaret would provide a safe place for the gang's rest and recreation in return for financial support. It would also allow Margaret to remain involved and help with communications, and with Jill's help, the money laundering.

Margaret was grateful for Keith's support and didn't want her son Frank to be entirely Spanish, so at eleven years of age in 1996 Frank was sent to boarding school in England. In Spain Frank spoke English at home as well as with the constant stream of visitors, but went to the local Spanish junior school where he became fluent in Spanish. He never knew his father and was told that he had died an accidental death whilst running his own business, so he reacted favourably when his mother and Keith became a couple.

Chapter Eight

1964 to 1996 Thomas Latimer

Thomas Latimer was clever and ambitious but knew nothing of his father Brian's corrupt activities in the Manchester post-war slum clearances. He was happy with the standard of living that had resulted from Brian using his ill-gotten gains to build a successful property business with the help of his mother Jennifer. Thomas had grown up in comfort in the family's detached house with grounds in Altrincham, which was in the catchment area of a very good school. As an only child both Brian and Jennifer spoilt their son but the only effect was to give him the confidence to speak up and behave in a manner that was ahead of his years. Brian's stories of his years working in the Manchester Town Hall created Thomas's first interest in politics. He realized that as a civil servant his father had not had any power then, only the frustration of watching it being wielded badly. Thomas was beginning to understand that the only way into power was through the political process.

He did well at school and took part in two mock school elections in 1974 and 1979, being the Liberal candidate in the latter election. He had no chance against the two major parties but was complimented on the quality of his speeches attacking them and proposing sensible alternative policies. Thomas did well at his O and A levels and was accepted by London University in 1979, where he took a Bachelor of Science course in Banking and International Finance. Following his growing interest in politics he joined the Liberal Party so that he could take part in the university debating society. The three year course included an extra placement year overseas, and Thomas was able to spend it in Hong Kong at the Chinese University, where he learnt to speak conversational Standard Chinese based on the Beijing dialect of Mandarin. Although Thomas arrived in Hong Kong with some prejudices regarding Asians and Communists he was too thoughtful to express them. As a result of his caution and his natural curiosity, he was able to make acquaintances and friendships that resulted in a greater understanding and admiration for the Chinese people.

Thomas's time at university saw him mature from a rather self-satisfied but not unsociable only child, into a mature young man confident in his own talents which included the ability to persuade others to co-operate and accept his guidance. He enjoyed sports provided they were accompanied by social interactions, and in fact he could have been better at tennis had not his love of conversation distracted him so much. It was the same with women, they loved the attention that he paid to them and were delighted to find a man so interested in discussing all matters that interested them, but felt that he was a bit distracted when it came to physical contact. Not that they doubted his heterosexual interest, it was just that his enthusiasm for debate continued just a shade too long.

Thomas graduated in 1983 and was employed by a merchant bank in their Manchester branch, a city with a long trading history with the Far East. From the Bank's office in Spring Gardens he was fortunate to be at the centre of a great city, and within walking distance of his grandfather's birth place in Ancoats. Horace had died when Thomas was fifteen but he was aware of some details of Horace's life, and had walked down beside the Rochdale canal in his lunch break to get some sense of what Horace's life had been like. Unfortunately the whole area had been completely changed by the slum clearances that his father Brian had taken advantage of. Fortunately Thomas knew nothing of his father's corrupt practices that had raised their status as a family. Back in his office he had a view down King Street but it did not affect his ability to concentrate, and he quickly assimilated the laws and practices of banking.

He continued his interest in politics by becoming an active election canvasser for the Liberal Party. Thomas felt that the power endowed on politicians by election could be the final link that could make a chain of economic manoeuvres possible, and he enjoyed debating which suited his ability to keep calm and always find a response to any argument. He was elected to the Manchester City Council as a Liberal Democrat Councillor for the East Didsbury District in 1988. The recent union of the Liberal Party and the Social Democratic Party had not affected Thomas's attitude to his chosen party as he had always found both the Conservative and the Socialist parties too dogmatic, and the middle ground was where he hoped to marry politics and business. Young for a councillor he concentrated on learning how power was exercised. His spread of contacts grew within the local leadership of the Liberal Democrats, and he was able to study the party structure from local cell through to annual party conference with its election of national officials. His life was very full and busy with work, politics, and social activities during his twenties.

Thomas's employer the Merchant Bank was grooming him to search for private equity investments in companies exporting to, or ordering manufactured goods from, China. Merchant Banks seek to provide capital to businesses that are seeking to expand or to take over competitors or suppliers. The bank can do this by lending to or investing funds in companies that seek to progress, whilst charging fees for providing the financial services involved. Thomas progressed from analysing companies to assisting senior staff as they managed agreed contracts with customers. The customers sometimes approached the bank with their business plans, but sometimes individual bank staff would recommend companies on the basis of their analysis. Thomas quickly gained a reputation as a creator of revenue for the bank, and his knowledge of Mandarin saw him specializing in businesses trading with the Far East. The reward for Merchant Bankers was based on the total profits that each individual brought in for the partnership, with a percentage of those profits being paid to the employee in the form of bonuses. Thomas was under this system accumulating considerable capital, and using his commercial knowledge to invest it for his further benefit. Still a bachelor his personal expenses were not that extravagant, although the amounts involved would have seemed like a fortune to any working family. Brian and Jennifer were themselves very comfortably off and very proud of Thomas as they enjoyed their retirement.

China switched to a market economy in the early 1990s and with Singapore and Hong Kong booming in support of the maturing economies of Japan and South Korea, the Far East was becoming the place for unlimited trading opportunity. Thomas's work took him back to Hong Kong and Beijing several times each year and he was able to build relationships with several Chinese contacts. As a politician he recognized the need for the help of communist politicians to authorize the clearance of goods for import or export and in the contracting of the Chinese manufacturing companies to produce the goods. It was part of Thomas's job to get to know the communist politicians and learn to deal with their bureaucrats.

Some of Thomas's Chinese political contacts were emphasizing their growing interest in access to the European Economic Community's massive consumer market. One way for Asian countries to get access to the European market was to set up manufacturing plants in one European country so that their products could be sold in all the other European countries without added duty. Thomas's expertise, knowledge and connections were in demand not only for bi-lateral trade between the UK and China, but now for tri-lateral trade between the UK, China and Europe. Thomas decided that it was now time for him to be elected as a Member of the European Parliament. He would retain his connection with the Merchant Bank but as a consultant rather than as an employee, and with their blessing he began his campaign for election in 1994.

European parliament elections have a notoriously low percentage turn out and very large electoral regions. Thomas first had to win selection by his party to be one of their candidates. His resolute campaigning for others in past elections, his many contacts within the party, and his recognized economic and management qualifications and experience all counted in his favour. European elections attract less media attention than general elections and walkabouts are less effective. Leaving the doorstep canvassing to his teams of volunteers, Thomas concentrated mainly on meetings arranged by local Liberal Democrat parties, at which he impressed with his command of economics and experience in trade and banking. He was elected as a Liberal Democratic Party MEP, one of eight from all parties for the North West region of the UK.

He now had access to the heart of Europe and soon gained a seat on the International Trade Committee of the European Parliament. His travel to China was now paid for by the European Union instead of by the Merchant Bank, and his time was divided between Brussels, China, and Cheshire. His social standing in the North West of England was very high and he was attracting the attentions of several eligible young ladies.

For a couple of years now Thomas had been pursuing a lady of high social status, and now in 1995 they were married in Chester. Susan was the daughter of a Cheshire landowner who was rich in assets but poor in cash. She had been sent to a private school and taken a degree in the History of Art at Oxford. Not a great beauty but she was tall slim and very elegant and was soon at the heart of Cheshire society. Susan ran her own interior decoration company and spent a lot of time searching antique shops and fairs in the UK and on the continent. She was as independent as Thomas and had met him when her father had invited Thomas to dinner to discuss EEC regulations regarding land management. Her mother had insisted that Susan attend the dinner to help her with the other guests. Susan had her own apartment in Chester and was quite happy to accept Thomas's invitations to the theatre, the cinema, to political meetings, or to play tennis. Susan found Thomas perfectly acceptable socially and was even physically attracted to him, but she didn't particularly want to be married or have children. She was very satisfied with her current life style and at twenty-eight was in no hurry to change. They had both had only a limited amount of sexual intercourse with other partners, which had not been very satisfying, so they were quite surprised to find that they were compatible in bed together. Susan's business activities were sufficient to meet all her basic monetary needs, but she realized that her social activity was partly due to assistance from her father, who would prefer her to rely on a husband for her extravagant lifestyle. Thomas had a substantial income and had accrued some capital from his work with the Merchant Bank. His social standing as a politician and businessman neatly complemented Susan's as a member of the minor landed aristocracy, and they both slowly came to realize that they could be a powerful married couple without losing much of their independence. They married when Thomas was thirty-four and Susan was thirty.

The wedding was a grand but stylish affair in the grounds of Susan's family's manor house. Thomas's guests included many political and business friends but only his mother and father as relations. Brian and Jennifer Latimer were delighted, their past was well hidden and their property business enabled them to contribute generously to the cost of the wedding, which as proud parents they insisted on. Brian however was not a well man having been diagnosed with, and being treated for, cancer. They were hugely proud of Thomas and he was delighted that they could mix with all the other guests as equals. Thomas took Susan to Hong Kong for their honeymoon, where he could demonstrate his mastery of Mandarin and his knowledge of Asian cuisine and customs. Susan was delighted with the shopping opportunities and purchased some stylish clothes for herself and lots of decorative items for her business. Her father could relax now that her husband had taken up the responsibility for her high maintenance lifestyle. The contented couple returned to the smart new town house that Thomas had bought in Chester.

Of the many contacts that Thomas had courted in China, the politician Wei Sung was one of the most fascinating. Thomas quite liked Wei whom he had known for several years now, from when he was on the party committee for a district of the city of Guangzhou in the province of Guangdong. His election was based on both his commitment to the party ideology and his education, which had been better than most as his father had trodden the same path before him in much tougher times. His father Bo was in his sixties now and still a senior official in the ministry of state security. Membership of the party and party committees were essential in order to be appointed to any public post, and Wei usually held positions that were influential in the promotion of production that the party introduced from 1986 under Deng. By 1996 China's production had quadrupled from the flat production graph of the post Second World War period. He was at the centre of the allocation of resources and permissions required to do business in Guangzhou but had recently started his own commercial enterprise.

Thomas didn't go around proclaiming that he and Wei were friends, and they didn't openly treat one another to lavish dinners in public restaurants, instead they met quietly in hotel lounges or Wei's office and did one another small favours. In January 1996 Wei Sung invited Thomas to his home and introduced him to his wife Shan and son Bo. They all three spoke some English and Thomas was almost fluent in Mandarin by now, so they had a pleasant dinner together in which Wei asked his son to speak only English. Thomas had his own opinion regarding the learning of foreign languages and proposed that,

"If Bo lapses into Mandarin whenever he can't find an English phrase, I will be able to give him the translation in English and that way, instead of limiting his conversation, he will be adding to his English vocabulary all the time." Wei and Bo agreed and the meal was a success. During the meal Wei mentioned that his wife Shan was an official in the ministry of state security and jokingly added that they had all better be careful what they said in front of her. Afterwards Wei took Thomas into his study and told him that these days he was concentrating more on his business enterprise than politics and that having his father and wife in the ministry of state security was a good safeguard against accusations of revisionism against the communist party's ideology. Wei explained to Thomas that he and Shan were of the same mind and anxious to send Bo to England to complete his education, believing that this would make him well trained to run their enterprises when he was older. Thomas realized how delicate this piece of information was and felt proud that he was being trusted with it. Only Wei knew how to negotiate the labyrinth of correct behaviour for a communist official, and the less said to the fewer people the better. Thomas indicated his willingness to help as a friend without reward, as he knew that discussing a fee would embarrass Wei. Wei for his part indicated that he would be able to assist Thomas with his consulting business in China on the same basis of friendship. Bo was called into the study and indicated his genuine willingness to comply with his father's wishes. On his return to England Thomas chose a boarding school in the Midlands without knowing that his cousin's widow had chosen the same school for his second cousin Frank Latimer. They would both start as eleven year olds in the autumn of 1996.

Thomas's father Brian died of cancer that summer and nobody from his Brother David's family even knew of his passing. Thomas had devoted as much time as he could to helping his mother care for his father since he had returned from his honeymoon, and watching his father die had been a distressing experience. It brought out all his own feelings about his own mortality and enabled him to convey his feelings of love and gratitude to his father. He revealed to him that he had taken a trip into Ancoats in search of Horace's background and that made Brian reveal more of his own life experiences, but he did not mention his corrupt involvement in the Manchester slum clearance business. Thomas worried about his mother's future but fortunately she was still quite active and well able to look after herself. The problem was that Susan had not had any time to form a relationship with Thomas's parents and being so independent it looked as though she did not have the inclination. She accompanied Thomas to the funeral and he resolved to have his mother over for dinner as often as possible.

Chapter Nine

1887 to 1996 from Helen Green to Emily Tang

Emily Tang had been as surprised as Frank when they discovered, some five years after they first became friends at boarding school, that they were in fact first cousins once removed. Now she wanted to know more about her family history. Her mother had died in 1996 just before she was sent to school in England, and her father Li Tang not had any real contacts with her Manchester relatives. She had however been in Manchester for the last three years and had learnt that her grandmother Joan had left Manchester in the 1930s as a Methodist Missionary, and the rest of her family story was in fact in China. Emily had discovered some relatives in Manchester but they knew little about her grandmother and even less about her mother. Strangely enough the suburb of Rusholme that her grandmother had left in the early 1930s now looked like a suburb of a city on the Indian sub-continent. It was mainly populated by Indian immigrants, something her grandmother could not have envisaged when she set sail for China over sixty years ago. There were some old letters and photographs that her father had and her two computer expert friends Frank and Bo had made sure that her computer skills were up to date for further research of her family tree. Her ambition now was to be a journalist in Asia, and that would give her the opportunity to finish her family research as she went along. On her return to Hong Kong with her father after their graduation dinner with Frank, his mother Margaret, Bo and Thomas in Manchester's Midland Hotel, she asked her father the question that troubled her most.

"Why did you never try to contact mother's relatives in Manchester once you had decided to send me to boarding school in England?"

"Because your mother asked me not to." replied Li; "As you know your mother was twenty-eight when she married me, and she was only fifty when she died of an infectious disease she caught whilst still on the Chinese mainland. She was deliberately vague about her work, but she had made me promise that if she married me she would always be allowed to work and keep her independence as is the custom in the West. She knew that in the East a wife is expected to obey her husband, but she didn't want to lose her freedom. I was a very progressive Hong Kong lawyer at that time, and trying to be as British as was possible because I admired Western ways. I went along with her wishes because I loved her and she made me very happy, and I hated the idea of having a subservient poorly educated Chinese wife. Before her last trip to China she told me her employer's employment conditions included the cost of boarding school in England for her children and we both agreed that was the best plan for you. She also told me that contacting any of her UK relatives could cause her, and possibly her employers', problems. I accepted these things because I knew that she did not want me to question her about them."

Emily was not much wiser for this answer to her question, other than it was all her mother's wishes.

"Well don't worry about it Dad, I enjoyed my time in England and an English education still gives me a great start here in Hong Kong."

Li was happy to hear Emily's words, but rather hoped that she would let sleeping dogs lie.

Rusholme was a quiet suburb about three miles south of the centre of Manchester when George Richards was born there not far from Birchfields Park in 1887. Three years later Helen Green was born only two streets away and they first met at the local Methodist Church's Sunday school. The class spanned several years of age with more than one teacher, and taught the children not only to worship a loving god, but to do so in straightforward ways that did not involve wasting money on ceremony. Their way to receive the protection of their god was to conduct their own lives in a manner that God would approve of, by being honest, hardworking, disciplined in their habits, obedient of the law, and by helping others who were less fortunate than themselves. Examples of other children less fortunate than themselves were always in evidence as Polio, TB, and other infections affected their classmates in those pre anti-biotic days. George was a believer and was determined to conduct his life in a manner that would bring him into God's favour, and Helen Green was one classmate to notice. Both their families were poor but hard working, sober, committed to socialism, and had a history in primitive Methodism, which had evolved into a strong religious belief, so the same values were in evidence at home as they were in church.

Not that the young were without joy or pleasure. Sport was encouraged and Manchester City FC's home ground was not far away. Education was valued and George's family made the sacrifices to enable him to get a good enough education to become a schoolteacher. Helen was trained as a dressmaker which enabled her to earn a small income after her marriage to George in 1912. It was Helen who made the decision as she came of age, that George was the man for her and the only way to get him was to be as good a Methodist as he was. She began to make her presence noticeable by her comments of support and her ready smile as she assisted him in his good deeds whenever she could. She knew that she could not attempt any fancy dressing up or make-up as George clearly expressed his opinion that simplicity of dress was best, but in fact she did not need any adornment as she had a handsome face and a healthy young body. George began to make it a habit to walk Helen home from whatever activity they had been engaged in, before continuing to his family's home. Eventually the question of a goodnight kiss arose, and after a bit of clumsy pecking Helen learnt to make her kiss meaningful. They married in Birchfields Methodist church and Helen gave birth to Joan in 1915 and Anne in 1922. George went on to become the Minister of the church that they were married in. The family's income was just sufficient and the two young daughters grew up in a happy home with religious belief at its heart.

Anne Richards the younger daughter of George and Helen, whilst a convinced Methodist Christian was easy going, pretty and enjoyed church rambling trips in the Pennines. It was on these trips by train that the church club's young men competed to sit next to her, and it was Warren Latimer who mostly won the tussle. Warren had grown up in Ancoats a poorer suburb of Manchester and had met Anne by accident. With similar ambitions they had become engaged before Warren served in the Pay Corps throughout the WW2.They were married in June 1947 and despite post-Second World War rationing, they manage to purchase a semi-detached house in Fallowfield, and start a family with the birth of Anthony Latimer in January 1949. They enjoyed a steady family life with Warren progressing as an accountant and Anne ensuring that he and Anthony were regular Methodist church attenders. They were able to run a car by the early sixties, and Anthony went straight from High School to employment in a bank. He was still in the bank when both his parents died in a car crash in October 1969. Anthony was left with a decent inheritance after selling the family home, and after quitting the bank, he set off to seek his fortune overseas.

George and Helen Richard's elder daughter Joan was seven years older than her sister Anne and much more serious by nature. Guided by her father she became an especially devout Christian who wished to save the world. She was attracted to The Methodist Missionary Society, which was formed in 1930 from the merger of several MM societies, and was in those days a separate organization from the Methodist Church, although of course it had their full support. The whole Methodist movement had been started in the nineteenth century by the Wesley family and temperance was an important value of the church. There were plenty of the sick and poor in England for Joan to minister to whilst she was trained by the MM society in London for several years. She was sad to leave her family in Rusholme but had her parents' blessing and encouragement, although her sister Anne was distressed at the prospect of missing her older sister and confidant.

Accommodation and food were provided with a small stipend which was sufficient for the trainee missionaries, as their time was taken up by providing social services for the needy. Joan's training was very practical and included, understanding the need for children to be protected from exploitation, nursing skills, alcohol and drug addiction treatments, and preventing the exploitation of females as prostitutes and domestic slaves. A thoroughly depressing kind of work that was relieved only by the conversion to the Protestant Religion in its Methodist form of those saved or protected. In fact the trainee missionaries' lives were lightened by their own cheerful companionship and good humour. Men and women together with no thoughts of marriage and with their sexual urges suppressed, they still managed occasional in-house feasts with their own kind of jokes, and earnest discussions as to how to make the world a better place.

Joan was posted to China in 1936 to assist at a mission station in the city of Guangzhou in the province of Guangdong. The journey by sea took several weeks on a freighter with accommodation for a few passengers. With little to do each day Joan was free to read the books that she had brought with her, having been advised that arriving at a mission station with several books would make her quite popular with the resident missionaries. To her surprise there was plenty of conversation with the other passengers, the manager of a company trading in China and his wife, a young salesman for a major UK manufacturer, and a Mr Benson with a military bearing but in civilian clothing, who indicated that he was a civil servant. Only Mr Benson had been to China before so their conversations were more of a general nature about the political and social positions of different nations. With Joan emphasizing moral and cultural attitudes, Mr Benson explaining the military possibilities, and the businessmen stating the case for international commerce. It was quite natural in those days for expatriate commercial representatives to express the racial superiority that their education as empire builders had prepared them for. Joan's education had emphasized that all God's children were equal of course, and she found herself defending the Chinese people as a race. To her surprise Mr Benson supported her position giving examples of the many fine intelligent and capable Chinese people that he had already met.

The central fact dominating their thoughts was that the Chinese province of Manchuria had been occupied by Japan since 1931. Mr Benson was careful to explore all possibilities without committing himself to any one end result. With Hitler already in power in Germany and allied with fascist Italy, they were seeking an agreement with Japan that would be known as the Axis. They were committed to opposing all communism, especially in Russia. China's communists were not yet in power in China but occupied certain parts of the country whilst the Republic of China controlled the rest of the country. If there was to be a war then Britain would rather have China freed from Japanese and communist occupation, whilst Germany was seeking living space in Eastern Europe, and the

Japanese would like the whole of China and all British and American controlled countries in the Far East. Behind all these manoeuvrings was the need for industrialized nations to control the supply of raw materials. Despite Mr Benson's contrived neutrality it was clear that he would prefer for China to be free of the attentions of Japan and the Chinese communists so that Britain could be the major exploiter of raw materials and trade in the whole area. Joan had been learning Mandarin from the moment that her posting to China was confirmed, and she was pleased to find that Mr Benson was already fluent in the language. He graciously agreed to help Joan with conversational practice in Mandarin and her voyage saw her arrive with a greater understanding of the political situation, and a useful language tool to help her understand the problems of the indigenous population. Of course communication in China was much more complicated than just learning to speak Mandarin. Chinese characters and Cantonese are only part of the many other methods of communication in China.

Joan arrived in Guangzhou in the autumn, as good a time of year as any, it was hot and humid but with less precipitation than the rest of the year. After a few days had passed since her parting from Mr Benson, she found herself reflecting on his influence upon her. At the age of twenty-one she had not experienced any feelings for the opposite sex and generally considered men to be more conceited but quite useful assistants in church activities. With Mr Benson she had felt something new but undefinable and it troubled her. Neither had said or done anything to suggest that their relationship was other than what was expected of them in their situation, and Joan did not even know if Mr Benson had formed a favourable impression of her. She found herself hoping so, but as they were unlikely to meet again, the only thing to do was put him out of her mind. Unfortunately that was the most difficult thing to do.

The resident staff at the mission station were kind and welcoming and eager to borrow any books that she had brought. Her work was of a nature that she had been trained to cope with, but it was the conditions in which she did her work that were entirely new to her. The sights and sounds all seemed to be as extreme as the weather. The Chinese people liked strong colours and strong talk and it seemed as though each speaker was trying to show that they were the most dominant personality by outshouting everyone else. In the streets the clamour, the colours, the varied design of each property, and the bustle of carts, bicycles, pedestrians and the occasional motor vehicle, all added to the heavy humid atmosphere. Fortunately Joan was good at sweating, which prevents the onset of prickly heat, a condition that irritates the skin of those who cannot perspire freely. The mission staff generally worked in pairs, seeking out the children who needed care and visiting their converts to offer assistance if it was needed, or to ask for their support and attendance on Sundays if they were prospering. Joan soon found her feet and was happy in her work with only an occasional thought for the welfare of Mr Benson.

Of all the children Joan helped in Guangzhou, Bo and Wei touched her heart the most. They were orphans in a strange city as their accents indicated that they came from further north. They didn't know or were unwilling to reveal how old they were although they knew their own names, but Joan thought that they were about five and three. Discovered sleeping on waste ground they readily followed Joan to the mission station as she fed them small pieces of sweetened bread every hundred yards or so. Once in the mission she cleaned them up, fed them properly and found a bedroom that they could use. The Chinese authorities were advised about their presence in the mission as was required, and over the next few days every effort was made to find the relatives responsible for these two boys. Bo was very protective of little Wei but would not or could not, add any information about relatives or how they came to be in Guangzhou. The local Chinese thought that the boys' accents indicated that they came from Shanghai. With nobody claiming them the local authority was happy to leave them in the care of the mission rather than waste its money on them.

For several months Joan acted as a mother to Bo and Wei and a sense of caring became mutual between them. She did her best to read to them and encourage informative play. It all came to an end when a man from Shanghai called Sung, claimed that Bo and Wei were the children of one of his relatives. The local authority made enquiries that confirmed that the boys had gone missing from Shanghai some months ago and instructed the mission to hand the two boys over to Sung.

Unknown to Joan, Mr Benson's main job in China was to promote the British Government's interests by warning the Chinese government of the intentions of the Empire of Japan. Japan's decades-long imperialistic policy had resulted in the invasion of Manchuria in 1931 and a series of incidents against China since then. Despite his best efforts the war that Benson had warned of started in July in 1937 before Joan had completed her first year in China. Fierce fighting saw the Japanese take Shanghai and by the end of the year Nanking. The Chinese resisted and with western help a stalemate was achieved but it left the country in a state of chaos. Both Japanese and Chinese generals acting as independent warlords along with several communist and local fiefdoms, took the place of the central government which had relocated to the north where it had little influence. Life in the mission station became difficult and married missionaries and their children were sent home. Independent Japanese generals occupied most of China's eastern seaboard including Guangzhou eventually, and they had little interest in the welfare of Chinese children.

Joan and several other European civilians were eventually interned in a Civilian Assembly Centre camp near Shanghai. Conditions in the camp were very basic and supplies intermittent, so with poor hygiene sickness became the internees' main problem. Joan, when not nursing the sick, tried to organize a committee to share supplies fairly, but those with possessions to bargain with, and some who had contacts outside, were reluctant to share. To her surprise Joan found that she had a contact outside the camp in the form of Mr Benson. He did not want to appear in the camp in case he was also interned, but was able to send some food and medical supplies in to Joan by a Chinese assistant. Of course this act of kindness stirred all Joan's strange feelings regarding him that she had so laboriously banished from her mind in the last couple of years. Not all the internees were selfish and some of the women helped Joan with the sick and some of the men worked on improving their accommodation. The camp was only loosely guarded as escape was into the even more dangerous environment occupied by warring armies.

In December 1941 the Japanese attacked Pearl Harbour, signalling Japan's entry into the Second World War allied with Germany and Italy, whilst China could now be openly assisted by Britain and America on a grander scale. This placed British and American citizens in even greater danger from the Japanese and conditions in the internment camp became even worse. Early in 1942 Joan was called over to nurse a badly injured British man who had just been dumped in the camp. He was barely conscious and had clearly been beaten and tortured. Tall and wearing the remains of a civilian suit Joan could only gently begin to clean his wounds. As she did so she finally recognized him, it was Mr Benson.

It was five years since Joan had felt the first stirrings of an unrecognized emotion as she and Mr Benson had voyaged together to China on a freight ship, and although it had taken some time, she had finally got him out of her mind. His recent kindness in supplying the CAC with food and medicines had reinstated those feelings, and now seeing him so badly injured those feelings came flooding back. She worked desperately to save him with the help of the Australian doctor in the hut designated as a hospital. They needed more antiseptic solution, bandages and clean water, but their main supplier was now lying unconscious in front of them. It was not clear whether or not Mr Benson had internal injuries but Joan work hard to prevent infections taking hold through his cuts and bruises. The big danger in the camp was from typhus and dysentery, especially for anyone who was already weakened by starvation or ill-treatment. Joan would not have been pleased to hear any suggestion that she did not treat all her patients equally, but even the Australian doctor noticed a special intensity when she was attending to Mr Benson.

John Lane had used the name John Benson only since given his current assignment. He was born in India where his father worked as a British official in the administration of the colony, and was sent to school in England from the age of eleven. With a keen intelligence and good at sport he set his heart on a career in the Army. His parents both died of an infectious disease before he finished his officer training at Sandhurst and the young subaltern joined the British Army. After several years of service in the middle and far-east and promotion to the rank of captain, John Lane was assigned to military intelligence and posted to Hong Kong in 1931. China in this period of its history was a place of utter confusion. Chiang Kai-shek's Central Government Army and Kuomintang, the Chinese Nationalist Party and National Revolutionary Army, had to contend with the Japanese Imperial Army, the Chinese Communist Party and Army, local Warlords and interventions by Foreign Powers which resulted in Shanghai becoming a demilitarised zone. Russia was interfering in the north of the country, Germany was trying to ally itself to Japan and Britain and America were trying to stop Japanese Imperialistic expansion. John's brief was to inform the British government of Japanese intentions, and their actual progress following their invasion of the eastern seaboard of China. He was also to facilitate the delivery of arms and supplies to Chiang Kai-shek, Britain's preferred ruler of China.

John had some discreet support from British embassies in the region but operated in civilian clothing and under the assumed name of John Benson as stated on his secret service passport. It was a stressful occupation and required a lot of travel around China, for which it was essential to know which faction was in charge of whichever area that he was traveling through. In such a confused governmental situation it is often the local criminal leaders who are best informed regarding the up to date situation, as they operate on a practical basis, and communicate with their criminal equivalents in each region as a matter of necessity to avoid conflict. John needed the help of these criminal bosses and made it his business to do them some favours. Arms and drugs were the main currencies during these troubled times, and they were imported from all directions with those facilitating their passage taking a good profit. With the intelligence that John Benson gathered he was in a position not only to satisfy his British masters, but to direct the suppliers of arms and drugs to the most lucrative markets via the safest routes available, thereby satisfying Ling Sung and his criminal associates. Ling Sung did not have any political allegiance, but his wife did as she was a dedicated communist. She wished to maintain contact with Mao Tse-tung's forces in Yan'an, and in the north of China. John agreed that Sung's wife could accompany him on some of his journeys and at other times he carried messages for her. In return he got protection from Sung's men and associates, and credit with the communists who were at that time co-operating with the Kuomintang and the British to oust the Japanese Imperial Army. John's luck ran out in 1942 when he returned to Shanghai just after the Japanese had suffered a reverse caused by the effective attacks of the Chinese Kuomintang Army, who had recently been re-supplied by the British and Americans. Nervous after Pearl Harbour and the declaration of war on Japan by America and Britain, the Japanese were keen to round up all remaining British and American citizens to prevent them from spying, and John Benson's travel record created great suspicion. They had no evidence against him but resorted to the age old method of trying to beat a confession out of him. When this failed they dumped him in the CAC where they expected him to die.

Ling Sung knew that his British business associate John Benson was in trouble, and he and his wife had come to regard John as a friend thanks to many occasions of mutual assistance. He therefore sent his two young servants Bo and Wei to search the CAC for him. They were the same Bo and Wei orphans that Joan Richards had discovered starving in Guangzhou in 1937. Ling Sung had eventually claimed them as relatives when in fact he knew that their parents were dead because he had killed them for stealing drug profits from him. He didn't know whether or not the oldest boy Bo knew about the murder, but certainly Wei was happily ignorant of the fact. Bo had in fact taken his brother and run away from Shanghai on a coastal vessel with the aid of his father's brother, but Sung had sent an assassin to kill their uncle for the same crime of drug theft. The boys had been ashore looking for food when the assassin had killed their father's brother and on seeing his body on their return, they had fearfully hidden themselves away on some waste ground, where Joan had found them starving.

When Ling Sung had claimed them back after they had enjoyed several months of loving care from Joan, they were terrified, but Sung simply kept them as servants/slaves trained to do his bidding on fear of death if they refused or failed. They were fed, clothed, and securely housed, but saw most of life's depravities whilst with Ling Sung. Bo had been impressed by Joan's Christianity whilst being too young to comprehend the whole idea of a church, and Wei was just now beginning to pick up on Sung's wife's communism, but they had little time for anything but obedience and day to day survival. They had observed Mr Benson on his visits and had little difficulty making their way into the CAC and locating the first aid hut. Joan recognized them immediately when they discovered her at Mr Benson's bedside, and she joyfully hugged them. They were surprised and unsure how to express their own emotions. They remembered Joan with gratitude for saving them from starvation and for her caring attitude, but with disappointment that she had let Sung take them away. Now Bo simply explained to Joan that Mr Benson had a friend outside the CAC who wanted to help him. Her prayers were answered and she quickly gave the boys a list of everything that she required. Gradually Joan's efforts were rewarded and John Benson slowly recovered if not to the full vigour that he had displayed on his voyage to China when they had first met, but to a point where he could look after himself.

The poor food, primitive accommodation and hard work in the CAC took their toll on Joan and by the time of her release in 1945 she was in a poor condition. It was only when they were safely in Hong Kong that Mr Benson became John Lane again and was issued with a passport in that name. Whilst they were together in the CAC for two years John carried a passport with the surname Benson, and to have even hinted that this was not his true identity would have put him in great danger of being arrested as the spy that he was. Any camp resident would have been happy to trade such knowledge for extra supplies by informing the Japanese. Once in Hong Kong John was able to tell Joan that his family name was Lane and that he had been working to get the Japanese out of China. Joan was not in any way troubled by this revelation as she had long since sorted out her strange feelings whenever she had thought about him. She decided that in the absence of any comparable feeling it must be love, although she did not rush to express this opinion. John re-established contact with his branch of the intelligence service and they de-briefed him and put him in his own flat in Hong Kong as his contacts in China were still a valuable asset, and they told him to rest and try and build up his strength for a return to work. Joan's Methodist Missionary Society decided that she was not well enough for a long sea voyage back to England and told her to recuperate in Hong Kong. Within a month of their release Joan gladly accepted John's marriage proposal and they were able to live together in his government-provided flat.

The head of the Methodist Mission decided to keep her in Hong Kong as the mainland was now in the throes of a civil war which was eventually won by Mao's communist party in 1949. There was plenty of work for her to do in Hong Kong but she soon became pregnant and gave birth to a daughter Florence in 1946. Joan still communicated by post with her family in Manchester who had all feared that she was dead until her first letter arrived after the war. She still did not feel well enough for the long voyage home when her father died of a stroke in 1946 just before she gave birth to Florence. Joan's sister Anne was still there to take care of her mother and kept up a steady correspondence whilst the Lane family struggled with ill health and bringing up their daughter. Joan continued to work at the Methodist mission station in Hong Kong and nursed John who was still advising the government regarding developments in China. John finally succumbed to the cumulative effect of his mistreatment by the Japanese and the deprivation of several years in the CAC when he died in 1957. His parents had died in India before the war and there were no siblings to attend his funeral. Joan had no sooner suffered the loss of her much loved husband than news arrived from her sister Anne that her mother had passed away in the same year. She struggled on bringing up Florence and tending to her Chinese converts until 1967 when she too succumbed to the hardships that she had suffered in the CAC.

Florence was just twenty-one when she became an orphan after dutifully nursing her parents through their years of ill health. Joan and John had put her education first and she was a natural linguist, but Florence was always willing to help with the housework and nursing duties when she returned home. Her mother's demise in 1967 made her an orphan and coincided with her graduation from The University of Hong Kong. This gave her the freedom to concentrate on her own future and she started work as a journalist with a Hong Kong English language newspaper. She soon found that because of her parent's contacts at the Methodist mission station and with the government, she was able to get visas to travel in China itself. It was however the time of the Cultural Revolution in China and there was much danger of being labelled a counter revolutionary. Fortunately Florence had absorbed her mother's strong socialist background which gave her credibility with the Hong Kong communists, and without joining the party she was accepted in their company.

After a few years learning the office routines her Hong Kong paper promoted her to reporter, and her reports began to be printed in both English and Chinese language newspapers. The British intelligence service MI6 had been keeping an eye on this daughter of their former agent John Lane and when she started making trips into China the time had come to recruit her. MI6 was short of information regarding the Cultural Revolution and they were not sure how to react to it. They needed to know which communist official retained enough power to be contacted in the event that there was a crisis, or when sensible discussion was required to solve day to day problems. Florence was intelligent and adventurous with her mother's naturally slim figure and her father's blond hair and handsome features. Amongst the Asian peoples she was very attractive and noticeable, not exactly how a secret agent should look. During her childhood she had spent many hours with her father, listening to his tales of travelling all over war torn China, and she did not for a minute consider refusing the approach from MI6. Of course she had to be trained as an agent, and this was arranged by her attending a course in London. As cover for her work colleagues and friends were told that it was a post graduate course in journalism. She already spoke more than one Chinese language and some of their dialects, along with the Japanese, Portuguese and English languages. She was a fit young woman who enjoyed swimming sailing and tennis but it was not envisaged that she would be sent on any clandestine operations, merely that she would be a conduit for information. Nevertheless she went through the self-defence training but the main emphasis of her course was on communications concealment.

She returned to work without trying to contact any of her relations in the UK partly because there was little spare time and partly because MI6 considered it unsafe to do so. Now she was to seek assignments in China and make as many contacts with officials as she could, in order to relate the moods of the people and await specific instructions from MI6. The Chinese Cultural Revolution continued for a good ten years until 1976 during which time Florence received and passed on several communications from and to agents in China. Her social life in Hong Kong was as full and exciting as would be expected for such an attractive young woman and in 1974 she married the Hong Kong Cantonese lawyer Li Tang, but they both carried on working and it was not until 1985 that their daughter Emily was born.

Emily's birth was delayed because Florence was eventually detained as a suspected foreign capitalist spy in 1978. The Beijing Spring was a period in 1977/8 when the Chinese were allowed greater freedom to criticize the government via the Democracy Wall Movement which was a reaction against the Chinese Cultural Revolution. Florence had been making regular trips to China for several years and returning with interesting stories for publication in the newspaper that she worked for. She visited Guangzhou and Shanghai several times and made contact with several Chinese who had known her parents, including a communist official Bo Sung. This was the same Bo who had been discovered with his brother Wei starving and sleeping rough by Florence's mother Joan in 1936.

After helping Joan and John Benson by smuggling medicines and food into the Civilian assembly Camp until the end of WW2 in August 1945, Bo and his brother Wei had fled from their enslavement by the Shanghai criminal gang leader Ling Sung, and joined Mao Tse-Tung's communist forces. The two brothers had several conversations with John Benson before they fled. They knew something of his spying activities and approved of them because his overall strategy was to get rid of the Japanese. Both brothers despised their master and wished to have revenge because they knew that he had murdered their parents. Joan's Christian socialist philosophy appealed to them and communism seemed to be the nearest thing available to them. Bo would have liked to explore Joan's Christian ideals more, but Wei was satisfied with the harsher disciplines of the communist ideology. John Benson owed the brothers his life and advised them of the best route to take to join the communist army in the north and gave them the names of some contacts who would help them on their journey. They were successful and in time to fight for Mao in the Chinese Civil War from 1946 to victory in 1949. But Bo was heartbroken when the little brother that he had protected from the

99

age of three was killed in a battle during the Huaihai campaign in late 1948. Bo was there to suffer the sight of his fallen brother and collapse emotionally at his loss. For a while Bo was careless of his own safety, almost wishing to die and join Wei, but gradually he learnt to live with the pain of his loss.

Still only eighteen in 1949 Bo's reputation as a fighter for the revolution got him an official appointment in Shanghai where he learnt how to progress from local to district committee whilst enforcing the laws and rules as set by the communist party leadership. Now was the time to avenge himself against the criminal gang leader Ling Sung who had murdered his parents, and at the same time enhance his reputation as an incorruptible official of the communist party fighting against crime. He knew all about Ling Sung's operation as he had worked at the heart of it himself. Bo recruited an informer who still worked for Sung and with the carrot of protection by, and work for the party, obtained the time and place of a drug drop that would be attended by Sung. Leading a police section Bo was happy to confront his old boss in possession of the drugs, and ensure him that the party would be executing him with a bullet in the back of his head as soon as he was convicted. Bo had worried that Ling's wife would be at the scene of the crime, as she at least had fed and clothed the two brothers and awakened their interest in communism. She was not there and there was no sign of her in Shanghai, so Bo assumed that she had fled from her cruel husband, or been killed by him.

With that matter settled Bo, who was still saddled with the family name of Sung, married in 1950 when he was only nineteen, the daughter of a veteran communist who had survived the long march, which of course brought Bo closer to the centre of power. The happy couple were not blessed with a child until 1960 when Bo named his newly born son Wei after his heroic uncle who died fighting for the communist cause.

Life in China was turned upside down by the Cultural Revolution from 1966 to 1976 but Bo's revolutionary background and his wife's family connections, combined with his modest life style and reputation for being incorruptible saved him from persecution by the Red Guards. During this period he met Florence and realized that she was Joan's daughter. He did take one private opportunity to express to her his gratitude to her mother, but knew that contact with foreigners was not approved of in this period and kept his distance from her after that.

Florence was briefed by MI6 on a more than usually difficult assignment. It was spring 1978 and the Chinese government was allowing some criticism by its citizens. Florence's handler explained that her father had recruited a Chinese communist official as an agent during WW2, and MI6 had been paying him and receiving information from him ever since. Unfortunately this official had been purged as a revisionist by the Red Guard during the Cultural Revolution. He had been labouring on a farm in the north of China but had recently been rehabilitated, and now wanted to leave China and be reunited with his savings in the UK. Florence was to deliver cash, travel documents, and verbal details of his route and the contacts who would help extract him.

She travelled to Shanghai to cover the story of the protest walls that were springing up in China and then made her way to the live drop meeting with the agent to be extracted. This was riskier than her usual dead drop assignments, but this agent had been out of contact for a long time and was not familiar with any of the current dead drop letterboxes. In fact he had already traded in his ability to lure a British spy into the hands of the communist government in order to get himself rehabilitated from hard labour on the farm, and to rejoin his family in Shanghai. He was waiting at the appointed meeting place but so were the state security officers who arrested Florence and confined her in a cell in Shanghai's main interrogation centre.

Bo, now forty-seven years old and higher up the chain of communist control by committee, knew the Chinese agent Song, whom Florence had been sent by MI6 to meet. John Benson had recruited him in the days when the British were allies of China and helping to get rid of the Japanese. Young Bo had admired them both, but it was Bo during the Cultural Revolution who suspected that Song was still in the pay of the British and a danger by association to himself. He had therefore directed the Red Guards to investigate Song's revisionist activities. When the Cultural Revolution ended Song was still working on a farm and it was Bo whom he contacted to try and arrange his rehabilitation. Sensing an opportunity to enhance his reputation, Bo agreed on condition that Song lure a British spy to Shanghai where he would be arrested, and exposed during a show trial with plenty of political propaganda against the capitalist west. In the event Bo was horrified when the British spy lured to Shanghai turned out to be Florence, and he took a few minutes to compose himself whilst viewing her through the one way window in the interrogation room. Turning to the two uniformed security men who were under his authority he said,

"She looks too composed, she's not ready for interrogation yet, lock her in a bare cell for twenty-four hours and prevent her from sleeping. Shove her around a bit, but no marks or bruises, only one bottle of water and one plate of porridge after twelve hours. I'll be back same time tomorrow."

Bo then went straight to the chairman of his security committee and told him about John Benson being a friend to China and that he thought that he could turn his daughter Florence to work for China. He was given permission to remove her to a training camp outside Shanghai. When Bo returned to Florence's cell he had the door unlocked and walked straight in to confront the dishevelled prisoner. Speaking English softly so that the guards would not understand he said,

"Do not show that you recognize me and I will get you out of here."

Then speaking in Mandarin he said,

"Get your things and follow me."

With Bo leading the way Florence followed him with the two guards bringing up the rear. A police car with a driver awaited them and Bo and Florence got in the back. As they drove off Bo said,

"I prefer to speak Mandarin with you as my English is not perfect."

"That's ok with me," replied Florence, "But where are you taking me?"

"I can't tell you that, but we have collected your belongings from your hotel and they are in the boot, so you will be a little more comfortable where we are going."

The journey took just over an hour without another word being spoken. Florence was shown to a sparsely furnished room in a large building, one of several inside a guarded compound. She was allowed to freshen up before being taken to an office where Bo was seated behind a desk. When the female guard had left Bo assured Florence that they were alone and not being overheard or recorded.

"I am the official who set the trap to catch a British spy but I was shocked when I saw that it was you, the daughter of my saviour Joan the missionary. You were caught carrying money, and instructions to help Song leave China, you do accept that don't you, you realize how serious your situation is don't you?"

"Yes." Florence was feeling a bit sick and wishing that she had never listened to her Dad.

"I indicated to you when we first met that I hold your mother in high esteem, and that I am grateful for the kindness that she showed to my brother and me when we were very young, but that is only half the story. You are safe for now as I have official responsibility for you, and if you co-operate I may be able to return you to Hong Kong, but first you must listen to the whole story regarding your parents."

For the first time since her arrest Florence felt a glimmer of hope, she had been berating herself for ever having signed up to work for MI6, what had she ever got out of it? The pay wasn't fantastic and she and her husband Li had good jobs and an enjoyable social life, so why had she taken the risk, why had she agreed to a live drop meeting when her normal mode of operation was to use dead drop letter boxes? She had not been allowed to tell Li what she had signed up to, and she would not blame him if he refused to have anything to do with her once he found out. She had just had her father's tales of derring do that had created a sense of pride in devotion to duty in her, so that she had willingly agreed to serve when asked. Now she was ready to clutch at any straw of hope and Bo was the only straw in sight.

"Yes, please tell me all you know, and I will be happy to co-operate all that I can," pleaded Florence.

Bo started back in 1936 when he was a five year old and he had discovered his dead parents. He knew nothing of Ling Sung and felt very afraid but determined to look after his little brother who was his only close family left. When his uncle said that he was going to Guangzhou and that they could go with him if they wanted, Bo thought that it may be safer there. When they discovered their uncle's body after coming back from searching for food, all he could think of doing was hiding. If Joan hadn't found them they would probably have died of starvation and exposure. For several months they were happy with Joan and recovered their health, and he began to understand a little of Joan's socialist attitude of everyone helping everyone else whilst relying upon a god for directions. But then Ling Sung turned up and he thought that maybe he was a relative and that they did have a family after all. It took a few years working for Ling Sung before he realized the truth, that Ling Sung was a drug dealer and had probably killed their parents. By the early nineteen forties John Benson was a regular visitor to Ling Sung and Bo understood that he was working to get rid of the Japanese, so he was a good man as far as Bo and Wei were concerned.

"I am sorry to tell you this Florence, but your father was a drug dealer as well as Ling Sung, they both worked together, but at the same time John still did his dangerous work for Britain."

Bo continued to explain to a dazed Florence that, "when the Japanese picked up John Benson as he was then known, it wasn't because he was a spy, it was because they wanted his drugs and the money that he had made dealing in drugs. They would have beaten him to death but he realized that he had to buy his freedom. In exchange for being released into the Civilian Assembly Camp he arranged for Ling Sung to make regular monthly payments to the Shanghai Japanese and he arranged for me to collect money from his bank account and reimburse Ling Sung each month plus twenty percent, as I could move freely around Shanghai. In return he taught me English and many other facts about the world before finally teaching us how to join the communists in the north. He was sure that after the World War, the communists would win the civil war in China, because they were better trained, better motivated, and would have the peasant population supporting them against the corrupt Nationalists. The Nationalists had a larger army and were supported by the west, but they did not relish a fight and the communists had the support of the Russians, who had shown just what motivated communists could do by winning World War Two. I was also pleased to help Joan the missionary during this period, and to see Wei grow strong and happy to believe in the communist cause. Unfortunately Wei died in one of the last battles of the civil war and I have progressed as a communist official, so I was a little worried when you first appeared in China as a journalist during the Cultural Revolution." Florence was upset by the revelations about her father but pleased that some more holes in her parents' past had been filled in. Finally Bo outlined his plan,

"So, now I have convinced my superiors that I can turn you to spy for us. You will stay here for a few days to be debriefed about MI6 activities in Asia. Be frank with them, don't lie, they will know that you don't know everything as you are only a field agent. They will then teach you our methods of communication, and how they will let you know what they are interested in in the future. We will then let you travel back to Hong Kong."

"What about Song," asked Florence, "If he doesn't exit China they will suspect that something went wrong and they will want me to explain what went wrong with my mission?"

"We will make it appear as though he followed the instructions that you delivered and then his body will be found showing that he was shot trying to leave China illegally."

Florence was not happy with her situation but she had no option but to go home and carry on lying to her husband and to everyone else.

Florence and Li continued their attractive social life together for several years despite the strain on Florence of keeping her secrets from her husband. Florence finally fell pregnant at the age of thirty-eight and she had no way of knowing who the father was. She had tried for a child with Li throughout their marriage but without success. They had both had fertility tests and been told that, whilst Li's sperm count was not the highest ever recorded, they should eventually be able to get pregnant. With Florence spending so much time in China and returning with so many interesting and commercially successful articles, she had eventually started an affair with Bo, who controlled her life. It wasn't just dependency that had caused her to respond to Bo's advances, she had genuinely come to admire his humanity. Bo had lost his wife to cancer in 1976 when they were both in their late forties and their son Wei was in his early twenties. He had had only concern for Florence when he first arrested her in 1978 but he hadn't failed to notice how attractive she was. Whenever Florence visited Shanghai Bo was there to de-brief her and assist her in finding stories that she could turn into interesting articles for the Hong Kong newspapers, but stories that did not upset the party. Florence would stay at the best hotels on her expense account but Bo would escort her to dinner at quiet unfashionable restaurants. In time he persuaded her to spend time in his home where their mutual affection had grown into an affair, and now with Bo in his early fifties, thirty-eight year old Florence told him that she was pregnant. She had no way of knowing who the father was but she was an accomplished liar by now, and assured Bo that Li was the father. They agreed that their affair should end and that Florence would be allowed to spend more time in Hong Kong to bring up her child. She also hoped that MI6 would also ease up on their demands upon her if she became a mother. Not that she had been able to find any information that was of great strategic importance to either side, as she mainly acted as a conduit of political opinions and intentions that enabled each side to prepare for negotiations with the other side. Nevertheless each side considered these evaluations, of prominent officials' status and intentions, as useful.

Li was delighted that Florence was finally pregnant and after an anxious pre-natal period when they worried about her being too old to give birth, daughter Emily was born in 1985. The added responsibility did bring the couple closer together and made them more conscious of planning for the future. With Britain's lease of Hong Kong coming to an end in 1997 Li, himself half English and half Chinese, was as a civil servant very busy with preparations for this event, but unsure of its effect upon himself and his job. Florence too wanted to ensure that Emily, not only maintained her right to UK citizenship, but that she would be brought up partly in the UK. She emphasised to Li that, as she had been recruited in the UK, one of her conditions of employment was that her employer would pay for the cost of her children's boarding school in England from the age of eleven to eighteen. This was in fact MI6's cost but payment would be filtered through her newspaper employer in order to conceal her connection to MI6. Li was happy with this arrangement but he did not realize that he would have to make the final decision as a widower.

It was not Bo's decision to eliminate Florence in January 1996 when he was sixty-five years old. He still maintaining considerable authority as an official of the State Security Service but he spent most of his time guiding his son Wei up the ladder of communist committees. Wei was now thirty-five, the same age as his English friend Thomas Latimer. He was well aware of Florence's relationship with his father, and that his father had revealed too much information about his past to her. He was not aware however that Thomas and Florence were distantly related. With the certainty that China would control Hong Kong by the summer of 1996, Wei decided that Florence was a danger to his family. Other communist officials might gain access to her or her records, or she might be indiscreet. Wei was named after his uncle who had died in the civil war, and had named his own son Bo in honour of his father, whom he knew had had an affair with Florence. He had his own commercial plans for himself and his son Bo and considered Florence a danger to those plans because she knew the whole history of his father. Wei's wife Shan was also an official in the State Security Service and he took her into his confidence. Shan had acted as an agent of her father-in-law Bo in contacts with Florence before and was able to socialise with her. On one of Florence's trips to China in 1995 Shan got her drunk before contaminating her food with Hepatitis B. It was then a simple matter for Wei to have Florence detained in hospital, sedated but not treated, until the infection had a fatal hold. By the time she returned to Hong Kong she was beyond help and died that autumn. Li Tang chose the same school in England for Emily that Thomas Latimer had chosen for Wei's son Bo Junior, and Margaret Latimer had chosen for Frank Latimer. All three eleven year olds started their first term at boarding school in the autumn of 1996 without any knowledge of the connections between them.

Chapter Ten
1996 To 2006 Thomas Latimer

Thomas at thirty-five years of age was at his peak. Life in Cheshire with his wife Susan was full of social events, many to do with horses. As a couple they were well suited to each other, satisfactorily intimate when together but happy to exercise their right to independence from each other that was occasioned by Thomas's travels. She owned and raced thoroughbred horses and ensured that they were one of the best dressed couples in the county. He collected Chinese artefacts and earned enough to maintain their extravagant lifestyle. Financially well rewarded but with few assets, life was good but still with a tremor of uncertainty as he knew that his wife had high expectations. Most of his wife's family were natural landed Conservatives and made him aware of their party's position on most political issues, despite knowing about his membership of the Social Democratic Party whom he still represented as a MEP.

He was welcomed onto the boards of a couple of British public liability companies sponsored by his father-in-law, and travelled to Brussels well briefed to make connections that would give him some influence through the European Parliament's committees. His seat on the International Trade Committee still took him to China where he could take advice from Wei Sung that was helpful to the companies and interests that he served back in Europe. If he was honest with himself he would have to admit that the majority of his efforts tended to serve commercial interests, but the rest of his time saw him struggling to effect measures that conflicted with the aims of his conservative relatives. Thomas did not want Britain to withdraw from Europe as it was clear to him that we needed to remain within one of the major trading groups in the world. Immigration had its irritations but the free movement of the peoples of Europe within the union was sacrosanct as a founding principle. Better efforts to control immigration from Africa and the Far East should be made, certainly better than the socialists had done since they ousted the conservatives. Variances in the standards of legal, educational, and social security services of the member states needed to be standardized over time, and it would take a lot of work and negotiation to achieve this. In the meantime the wealthier nations in Europe would suffer minor irritations, but the end result would surely justify the wait. Of course Thomas knew that it would have been better for the European Union to achieve political union before they attempted monitory union, but the hasty introduction of the Euro first, had at least allowed Britain to keep the pound. Another weakness was that when a country applied to join the European Union they could be made to clean up their monetary and political acts, whereas once they were in, they could revert to dictatorship and corruption without any clear disciplinary procedure to punish them. Despite all these problems, Thomas was in favour of Britain staying in the European Union because of the clear commercial advantage and, for the first time in history, the chance to progress by negotiation rather than by war.

Thomas accompanied Bo Junior to his new English boarding school with its outdoor philosophy but structured lifestyle. Bo had passed the entrance examination without any trouble and was pleased with its location in the countryside. Thomas noticed Li, Emily's father, because of his Asian features, and conversationally let him know that he visited China frequently and spoke Mandarin. So immediately Bo and Emily found that they had a common bond of the Chinese languages. They were of course directed to different houses for their accommodation, and Bo found himself in the same house as Frank. Friendships are easily and necessarily made at the age of eleven to combat any homesickness. They weren't the only two new boys in their house and relationships between them ebbed and flowed, but the discovery that both Frank and Bo were computer nerds, computer games players, and Dungeons & Dragons fantasists cemented their friendship for life. Frank also formed a friendship with a lad from West Africa. Mambu Koroma was the son of an officer in his country's army and being physically well made and fast he joined Frank and Bo in their interests in sport. Bo kept on coming across Emily and they always had something to talk about from their childhoods in China and Hong Kong, so she was slowly added to the close knit gang of three. Thomas, Margaret, and Li regularly appeared to collect their charges at the end of term, and from comments overheard and conversations held, Thomas and Margaret eventually worked out that they were related by marriage. Neither had the slightest idea that Emily was related to both Thomas and Frank.

Whenever Thomas accompanied Bo Junior back to China, he and Wei would plan the next step in expanding Wei's enterprises. Wei had already opened up regarding his philosophy to Thomas, and without betraying the communist ideology, expressed ideas for the future that were similar to Thomas's. Wei explained that he expected China to want to move into exports in future years as well as importing western technology and science, and that this would not just be manufacturing cheap mass produced everyday goods, but would include high margin technologies. China was going to really develop its infrastructure and Wei and Thomas could be at the heart of China's entry into world trade. Over the next decade this all came to fruition and both men prospered from it. Wei had already entered the mobile telephone industry and Thomas was able to interest the merchant banks to help fund him. The Chinese market was huge and Wei's company was busy signing up subscribers with both imported mobiles and cheaper ones developed locally, all connecting to the national network. Thomas had little difficulty finding funding from banks and potential partners. A year later on Thomas's recommendation Wei entered the Chinese property market. Land belongs to the state in China but is leased to businesses and even to some individuals for approved purposes, even those with a profit motive. The new law regulating these matters did not get passed until some years later but many of China's newly wealthy individuals took a chance, and profited when they were finally legitimized. Almost every year Wei got into some new business much to Thomas's benefit but to the alarm of his father Bo Senior. The family back-up in the State Security Service was crucial to enabling Wei to negotiate with the bureaucracy and make sure that the right officials approved his requests. Finally Wei took some of his businesses and cash abroad and into Europe and in these endeavours Thomas was a great help. The crucial green light to such a move came when China's membership of the World Trade Organization was agreed upon in

2001, after a long period of negotiation and many adjustments to China's economy.

In 2003 after seven years at the English boarding school the three now close friends, Frank, Bo, and Emily, guided by Thomas, all decided to apply to Manchester University. Frank for the computer science course at the birthplace of the first electronic computer, Bo for the Business School as his father wished, and Emily for Modern Languages. They were all accepted and Thomas, at a celebratory dinner told them all that Bo's father would be funding a flat for the three of them not far from the centre of Manchester. Leaving the leafy countryside with its outdoor pursuits available on the doorstep, and its disciplined structure of school life with lessons, sports, meals, housework, and hobbies, they were now to enjoy new freedoms, new friends, and the excitement of the big city.

Wei Sung resided mainly in Hong Kong now that his businesses were prospering but his wife Shan had remained in Shanghai, where she looked after Bo senior and Bo junior whilst still working for the state security service. Thomas had always delivered Bo junior back to Shanghai and became very fond of Shan and enjoyed her company. Shan was still loyal to Wei but Thomas noticed when he visited Wei in Hong Kong or met him in Europe, that he was always accompanied by a very attractive PR woman. Wei made his attitude clear to Thomas; that wealthy Chinese businessmen were entitled to sexual relief when their number one wife was not available. He even gave the impression that his wife should be able to make some arrangement herself without it affecting the marriage. Thomas had thought about it but didn't want to strain his relationship with Bo junior or his own wife. After business had been conducted Thomas and Wei were enjoying visits to Royal Ascot and social events in Europe and America, and they both developed an interest in tennis and horse racing. Thomas's wife Susan wasn't a race horse trainer but was happy to manage the few horses bought by Wei and own those bought by Thomas.

Wei's businesses was making good profits all the time, and Thomas wondered where he had got his initial start-up capital from before he brought Thomas with his Merchant Bank connections into the business. After several years trading in China Wei had shown Thomas his business plan for the next five years based on his already proven turnover and his desire to build up his business outside China. That was where Thomas had been such a help to him, as he was able to persuade the banks to start funding Wei's businesses. After a couple more years Thomas was made a director of Wei's holding company, which controlled an electronics manufacturer in Scandinavia, a mobile phone network in Italy, and property holdings in America and Britain. He taught Wei the value of good management, delegation to the right properly trained and experienced employees, careful examination of monthly management controls, and when a problem was identified, contract the right consultants to devise a solution and supervise its implementation. Finally he persuaded Wei to envision a strategy for the business's future. Wei himself was a driving force because he loved the involvement with what he considered his creation, and he used his fellow citizens who were hard working and loyal employees at home and overseas.

Chapter Eleven
2007 to 2011 Frank, Bo, Emily and Thomas

Frank Latimer relaxed on the reasonably quiet beach and in the bars of San Carlos de la Rapita, Spain, until the new year of 2007. He wasn't getting drunk or even seriously chasing girl tourists, but reflecting on his father's fate and how best to use his computing software skills to achieve closure on the former and progress on the latter. In January he moved to Manchester in England and rented an apartment in the city centre which would double as an office while he prepared software for his website. He contacted Keith only through his mother as they had agreed, playing safe by ensuring that there were no links tying him to the drug gang when it wasn't necessary. His mother Margaret and Keith had already explained to him that his father and grandfather had mastered the problems of storage and distribution of dangerous substances which had been profitable, but the laundering of those profits had always been a problem. He now started to design his own websites for internet sales companies, not on the scale of Amazon the American giant, but multiple wholesalers with storage, transport, and international banking facilities. The capital to start or takeover established medium-sized companies would come from Keith's operations via several banks and his mother in Spain, until they had sufficient legal business to attract investment. The sheer number of businesses and banks would make it impossible for the authorities to trace a parasite operation freeloading on the legal businesses and controlled only by Frank, who would split the records between several office locations in different European countries. Physical control of the legal products would be directed by employees and managers already recruited by Frank who was training a new generation with better educational qualifications and computer skills. Keith and his old gang members would have physical control of the illegal substances as they infiltrated the businesses as warehousemen and delivery drivers. By the end of 2009 they had majority shareholdings in six start-ups and had their own automatic computerized warehouses in England and Spain.

Keith was in his sixties now having been only three years younger than Frank's dad. They had been good mates and knew the risks of their business. Frank only met Keith in Spain now to avoid any contamination of the modern businessman by the old drugs gang leader, and finally he managed to extract the full story of his father's murder out of him. A young woman had been found dead of an overdose in a flat in Chester. She turned out to be the daughter of a family of criminals who operated in Liverpool and they quickly established that she had been seeing a Pakistani, and that he had roughed her up and supplied the heroin that killed her. Unfortunately he was one of William's lieutenants and he realized that he was in danger of a revenge attack. William suggested that he carry a tracker device and when he was abducted he managed to switch it on. William with Keith driving tracked them to the Delamere forest but they arrived too late. They were both armed and stumbled upon the scene of a murder in which shots were fired. William was shot dead and the Liverpool family had one wounded man to take care of. Keith was left alone and feared for his life, so he agreed when the Liverpool gang's leader suggested that, as they would all be in trouble if the police found the bodies, he should withdraw and allow them to clean up the site. They did and left William's body in a stolen car on the outskirts of Manchester for the police to find. There were no clues and it remains an unsolved crime. When William's body was released for burial he was quietly cremated and his ashes scattered in a garden of remembrance. Shortly afterwards Margaret retreated to Spain with her newborn son Frank. A visit to Delamere Forest did not bring about closure for Frank regarding his father, as he was still intent on experiencing the same risks that his father had chosen to accept. There was no case for revenge against the Liverpool gang as all the blame seemed to belong to the Pakistani, who had already received the ultimate punishment anyway. Frank finally quizzed his mother about what sort of a man his father had been. Margaret of course was nostalgic about the love of her life, but she was not going to embarrass her son with details of her parent's real romance. Instead she explained to Frank about her family's life as market traders and how she had brought the same amoral attitude that he had into their marriage, and how they had both accepted the risks and revelled in the excitement as they both enthusiastically built up their business. Frank was inspired by this revelation and returned to work on his plans with renewed enthusiasm.

With several sales and distribution businesses to direct and more being investigated for possible takeover, Frank was busy but all real work had been delegated to managers. In each business there was one representative with executive powers, like a communist political commissar, who was responsible for the one extra box or crate or package that contained the illegal substances being stored or distributed under Frank's overall control. Paper trails were split between companies to confuse any trace investigation, and even computer records slipped from machine to non-linked machine that only Frank could piece together. The end of the line pushers were of course still at risk of police action, but they were supplied by one cut out delivery gang member, who knew only one company that supplied him, and good legal and family support bought their silence on the rare occasions that arrested pushers pointed a finger at them. The illegal profits rolled in and disappeared by interbank transfers into elaborate tax avoidance schemes. Each company was meticulous at complying with all laws and regulations regarding the modest profits from the genuine business operations, and was unconnected to any other business under Frank's control, so any investigation into one company could be isolated to prevent the investigation extending to the others. Professional legal and accounting partnerships provided the expert advice for the legitimate businesses and it was Frank who ensured that their recommendations were acted upon, whilst he alone controlled the illegal activities that were parasitically infecting the whole conglomerate without harming it.

Just as the point of sale created great risk, so the point of supply was equally risky. Frank's main deputies, with Keith now mainly retired to Spain with his share of the profits, dealt with the international suppliers of dangerous substances. Payments had to be made and the product inserted into the storage and distribution system. Frank's deputies purchased only in the UK and Western Europe, where prices had been marked up to reflect the difficulty and danger of importation from South America, Russia, Asia and North Africa. A new supplier was needed whose product could be sold at a higher margin giving the business greater profits to fund expansion, which would allow for even greater complexity that would provide even greater protection. Still wanting to isolate himself from contact with most of his own gang, as his own system of self-protection required, he was forced to get more involved when one of his deputies reported an approach from a Chinese outfit. They were looking to supply large quantities of drugs to an organization capable of distributing them in Europe. Despite the obvious risks Frank decided that he should personally attend the arranged meeting, after receiving assurances that neither weapons nor drugs would be allowed or required in Hong Kong.

With Bo's return to China after completing his English education his father Wei was delighted and ready to put him to work, but like Frank at the start of 2007 after a couple of months' rest and recreation. The plan was for Bo junior to take over Wei's conglomerate one day and being a dutiful son he was proud to be asked. It was exactly what his qualifications had prepared him for, but first he had to complete some line management tasks around the world in each of his father's companies. The first six months were spent at the newly acquired Chinese transport company, followed by the same amount of time at the Hong Kong mobile telephone network where he was tasked with increasing the number of subscribers in South East Asia. There followed three months at the electronics manufacturer in Scandinavia, before moving to Italy to spread the mobile phone network there to the Balkans. The property business with holdings in China, America and Britain, involved a lot of travel as he was tasked with reporting back to Wei regarding national price cycles and whether they were rising or falling, which city suburbs were likely prosper or collapse, and in conjunction with their local estate managers, any properties that were ready for purchase or sale. This was just the life and work that Bo had hoped for, and had been prepared for by his excellent education. Finally he returned to Hong Kong to find that his father had purchased a rundown Indonesian shipping line and was about to order some new ships.

By 2010 Bo junior had been appointed Chief Executive Officer of the Electronics Division of his father's enterprises, Bo senior was CEO for the Transport Division and Wei was Chairman of the holding company. Young Bo, whilst still traveling on business a lot, had settled down with his own apartment in Shanghai with plenty of girlfriends to escort around the emergent night life of the city. He had become aware that his parents now led separate lives. He was close to both his parents, and in accordance with the country's one child per family policy, he was an only child and the focus of all their emotions and generosity. Since leaving university his base had been Shanghai and he had developed a relationship with his grandfather, listening to all his tales of hardship from his youth and during the civil war fighting for the communists. Gradually the tales of the now seventy-nine year old powerful head of the State Security Service for the Shanghai Municipality, began to ring bells of familiarity. Grandfather being saved from starvation by an English lady Methodist missionary and Emily at school had mentioned a grandmother going to China as a Methodist missionary! Grandfather making friends with an Englishman who had been looked after by the same Methodist missionary when they were both put in the Civilian Assembly Camp by the Japanese, and Emily had mentioned that her grandparents had been interned by the Japanese during the Second World War! Senior Bo hadn't mentioned anything about Florence, the missionary's daughter and Emily's mother, because that was a state secret and was much too delicate a subject for him personally, but Emily had told Bo junior that her mother had died when she was quite young from an infectious disease that she had caught in Shanghai.

"Grandfather, I was at school and university with a girl from Hong Kong whose mother Florence died young of an infectious disease, and her grandmother came to China as a Methodist missionary and married an English diplomat when they settled in Hong Kong. Her name is Emily Tang and she shared the flat that Dad rented for me in Manchester." Do you think that it is the same family?

The old man paused, lost in thought, what did this Emily know, would they have to eliminate her as well? No, she was only ten when her mother died and her father didn't know anything about his wife's activities, not even that she had worked for MI6.

"In China you would not have been allowed to share a flat with an unmarried woman, but yes her grandparents fit the bill. Ask her if her grandfather was born in India with the family name of Lane, but used the family name Benson when he was in China. If so then it is certainly the same family. Are you still friends? Do you still see her when you go to Hong Kong?" Young Bo was astonished at the coincidence that had emerged from their conversation.

"Well I will certainly arrange a meeting with Emily soon, she will be as fascinated as I am to hear of the connections between our two families." Senior Bo was thoroughly alarmed by now; there was a possibility that Emily was his grandson's aunty although they were the same age. He didn't want any romance between them, the consequences would be horrific.

"Can't you just e-mail her?" He asked hopefully, the less contact between them the better.

"I could, but something as exciting and interesting as this and I would rather have a good chat with her face to face." Grandfather Bo had been working towards an even greater revelation in the course of these chats with his grandson. Now in order to divert his grandson's attention from Emily, he decided that it was time to come to the point.

"How do you think your father has done in building up his conglomerate business?" he asked young Bo.

"I think that he has done fantastically well, especially as he started from scratch, and I hope that I can keep it profitable and expand it myself," he answered.

"Well it didn't happen by chance, and as you are going to take over as CEO one day, you need to know every detail of its creation. When I and my brother Wei were enslaved by Li Sung we were at the centre of the drug scene in Shanghai as he was the main gang leader who dealt in drugs. He provided food and accommodation for us and we did his every bidding. I didn't mind so much as I was intent on finding out who had killed our parents. Mainly through John Lane I discovered that it was Li Sung who had killed them. We were too weak to do anything about it then, but when I returned to Shanghai with the triumphant communist army, I set about establishing myself as an official in the State Security Service and used my knowledge of Li Sung's operation to catch him red-handed dealing in illegal drugs. I didn't try to kill Li Sung instead I arrested him and let the state punish him. To my surprise the party asked me to continue running Li Sung's illegal drug business as a tax collector. The buyers and pushers remained in place so long as they handed over most of their profits on pain of death or arrest. The money couldn't go straight to the party but they instructed me on how it should be spent for the good of state. Once the Cultural Revolution was abandoned and Deng began to reorganize China so that it could join the World Trade Organization, the party told me to feed the money into a commercial business that they could tax for the benefit of all. More recently they are using Wei's conglomerate to feed drugs to the West to help undermine their societies. So that's going to be your task in the future. Didn't you ever ask yourself how your father funded such a rapid accumulation of asset rich businesses?" Young Bo was dumbfounded but muttered,

"I thought that Thomas Latimer with his bank connections had arranged funding." His grandfather further enlightened him.

"Western Banks won't look at you until you have several years of successful trading with a provable turnover. Prepare yourself from now on to see the whole organization and how it functions, and remember that we always have to satisfy the party at its highest level. You will need a strategy that keeps them happy but allows you a back door in case you need an exit in a hurry." His grandfather seemed to have exhausted himself and Bo had a lot to think about. Torn between family loyalty - after all his ancestors had been swept along by events beyond their control - and his respect for free enterprise within the limits set by the law that he had learnt about in England. He decided to seem to accept his lot whilst he had time to think it all over but he was troubled by this revelation.

Emily Tang with good language and business skills and with her family connections, soon found herself a job as a journalist after her return from boarding school and university in England. Her father as a successful civil servant in Hong Kong had survived the transition from Crown colony back to Chinese sovereignty, and now wanted to be closer to his only child. He helped her review all the old letters and photographs that they had so that Emily renewed her familiarity with the details of her grandmother's and her mother's lives in the east. She knew that her grandparents had been interned in a Civilian

Assembly Camp in Shanghai during the Second World War and that its effect on their health had shortened their lives. It was however a sanitised version of her grandfather's and her mother's lives as she and her father knew nothing about his involvement with MI6. There was however a mention in one of her grandmother's letters of a Mr Benson, and in another letter the revelation that Mr Benson was in fact Mr Lane her grandfather. Emily was herself one quarter Chinese, although it was perceptible in her appearance only in her black hair. She knew about her father's parents and their backgrounds which left two puzzles: her mother's untimely death and the missing relative Anthony Latimer. Her female line had been brought to Asia by the Methodist church whose philosophy of service and equality was not all that different from the communist party's, although in execution of that philosophy the Church and the Party were very different. Emily joined the communist party as she had vague political ambitions which she visualized as bringing peoples from different cultures together by negotiation. Her ambition might have been better realized if she had joined the Methodist Church.

With dual nationality, Hong Kong Chinese and British, Emily was able to travel in China just as her mother had done. Search as she did she could not find any record of her mother's medical treatment in Shanghai or Guangzhou, and in Hong Kong the records showed that she could have been better treated if she had arrived back earlier in the infections cycle. Hepatitis B is endemic in China and half a million citizens a year die from the infection, but that is quite a small percentage of those who are infected. Emily was unhappy that there had been a delay in her mother's treatment for Hepatitis B, but there was no evidence that the delay had been whilst she was in Shanghai or Guangzhou.

Emily had been kept up to date with her computer skills by her two friends Frank and Bo, and with their and the internet's help, had been able to fill in the blanks in the family tree when she started at Manchester University. She knew about her grandmother's sister Anne from her letters to her mother Joan that her father still had, and she had found out that Anne and her husband had died in a car crash in 1969. Following the paper trail she knew that Anne had a son called Anthony who was twenty-one when his parents died, but she could not find any marriage or death certificate for him to date. Emily still wondered what had happened to Tony Latimer.

The three friends Frank, Bo, and Emily had of course, when they parted after graduating from Manchester University, sworn to keep in touch and meet as often as they could. Many e-mails had passed between them of course, but now Emily decided that it was about time that they met face to face and caught up on all that they had learnt since 2006. She reached this conclusion at about the same time as Bo Junior decided that they should meet and reconcile his father's revelations regarding his experiences in the Second World War.

Thomas had been freed from his responsibility to Bo but was even more involved with Wei and his conglomerate. He was now a very influential politician in Europe and the UK, and consultant in Asia with good political, banking and business contacts, and Director on the Boards of several businesses. He was a skilled negotiator but quite capable of taking dubious practical action if he thought that it would lead in the long term to an achievement within the bounds of his political philosophies. Thomas and his wife Susan both enjoyed their lifestyles with plenty of work and plenty of socializing of the type that they enjoyed.

Susan's business was making good profits and she enjoyed the company of those involved in the fashion industry. Thomas did a lot of travelling and it did occur to him that Susan might sometime enjoy the excitement of an extramarital affair, as was quite common amongst her creative friends. He was confident that she would be very discreet if she did, and that she would ensure that he would not suffer the embarrassment of knowing anything about it.

He and Wei still enjoyed social and sporting events together, but more and more Thomas found himself drawn to Shanghai and the company of Shan. Wei's old fashioned attitude based on unrealistic assumptions was that wealthy Chinese men were entitled to a mistress if their number one wife was not always available, expressed to Thomas some years ago, and was, unknown to those same wealthy Chinese men, totally unacceptable to their number one wives. Indeed this is a misconception held by men in many parts of the world, and has always caused unhappiness for the wives, although many of them have to accept the situation for economic reasons. Shan knew about

Wei's personal assistant escorts and had been resentful of them for some time now. She greatly enjoyed Thomas's attention and their affair when it started was an enjoyable extension of their genuine friendship.

Bo was restless and found it difficult to sleep following his grandfather's revelation that his father was trading in heroin under cover of his business conglomerate, the same business that Bo was being trained to take over one day. His Grandfather Senior Bo had had no choice when you consider the path from poverty that he had followed, and his Father Wei would have preferred not to have the communist party on his back, but family loyalty was as strong a factor as party loyalty, in making him accept what in fact he could not refuse. Now it was Bo's turn and he could not see any way out of the situation just yet, but he would accept his grandfather's warning and look for an exit for himself in the future. With his mind made up he tackled his father regarding the details.

Wei was relieved that his father had enlightened his son, and now explained to him how important it was to keep the State Security Service happy and that meant keeping his grandfather and mother happy. Wei explained just how the system worked and how the recent acquisitions of a transport company and a shipping line would help with expanding into Europe. To that end Bo was to meet and negotiate with the boss of an English organization who could handle the distribution and sale of large quantities of drugs in Europe. Bo was prepped by Wei's managers regarding minimum and negotiation starting prices for their various products, and how various delivery points would affect those prices. Finally the time and method of payment must be agreed. The English organization had been chosen because it was believed that it was backed by considerable assets, so a payment up front would be confirmation of their good standing.

Frank arrived in Hong Kong early in December 2011 with two of his lieutenants, a password, and a telephone number for making contact. He called the number as soon as they had checked into their hotel and after hearing the password, requested a meeting in a public place. They agreed on the Victoria Park near the swimming pool, which was just across the road from their Park Lane Hotel, in an hour's time. For recognition Frank was to carry a folded newspaper and he would be approached and given the password again. His friends should stand off at least fifty yards as would the negotiator's friends. As previously agreed no weapons or drugs to be carried by anyone. Frank's main worry had been a police sting so he was determined that the words drugs or heroin or any similar slang would not pass over his lips. If he was meeting the organization that he thought that he was meeting, then as this was a preliminary meeting to try and reach an agreement, and whether they agreed or not, both parties could walk away no harm done. Having taken up what the Englishmen considered to be casual positions with Frank fifty yards out in front on his own, a familiar figure appeared walking towards him. Bo quickly got his words in first.

"Don't show that you recognize me and if we keep our voices down our companions won't know that we know one another." Frank could only say,

"Jesus Christ Bo what are you doing here?"

"I will give you the password if you like, but yes, I am in the same business as you, and no, I didn't know that I was going to meet my best buddy here in Victoria Park." Frank recovered his composure and they agreed to meet later that evening. Bo would send a car to pick up Frank from his hotel and they could explain to each other the events of the past five years that had brought them to this meeting. It then took only about ten minutes for them to conclude the business that they had come for. Bo's prices were cheaper than Frank had been paying for delivery to Western Europe, and were even cheaper for delivery to Turkey, and cheaper still for delivery in West Africa. Frank asked for and Bo confirmed the quality of the product being supplied, and Bo gave Frank a card with details of a bank account in Pakistan for payment. A five million dollar order was placed and Frank agreed a fifty percent payment in the bank account before the end of the year. With that settled they shook hands and retired to their companions. Frank assured his lieutenants that the deal was done and they walked back to their hotel.

Frank told his lieutenants that he knew a woman in Hong Kong and that they should enjoy themselves on expenses. Bo was as good as his word and Frank was chauffeured to his apartment that evening.

As he settled back in the comfort of a luxurious vehicle Frank pondered how Bo had become involved in the drugs business. From what Bo had mentioned when they were at school and university together, his father had been an influential communist politician. Later on both Bo and Frank's cousin Thomas had mentioned in casual conversation Wei's business activities, and his gradual expansion into a worldwide conglomerate. Frank and Bo had both casually indicated in their last year together at university that they would probably return to the family fold and help out with the family business, but neither had known that their family business was involved in illegal drugs. Once they were alone in Bo's apartment and had greeted each other with a man hug, they settled down with a cold beer and Bo broke the ice.

"What did you think Frank when you saw me walking towards you in the park this afternoon?"

"Think! I was speechless, and I have been thinking about it ever since. Are you the boss? What about your dad's business? Wait a minute what about bugs?" Frank was twisting uncomfortably in his chair as he helplessly looked around the room."

"Don't worry, I have this place swept every month and I apply my own personal security measures to it, so that I would know if anyone got in here without my permission." Bo was anxious to maintain his special friendship with Frank, and went on,

"After we left Manchester I began my training to learn all about my father's business, as I have told you in e-mails over the past five years, and it was only a few months ago that my grandfather enlightened me about the facts of my family's history and its relationship with the communist party. I can tell you, I was shocked, but what can you do when you learn that to pull out would harm your whole family?"

"I suppose that I had more choice than you," replied Frank, "I always suspected that my father's death was gang related, and when given the choice I decided to take over the family business with some cockeyed idea of avenging or justifying him." Bo was pleased that Frank seemed to have faced a choice similar to his, and went on,

"My father has built up a good business that he is proud of, and I want to carry it on because it is fascinating. The drugs are inserted by the State Security Service and our only job is distribution to rich markets like Europe and America. My father keeps it all at arm's length, as I plan to do when I get full control."

"Yes," replied Frank, "I make sure that I never handle the product, but it was imperative that I as a leader negotiate with the new source of supply from China. I, like your father, built up legitimate businesses and then gradually inserted my father's old business into them for better cover, so I knew all along what kind of business I was in. I believe that all dangerous substances should be legalized, and that would remove the criminal activity from both the supply and the sale ends of the business. As a legitimate business it could be properly taxed and that tax should not go to the treasury to be mixed in with all the other taxes and then spent on what the politicians feel like spending it on in order to get themselves re-elected. It should be kept separate and legislation passed to state that it could only be spent on two things. Firstly half should be spent on the care and cure of addicts, and secondly the other half should be spent on educating the young on the real dangers of drug and alcohol use. Of course the politicians will never accept such an arrangement because it reduces their power, the power that comes from having control of the expenditure of all taxes collected and stuck in one general purpose pot. The police, the agencies currently involved in the care of addicts, and the criminals that make their living from the production and sale of drugs, they all don't want legalization because they all make their living from the whole business. They all hide behind the mantra, have you seen the devastation caused to individuals who become addicted. Well even if you still have those devastated individuals after the legalization of drugs, then the benefits are still less crime and more tax to help those addicts. Another benefit could be even more important because the terrorist organizations are now funding themselves by dealing in drugs"

"Wow Frank, you really have been thinking about this, but as you say it won't happen because the vested interests don't want it to happen. For the time being we are involved and backing out would be very dangerous, so we should only discuss this matter when we get together alone in a secure environment, right?" Frank agreed and then Bo sprang a surprise on him. He had been in touch with Emily and they were all going to have a sumptuous dinner in a very good restaurant right now. Although the two boys had treated Emily as an irritating sister when they were all at school together, once they had moved on to university Bo had become closer to her. They had dated and kissed but both held back from expressing any stronger feelings. Once they had parted they were both very busy with training for their new jobs but had kept in touch by e-mail. It was Bo, after his grandfather had enlightened him about his father's business being involved in drug dealing, who, feeling the need for something pure in his life, had sought out Emily and after several dates had taken the relationship to a new level. Emily had responded favourably but still both held off from full commitment. Leaving out any mention of illegal substances the boys exchanged experiences with Emily and listened to her puzzlement over the early death of her mother, and the disappearance of Anthony Latimer. Bo promised to investigate to see if he could find out anything about her mother's treatment in Shanghai for Hepatitis B. Frank thought that cousin Thomas had already made some enquiries about Tony Latimer, and he would contact him and find out what progress Thomas had made.

Before Frank managed to contact Thomas, they found out all about Tony Latimer after he died in a plane crash on the 27th December 2011.

Chapter Twelve

Spring 2012 the settlement of Anthony Latimer's Billion Pound Fortune

In his office in Sandyhill Fergus Logie received the family tree from the genealogist, whom he had appointed to do the job in March 2012, and immediately set about contacting the three beneficiaries. They were Thomas Latimer, Frank Latimer, and Emily Tang, who were going to be worth some two hundred million pounds each after tax. Fergus had little difficulty in tracing their current whereabouts and sent out the usual communication by every method available.

"Would the recipient of this communication please contact Coldstone & Logie, solicitors in Sandyhill, where they will learn something to their advantage regarding the estate of Anthony Latimer" Telephone enquiries from Thomas, Frank, and Emily were answered by being told that they had inherited a considerable fortune from Anthony Latimer and that the details would all be explained at a meeting at The Fallowfield Estate in the first week in April. They were also advised that a luxury apartment had been booked for them at The Fallowfield Estate Hotel for two nights, or longer if they so choose. Coldstone & Logie also invited Lady Sarah, and all Tony's children along with a friend or partner if they so choose. The legal firm of Fortune & Fulbright would also send a representative to explain the tax situation.

Fergus and Peter Coldstone took a copy of the full family tree to show it to Lady Sarah. Of course they had no idea of the details that made up the life of each individual on the chart, only some cursory locations and employments. It was nevertheless fascinating to see the three different lines that led to the lucky three beneficiaries and note that, whilst they all originated in Manchester, Emily Tang's grandmother had diverted her family line to China. There was no indication of the beneficiaries' current wealth or social status, but Fergus was quietly confident that they were probably already well off, as luck like this rarely happens to the poor.

Emily was the first to contact Frank, carefully fishing to see if he had received the same letter from Coldstone & Logie. Frank readily confirmed that he had and wondered how much this Anthony Latimer had left them.

"Maybe he struck gold in Africa or something," laughed Frank. "Anyway I guess that we will meet at The Fallowfield Estate Hotel very soon, right?" Emily confirmed that she would be there. Frank had not had much contact with Thomas since leaving university but knew all about his business activities with Bo's father, and a quick telephone call confirmed that Thomas was also a beneficiary and would be attending the meeting with Coldstone & Logie. Thomas added that his father had told him that Anthony had taken a job in oil in Africa, but he had no idea how his cousin had fared since.

Frank then called his best mate Bo, who had already heard from Emily that she had an inheritance coming. Being careful not to say anything about their drug deal on the telephone, they both hinted that this might be a chance for Frank to change direction in his businesses. Bo said that he would come along to The Fallowfield Estate anyway, as he knew that he could cadge a few free dinners from Frank at least. Bo too was spending his spare time planning the back door escape from drug dealing and communism that his grandfather had advised him about.

Thomas arrived first at The Fallowfield Estate and was met by Lady Sarah who explained who she was and that the meeting with Coldstone & Logie was scheduled for the next morning.

"So you were living with Anthony when he had his accident, I am really sorry for your loss." Lady Sarah accepted his sympathy with a smile and said,

"Yes, it has greatly saddened a lot of people, he was a wonderful man." Thomas had only one memory of Tony.

"I haven't seen him since 1969 at his father's funeral when I was only eight, he just disappeared overseas working for an oil company according to my father. Some of my cousins have recently been wondering what happened to him, and sadly we are about to find out. You weren't married to him then?" Curiosity had overwhelmed diplomacy as Thomas knew that Emily had tried many times and failed to find evidence of a marriage for Tony on the internet.

"No, he bought what was my then husband's estate in January 1999 and employed me as his property manager. We just came together over the next few years, but he has taken care of me and all his children financially, so we don't figure as beneficiaries." Thomas was surprised and found himself responding,

"All his children, so Anthony has children?"

"Yes he has four children by four different mothers, but I was not one of them."

Sarah thought that maybe she had said too much so soon, but there would have to be lots more explanations tomorrow anyway, so she answered a few more general enquiries from Thomas as she showed him to his room.

Frank picked up Emily and Bo at Heathrow and they all checked into their own rooms in The Fallowfield Estate Hotel at around six in the evening. Sarah told them that Thomas had already arrived and after freshening up they all met in the dining room.

"Four illegitimate children with four different mothers, we really did lose track of cousin Tony didn't we?" declared Frank.

"Wow, and Lady Sarah wasn't one of them and never married him?" Responded Bo.

"That's right, but Lady Sarah has a grown up daughter from her marriage, but she was widowed before she moved in with Tony." That was the extent of Thomas's knowledge so they drifted into conversations about Hong Kong and business. Thomas noticed a certain affection seemed to exist between Emily and Bo, and for some reason it irritated him. After a couple of glasses of wine he couldn't concentrate sufficiently to remember why it irritated him, and they all decided on an early night so as to arrive fresh at the ten o'clock meeting in the morning. Not wanting to anticipate that they were about to inherit a large fortune in case that was not the case, the three beneficiaries like most humans would, allowed themselves a little imaginative speculation as they drifted off to sleep. Frank didn't really need more money except as a business tool that would allow him to exit the drug business. Thomas would be glad of sufficient funds to allow him to stand tall amongst his wife's family by buying land. Emily was the most ambivalent, she and her father were comfortable meritocrats, and would be content to remain so, leaving her with mild fantasies oscillating between minor technological gadgets and helping the needy. Bo wasn't a beneficiary but his thoughts were similar to Frank's, he was working on a safe backdoor for when the State Security Service came in the front door.

Sarah also greeted Tony's two eldest children, Per from Norway and Gina from Italy, and did her best to describe the three beneficiaries to them over dinner at her home. Sarah had been advising the other family members about the family tree of Tony's family, but now Per and Gina could see for themselves the tortuous branches that led to Thomas, Frank and Emily. Per's first thought was that Frank and Emily were very young and he wondered what sort of education they had. Gina wanted to know if Emily was beautiful and how Asian were her features? Sarah assured her that Emily was beautiful with black hair but didn't know any more about the men, but the questions were beginning to pile up for tomorrow.

Fergus Logie was ready with what was a fairly simple presentation backed up by quite a thick folder detailing the transfers of Anthony Latimer's fortune into the probate account, with one for each of the three beneficiaries and one each for Lady Sarah the appointed administrator, Coldstone & Logie, and Fortune & Fulbright. Lady Sarah did the introductions and gave everyone a copy of the family tree so that Anthony Latimer's four children could see the family background of the three beneficiaries. The three beneficiaries could see the names and ages of the four children but not their mothers' names or their different nationalities. Clearly there would be plenty of questions to be answered after the meeting was over.

Once they had all settled down Fergus announced that because Anthony Latimer had died suddenly in an accident there were no messages from the deceased to be read out, and indeed no last Will and Testament. However Lady Sarah wished to say a few words. She reminded them that, although it might seem strange for such a competent and organized man as Tony to not make a will, she was sure that he had done this intentionally as he had taken care of everyone that he cared about anyway. She knew that he loved all his children and was sure that they loved him, and the main thing was for them all to remember him lovingly for the rest of their lives. Fergus than announced that the total sum in the probate account was just over one billion pounds. Frank, Thomas and Emily looked at one another with raised eyebrows and Frank let a slight whistle escape from his lips. Fergus continued to explain that Fortune & Fulbright in discussions with HMRC had established the amount of Inheritance Tax due at between three hundred and fifty and four hundred million pounds. This would leave each of the three beneficiaries with just over two hundred million pounds each. No one amount would ever be the exact final amount for each beneficiary as the probate account was earning interest, legal fees had to be deducted, and the tax total had to be finalized according to the individual's circumstances. Two hundred million however was a good number to work with and that amount could be paid out immediately.

Fergus went on to state that there was also the question of the Provision for Family and Dependents Act 1975 which allowed claims for sufficient provision for cohabitees and dependent or step children without questioning a will. It was Coldstone & Logie's considered opinion that Lady Sarah and Anthony Latimer's four offspring could claim maintenance of at least two hundred thousand pounds per annum and that this could be achieved by a trust fund of twenty-five million pounds. He also explained to the three beneficiaries that The Fallowfield Estate country club and racing stables with all properties thereon, were owned by a trust, and this was outside their sphere of interest. Fergus then asked the three beneficiaries to take some time to consider all this information as they had decisions to make. To assist them he gave them each a slip of paper with each point that they needed to decide upon. First, would they accept the provision for dependents or dispute it in court? He recommended that they appoint their own legal representation with whom Coldstone & Logie would be happy to co-operate. If they accepted the administrators probate as explained to them, payments could commence as soon as they advised Coldstone & Logie as to the destination of the funds. With that they all retired to the lounge bar to study the family history with the aid of the family tree.

Thomas, Frank and Emily were joined by Bo and huddled around one table. They quickly agreed that they would not dispute any of

131

Coldstone & Logie's decisions, and that they would instruct their own legal representatives to get in touch with them to inform them of this fact and arrange settlement. Thomas recommended a London law firm for Emily and said that he would introduce her to them as she had not had any need for legal representation before.

They then joined Anthony Latimer's family to be acquainted with the rough details of Tony's life, and found out that he had indeed been a lucky banker. Sarah first introduced Per as Tony's thirty-seven year old oldest son, whose mother Marit had formed a jointly owned property company with Tony in Stavanger Norway in the 1970s. Next she introduced Gina as Tony's twenty-six year old eldest daughter, whose mother Fabia had formed a jointly owned antiques business with Tony in Milan Italy in the 1980s. Then she introduced Becky as Tony's fifteen year old youngest daughter whose mother Linda had formed a jointly owned Computer Services business with Tony in Houston in America in the 1990s. Sadly Linda had died in the twin towers terrorist attack on nine eleven. Finally she introduced nine year old Harry whose mother was Sarah's daughter Pamela. An embarrassed silence fell over the beneficiaries until Sarah explained that Pamela had married her partner Barbara and that their best way to have a child was by using Pamela's egg and Tony's sperm. This was after Tony and Sarah had started co-habiting and she was pleased to bless the laboratory fertilization. She then explained that Tony's three Personal Assistants, Fiona, Nicole and June had all been part of the development of The Fallowfield Estate into a luxury country club with sporting facilities and a first class racing stables. They all lived and owned properties on the estate except Per and Gina who lived with their families in Norway and Italy. They were all also trustees of The Fallowfield Estate Trust, and therefore didn't have any problem with the beneficiaries inheriting Tony's cash, as they had been well taken care of. Thomas hadn't mentioned that he was an MEP and when Sarah introduced Gina her mother's details had struck a chord with him. He knew an Italian MEP who was from Milan and had an antique business but decided not to enquire any further just now. Frank was the first to re-act,

"Well, our cousin was a well-travelled man." Which prompted Sarah to complete the story.

"That's not half of the story; Tony was constantly travelling from the age of twenty-one until he settled down here in January 1999 when he was fifty-eight. He had property businesses in Aberdeen, London and Houston, and investments all over the world. He forecast the 2008 bank crash and several major increases in the price of gold, which led to him being involved in an American court case, which he won. When he settled down here he built up a stable of top class race horses that Pamela trained for him, but he never mentioned any family, other than his parents who had died in a car crash, and that he did not have any siblings." Thomas responded this time,

"It's partly our fault because we didn't make much of an effort to find Tony, although Emily was just beginning to get interested in her missing cousin. It's not uncommon for first cousins once removed to lose touch with each other, so perhaps you are surprised that we beneficiaries and our friend Bo here, seem well acquainted, so perhaps I should explain our connections."

Thomas then went on to explain how they had all been brought together when the three youngsters started at the same boarding school on the same day, and that he had accompanied Bo, the son of a Chinese business acquaintance of his. Frank had been accompanied by his mother Margaret who had the same surname of Latimer. He and Margaret, who was a widow, had worked out their relationship to one another over the next few meetings, but Emily had come into the picture only because she spoke Mandarin and came from Hong Kong after it was returned to China. Of course Bo who came from Shanghai and also spoke Mandarin, had brought Emily into the triumvirate of friends. It was only later after all three of them had moved on to Manchester University, that Emily had researched her grandmother's family, which she knew came from Manchester. To her surprise she discovered that she was related to both Frank and himself, but also that she had another missing cousin called Anthony. Frank and Bo had gone on to work in their family businesses in England and China respectively, and Emily was a journalist living with her widower father in Hong Kong. Thomas was from an older generation and although married still did not have any children. He was a business consultant specializing in Asia as he too spoke Mandarin.

Afterwards they mixed together and satisfied their own curiosities during a celebratory dinner. The next morning they all took their leave of one another. Per went back to Norway happy with his annual maintenance allowance and his trusteeship of The Fallowfield Estate, although he was proud of the fact that he had always earned his own living, it was nice to have a little extra. Gina was in the same position as Per only her family was her work, and her mother was on her way to join her in London to celebrate. For Sarah, Becky and Harry it was life continuing as usual only now Sarah was even busier and they all still felt the loss of Tony. They were however happy in the knowledge that they had healthy bank balances and a secure share in The Fallowfield Estate Trust, which was now a one hundred million pound asset. The three beneficiaries and Bo retreated to London to call their families and lawyers and discuss their future.

Part III Family Misfortunes
Chapter Thirteen
The International Conglomerate

Emily met her father at Heathrow and took him to Bo's father's company flat, a luxurious four bedroom apartment in Mayfair, where Bo and Frank were discussing their mutual problem whilst they waited. Frank wanted to get out of dealing in drugs but wanted to continue to build his successful non-drug businesses using his newly acquired capital. Frank however, had a contract with Bo's father's businesses to fulfil, as he now pointed out to Bo. Bo understood and told Frank that he would help him in every way that he could, as he too was looking for an escape route from both the drug business and the tentacles of the Chinese State Security Service. They both agreed to start looking for ways to separate the drug involvement from the rest of their respective businesses, and keep one another advised of their progress.

Once Emily and her father arrived they all turned their attention onto Emily and how she should handle her inheritance. Li Tang was not ecstatic when Emily telephoned to tell him how much she had inherited, and had rushed to join her and help her with the administration of two hundred million pounds sterling. On the twelve hour flight to London he had time to reflect and in the cab from airport to apartment, he had suggested that he and Emily should become resident in the UK. As for the money, it was best to invest in low risk interest or dividend paying accounts and use the income to support good causes. His one special interest however, was supporting the shaky democracy that Prime Minister Thatcher had managed to bequeath to the people of Hong Kong. Already the communist party that ruled China was trying to undermine the principle of 'one country two systems for fifty years', as they had agreed with Mrs Thatcher's British Government. Li knew everyone worth knowing in Hong Kong and thought that from the safety of the UK, and with some funds he could keep the communists out of Hong Kong until they were forced to accept democracy for the whole country before the fifty years were up. Emily listened to her father's advice and was pleased as she had been thinking along the same lines. She could continue the good works of both her grandmother and her father, and that would give purpose to her life.

Emily and Li didn't immediately mention any of their plan when they arrived at the apartment, and it was Bo who, after they had all settled down, asked Emily if she needed any help with collecting her inheritance. Emily had been in a bit of a daydream since the announcement of the amount of her inheritance and was pleased with Bo's masterly manner, taking care of their accommodation and addressing her practical problems.

"Thomas introduced me to a firm of lawyers before he left to visit his wife and I went to collect Dad from the airport. The legal firm have agreed to act on my behalf, on the understanding that I do not wish to dispute anything. You can help me open a current account here in London and then I will advise the lawyers of its details, along with my personal details so that they can keep me informed of their progress." Emily had a first class honours degree in Modern Languages and Business & Management (Chinese), so she was not incapable of handling her newly acquired wealth, it was just nice to have Bo offer to help, and it gave her a warm feeling. Now with a smile in the direction of her father, she decided to reveal a little of his plan.

"With such a huge inheritance I don't need to work but I want to, so I will find some good causes to support with my money. Father and I are thinking about becoming UK residents but we will spend some time in Hong Kong each year." Bo was pleased that Emily was already making plans as he was becoming more and more infatuated with her.

"You and Li can stay here as long as you like and I will help you with your plans if you like, you only have to ask."

Emily was a sensitive woman who felt distressed when seeing or hearing about the misfortunes of others. Her membership of the communist party was an anomaly now that she was a multi-millionaire, and her search for her mother's life and death had brought her into contact with the Methodists who had known her mother. This form of Protestant Christianity was sympathetic to the communist aims of equality and sharing to help the poor, but varied radically from communism because of the Methodists' abhorrence of rule by a wealthy elite priestly class, and any form of violent enforcement that a one party system required. Emily's father Li Tang was a recently retired Hong Kong civil servant, himself half Chinese and half English. He had survived the end of the British lease of Hong Kong and its return to Chinese sovereignty, and was happy that the one country two systems would last beyond his life time. The Tangs were essentially carers and administrators whose main aim in life was more equality for the world's citizens. They acknowledged the usefulness of capital if used for the benefit of all, but it was not something that they had deliberately sought.

Bo was entranced by the Tang family, who were so confident and optimistic. They didn't seem to suffer the same anxieties as everyone else and were satisfied with working hard towards what they believed in. Nevertheless he wanted to show his affection by teasing Emily.

"You could also donate some money to supporting your old school and some of its pupils, those who have fallen on hard times and haven't received an inheritance," he said smiling. Emily recognized his intention to convey intimacy, by joking about a suggestion that would embarrass if there was no intimacy.

"Oh alright, I will give you a couple of grand if you are broke," and Emily gave Bo a look that melted his heart. That night Emily went into Bo's bedroom and climbed purposefully into bed with him. Their first ever love-making left them both in no doubt that they were meant for each other. Even if it hadn't been so successful Emily would have persevered as she had made up her mind. She needed the strength and comfort of a good partner and the children that they would produce.

The lovers didn't mention their commitment in the morning and Frank took off for Spain to inform his mother and Keith about his good fortune. Frank Latimer was in a quandary; why would a man worth more than two hundred million pounds risk prison by dealing in illegal drugs? He was proud of the legitimate businesses that he had built up and would now love to expand them with the aid of his newly acquired inheritance. He couldn't just drop the whole drug business as it would upset too many people, and even if they didn't decide to protect themselves by eliminating him, they might inform on him to the authorities. Frank was well protected by his Captains who acted as cut outs between himself and their Lieutenants. His legitimate businesses had been funded by the profits from the purchase and sale of illegal drugs, with ownership and the dividends that they earned, shared forty percent to Frank and his mother, forty percent to Keith and twenty percent to other investors, managers, and employees who knew nothing about the drugs. Frank's problem was that the drugs infected the legitimate businesses like a virus, with disguised packets of various quantities of illegal substances inserted into the storage warehouses. Each package was extracted under the supervision of the Captains and transported to seemingly legitimate purchasers, who were in fact the Lieutenants. One Captain in each business monitored and instructed the entirely innocent warehousemen and delivery van drivers. If Frank suddenly stopped providing the drugs, denied access to his multi company storage, transport, and secure administration facilities, his Captains and Lieutenants would be very upset. Then there was his agreement with Bo, to purchase large quantities of drugs on a regular basis from Wei's Chinese business.

Upon his arrival in Sant Carles de la Rapita Frank told Margaret and Keith about his good fortune and they were delighted. His mother immediately said that this was his opportunity to get out of the drug supply business. Frank looked at Keith as he knew that was where the solution to his problem lay. Keith was confident that he could persuade the best Captain, Chris, to take over Frank's position and re-organize the other Captains. Frank would incentivise Chris by giving him his first two major purchases, one from Europe and one from China. He would introduce Chris to his two remaining European contacts and to Min Kuang, Wei's Chinese front man for the supply of drugs. Finally Frank would separate one warehouse in Europe and one in England, each with its own Internet sales website, staff, and Frank's computerized control system. The control system identified the whereabouts of the drug packages only to those who could recognise it. All that was needed after that, before Frank could became free of the drug supply business, was to organise a buyer for this Chris-controlled outfit that was still forty percent owned by Keith, forty percent owned by Frank and his mother, and twenty percent owned by the other investors, managers and employees. A legal sale was crucial to finalize Frank's detachment from illegal activities, and to satisfy the twenty percent of shareholders who knew nothing about the drugs. Because of these shareholders Keith and Margaret and Frank couldn't give that part of the business away at a knock-down price, but would accept an offer at moderately less than the market price, and make up the difference to those minor shareholders from Frank's inheritance. Keith would try and put together a bid consortium of people and funds that he had contact with, Frank would give a quarter of the money that he would be due from his forty percent share of the sale price, to Chris in the form of shares in the new company so that he would have a place on the board. He would also instruct Chris on the understanding of the computerized control system, so that he would have credibility as being in control of the business. Keith would also reinvest some of his profit from the sale of the old business into shares in the new consortium, in the name of his son from his first marriage. This allowed Keith to keep in touch with the business and satisfied Margaret that he and Frank would be clear of it. Keith and Frank agreed to set about organizing this planned sale of what was in fact only one quarter of the whole business that Frank had built up. The remaining three quarters of the business, renamed Delamerenet plc. Would continue under Frank's management with the same share ownership, but it would be free of any connection to the purchase and supply of illegal drugs.

Bo was in London and agreed to join Frank at Aintree to watch the Grand National. The two good mates had a drink together and backed their fancy in each race with careless abandon and no success. In between races there was plenty of time to discuss business and their private ambitions. Bo started by confessing,

"Emily and I have started an affair and we are both head over heels in love." He was pleased to get their secret out in the open, and continued,

"I always had a special feeling for Emily, one of those things that it's hard to define, but it was Emily who made the first move. It's so much different for women, they seem to sense that something is right and necessary for them, and then they go for it as though their life depends upon it. Anyway I was glad that she made her feelings clear to me as that made it much easier for me to abandon my attitude that she was an untouchable friend." Frank wasn't expecting this outpouring and for a moment searched for a response, his two closest friends from his teenage years would now be closer and more intimate with each other than they were with him. Of course he had fancied Emily, what young man wouldn't, but he had always managed to persuade himself that she was one of his mates and had to be treated as such. Now he felt a little bit jealous and betrayed by both his best mates, but he persuaded himself to hide his new feelings.

"That's wonderful," he blurted out, "So what are your plans?" Bo realized that Frank had called this meeting because his situation had changed since he had received his inheritance.

"We don't have any just yet it's all so new. Emily doesn't know about the illegal drug side of my businesses. My Dad is Chairman and I am now the Chief Operating Officer of the conglomerate and see no way out of that situation. We both live mainly outside China proper and I am going to set up more security so that I can disappear myself if the party, or the Western security services, decide that I am a problem. What about you Frank, now that you have a fortune?" Frank liked Bo's security idea and he had more than enough money to keep a helicopter handy, maybe even learn to fly one. He was now busy working on his plan to separate his drug business from the legitimate one and sell it, but believed that his plan could be further enhanced if he solved Bo's problem as well.

"I'm in the same boat as you Bo, but like you a lot of people depend upon me, including your outfit, and they wouldn't be happy if I just dropped out. Anyway I don't want to sit around spending money and getting fat, I want to expand and develop my legitimate businesses. I have the inkling of an idea! What if your outfit Bo, made a takeover bid for my legitimate business? I am already arranging the separation and sale of the part of my business that deals in drugs, and you could isolate the drug dealing parts of your business, leaving your international conglomerate free to take over my profitable business with good access to the European market. I would take shares in your conglomerate as the price for my business and I could become your Financial Director, which would ease your burden and allow us to work closely together to avoid any problems with the authorities. What do you think about that?" Bo felt a sense of relief, there was hope after all,

"Wow Frank, that's quite a plan, I always knew that you were a clever boy. Let's think about your idea and develop it."

With a few beers downed and now starting on the wine with a nice meal in the restaurant, the two good mates began to see the light and to cheerfully plan Bo's and Emily's wedding sometime in the future.

Thomas thought that his wife had had one or two affairs whilst travelling to fashion weeks around the world, he thought that he had noticed little changes in her, but as he expected she had been very discreet and he had suffered no embarrassment. He had told his wife that he was about to inherit a small amount from a cousin, who had lost contact with the rest of his family in 1970 when Thomas was only nine. Of the three inheritors Thomas was the one who had known the most about Anthony Latimer. Once Emily had started constructing her family tree when she started at Manchester University, and had discovered that Tony had disappeared to Africa in 1970, Thomas had done his own research. He discovered that his cousin owned The Fallowfield Estate near Cambridge, and to his own surprise, that they had shared a mistress. Fabia, the mother of Tony Latimer's second illegitimate child Gina, whom Thomas had just met at The Fallowfield Estate when collecting his inheritance, had become an MEP in 2006. This very attractive mature woman only two or three years older than himself, must have noticed his Latimer surname and decided to seduce him. This was her nature as it had been all her life, and she would have found satisfaction and amusement in their short lived affair in Strasbourg, without letting him know of their connection. Thomas knew that The Fallowfield Estate had been gifted to a trust and because Tony Latimer had always been secretive regarding his other assets, Thomas had no way of knowing that he had one billion pounds stashed away in liquid assets. Now he hesitated to tell his wife how much he had inherited; two hundred million pounds after tax was a lot more than he had expected. It would be handy for him to have more than her family thought he had, as it would give him flexibility, an advantage that politicians love to have. He now told his wife that he had inherited about one hundred million pounds, but it would take a couple of months for the money to be deposited in his account. In the meantime she could start looking at buying a place with some land in the countryside, as he had to go and take care of some business in China.

The business in China was to gently break off his affair with Shan, Bo's mother, but not until he had extracted some more information from her about Emily's mother. During their affair Shan had already let slip that Florence Lane had been caught spying for MI6 in China, and that it was Shan's father-in-law, Bo Senior, who had caught Emily's mother. Bo Senior had himself been saved from starvation as a child by Emily's grandmother the Methodist missionary and Thomas had already made some assumptions regarding these bare facts before he took off for Shanghai to see if Shan would confirm them.

Thomas checked into the same Park Lane Hotel that Frank had used when he first met his Chinese suppliers and found out that Bo was their boss. He had stayed there before and was recognized at the reception counter. Fluent in Mandarin he chatted politely before taking his key to his room and tipping the porter who delivered his bags. Tired after the long flight from London Thomas found the energy to telephone Wei in Hong Kong and discuss the forthcoming board meeting that was the main purpose of his trip. Wei indicated that Bo had an interesting motion for discussion by the board, a takeover bid for a British business managed and part owned by a certain Frank Latimer. Thomas's brain went into overdrive, he knew that his father Brian had deliberately steered clear of his Brother David's family because of his involvement with drug dealing. Similarly he had avoided his cousin William, Frank's father, who had been murdered. His own familiarity with Frank had only come about because of his sponsorship of Bo at the same school. He had heard that Frank had started his own internet based companies since leaving university, but had never had occasion to investigate them. Now it looked like he would regret his failure to do so, and responded to Wei's revelation with,

"Bo and Frank are best mates, they were at school and university together, but you know that right?" Wei was well aware of the friendship between his son and Frank although he had never met

Frank. He had deliberately slipped the surprising information about Bo's motion into his telephone conversation with Thomas to see if Thomas would let slip something that he didn't know about Frank Latimer.

"Yes, but how close have they been since they left university, have you heard anything about Frank's activities during the last five years?" This astute question sent Thomas's mind into convulsions once more. Bo knew all about their inheritance, but would Bo have told Wei. If Wei knew he would surely have congratulated Thomas on his good luck when he first started this telephone conversation. Thomas decided that honesty was the best policy for maintaining trust.

"We all recently met when Frank, Emily and I inherited a great deal of money from a cousin, but Bo must have told you about that right, he was there. We will have a chat before the board meeting so that we can discuss it all fully then. I am a bit jet-lagged now so I will see you on Friday." With that Thomas rang off but found it hard to sleep for an hour or so, before fatigue finally overwhelmed his mind.

The next day, Wednesday, Thomas was up late and enjoyed a good breakfast before settling down with the telephone and his laptop. Frank's business webpage reflected a prosperous business retailing and delivering many lines of consumer items. He telephoned Frank's mother Margaret in Spain, asking after her health and reminiscing about their trips to Frank and Bo's boarding school. She congratulated him on his inheritance and he asked her what Frank was likely to do with his two hundred million pounds. She replied that he was thinking of investing some of it in his business, and issued an open invitation for him and his wife to visit her and Keith in San Carlos de la Rapita. So nothing revealed there then. He then searched for court convictions in Frank's name but drew a blank with that enquiry. He tried a couple of social friends whom he knew used drugs recreationally but they had never heard of Frank Latimer, and had no idea of the identity of their own supplier. Five years to create such a thriving business? Where had he raised his capital? Even if it had come from his father and mother's time in the drug business, that didn't prove that he had carried on with his own drug business. There was no option left but to talk to Frank as he had his mobile number following their meeting at The Fallowfield Estate.

"Hi Frank it's Thomas, what's this I hear about Bo proposing a takeover bid for your business at Friday's board meeting?" Frank had never received a telephone call from Thomas before and assumed that as a director of Wei's consortium, Thomas was fishing for information before the board discussed the motion.

"Hi Thomas, well it's all confidential until your board votes to do due diligence, but as you're a director perhaps I can convince you to vote for the motion. We have a good fit with Wei's shipping and transport interests, which could be brought together with my software control of the retail end of my business in a separate division with some nice cost savings. I might take shares in Wei's business conglomerate outside China as payment and then invest half my inheritance in expanding that division side by side with Bo. What about you Thomas, why don't you invest half of your inheritance with us, we know you have the experience and the contacts that we need?"

Once again Thomas was surprised by a new proposition and could only answer that he would think about it. Afterwards he wondered about the division of Wei's business that was to remain Chinese and in which Frank would not be investing. Was this where the drug dealing would be hidden?

Thomas finally got round to calling Shan and arrange a tryst for that evening. He was still sexually excited by Shan's small but exquisite face and figure but Thomas was fifty now, and Shan only a couple of years younger. They no longer felt the same urgency or frequency for one another, but with careful stimulation and attention to one another's needs they could still reach the ecstasy of mutual satisfaction at the climax of their intercourse. Thomas picked Shan up at her home in a hired chauffeured limousine and they drove to a suitably expensive and discreet restaurant. In fact there was no need for discretion as Shan was one of Shanghai's richest and most powerful women. She was proud to display her distinguished western businessman, who was fluent in Mandarin, as her escort, and was quite happy to acknowledge greetings from other prominent dinners. Once settled at their table in an alcove Thomas decided that he would not tell Shan about his inheritance, but would relax her by talking about her son Bo.

"I have to attend a board meeting with Wei and Bo in Hong Kong on Friday and I understand that Bo has an exciting new proposal to expand the business." Shan already knew about Bo's motion and was worried about the connection with Frank whom, like Wei, she had never met, but she knew full well that he had been Bo's good friend at school and university.

"Yes I know, but you know Frank Latimer well; I believe that he is your first cousin once removed, so what do you think about a tie up with him?" This was Thomas's chance to make a confession and maybe extract one from Shan.

"Frank is a clever lad just like Bo, and I think that they will make a good business team, but there have always been rumours about Frank's side of the family being involved in dealing drugs. His business has been very successful and grown very quickly over only five years since he left university, and I don't know where he got his capital start-up funding from. He certainly didn't approach a bank or I would have heard about it as I have an office in Manchester where he is based." Shan was caught by surprise at the mention of drugs and quickly assumed that her clever son Bo knew that Frank was involved in drugs, and that Frank's business could be a good match for that part of her and Wei's business that also involved drug dealing.

"That's interesting, drug use in China is not unknown, even my father-in-law Bo senior had some involvement when he was very young." That was a perfect lead-in for Thomas, who replied,

"Do you remember Emily Tang in Hong Kong who was also at school and university with Bo and Frank, and became a good friend of theirs? You once told me that Bo Senior caught her mother on a mission for MI6 in Shanghai. You also told me that her grandmother had saved your father-in-law's life when he was a child. Did Bo Senior free Emily's mother because he felt that he owed his life to her grandmother?" Shan was beginning to relax as the expensive wine they had been enjoying began to take effect.

"Yes but he couldn't just let her go as he had to satisfy the party, so he turned her into a double agent and had her going back and forth to Hong Kong carrying instructions for and making deliveries to other agents. I don't think that she produced any great revelation for either side, but she had an affair with my father-in-law. When it became apparent that China was going to get Hong Kong back, Wei was worried that she knew too much about our family, and could be used by other party members against us once they had access to her in Hong Kong. Wei decided to get rid of her and had her infected with an infectious disease." Back in Shan's home Thomas was already on the couch up against Shan and beginning to enjoy lightly caressing every gentle curve of her body. They kissed but then Thomas pulled back away a little with a sigh. Shan's mind was troubled by some indistinct thought but her body was getting ready for pleasure.

"What's the matter darling," she murmured.

"I would love to go ahead but I really came to visit because I want to simplify my life. We are getting older and my wife is getting more demanding, so perhaps it would be better if we were just friends in future."

"That's all right darling but now we have started please continue and we can break up tomorrow." Thomas could not restrain himself as Shan began to move her body against his and for a while they gave themselves up to their feelings until they were drained and ready for sleep. Their dreams were disturbed but it was only when they awoke that they could concentrate on Shan's revelations. Shan made Thomas promise never to mention her indiscretions to Wei as she feared that he might eliminate her if he knew that she had let his secret slip out.

As Thomas returned to his Shanghai hotel room that Thursday morning he had a lot to think about and a niggling worry that too much knowledge can be dangerous. He had a security man and a personal assistant with him now that he was a multi-millionaire and he called them to join him for breakfast. He advised the security man that he had some sensitive information on his person and that he should assume that there was a slightly increased risk that he might be approached or threatened. Thomas told him to stay with him at all times until they got back to Europe. His PA was to arrange the charter of a private jet for the trip to Hong Kong that afternoon, and a hotel suite with two bedrooms and a sitting room for the three of them in Hong Kong. Thomas relaxed a bit as he realized that he was beginning to enjoy being filthy rich. He then composed a letter and sealed it in an envelope addressed to-whom-it-may-concern. He put the sealed envelope in another envelope with a cover letter to his lawyers in London. He made two more exactly the same and gave them to his two companions with instructions to post their envelopes on their return to Europe. He intended to post his letter as soon as they landed in Hong Kong. Thomas then made a phone call to his wife and told her he would be home by Sunday but if he didn't show up she should start searching for him on Monday at the latest. This of course alarmed Susan and Thomas had to start reassuring her that the risk was minimal and concerned some delicate commercial information that he had gained.

Frank flew in to Hong Kong on Thursday and was met by Bo's limousine and driver who took him straight to Bo's apartment. They wanted to present their proposal to Wei the major shareholder as an agreed deal just before the board meeting. Frank had brought the audited accounts of Delamerenet showing that the three-quarters of his legitimate retail business, remaining after the sale of one quarter of the business to a drug dealing consortium, had a turnover of 35M, 40M, and 47M over the last three years, with a net EBITDA (Earnings before Interest, Tax, Depreciation and Amortization) of fourteen percent. That would be worth a 50M pounds Sterling bid of anyone's money, or £5- a share for the 10M shares issued. (A hostile takeover would probably have had to go to 60M, but there was added value for all parties in a friendly merger.) For payment Frank and the other shareholders would accept shares in Wei's non-Chinese conglomerate that Bo Junior had now registered as an entirely separate business in Switzerland renamed Oxysung International. Frank would also make 100M pounds of his inheritance available, either as a loan to Oxysung Int., or for a share issue by Oxysung Int., whichever its board decided upon. This commitment to the company would come as soon as Frank was appointed the Financial Director with the appropriate salary and benefits. Bo was already the Chief Executive Officer (CEO) and the two friends knew that Wei would be happy to reduce his involvement in the day to day running of the business, but as he was still the majority shareholder he would be Chairman of the Board. Bo and Frank were ready to put the deal to Wei.

There was no chance of the other shareholders of Delamerenet refusing the takeover offer, as Frank had Keith's assurance that he would vote his forty percent to accept the offer. Frank had also assured all other shareholders of Delamerenet that he would buy their new shares in Oxysung Int., at the takeover value as soon as they received them, if that was what they wanted.

That left Wei's China-located businesses, which included: the mobile phone network, property, the land transport company, and the shipping company, which he had effectively handed over to the communist party under Bo Senior's management. It would still be used to supply drugs to Europe as a means of weakening the West. Wei would still help and advise his father from his office outside China, especially with regard to the shipping line and the control of the drug dealers. Frank assured Bo that both he and his business were now entirely free of drug dealing, but that they should explain to Wei that Chris would be lined up to connect with his Chinese manager to ensure the continuation of the flow of drug supplies from China to the UK.

On Friday morning Bo met with Wei and laid out their plan in detail. Wei was quite happy to accept the proposal and at the following board meeting Bo's motion was passed unanimously. Of course no mention of the drug business was made as this was known only to Frank and the Sung family, although Thomas was beginning to put two and two together. The board consisted of Wei, Shan, Bo Senior, Bo Junior, Thomas Latimer and four respected businessmen, two Chinese, one British, and one American. Frank had been comfortably installed in the visitors' lounge by Bo prior to the meeting and was now fetched by Bo to be introduced to the board members and receive their congratulations. Papers were cleared away and a splendid lunch served as Wei started to assess Frank his new partner.

"I have heard nothing but good things about you during your schooldays with Bo and it was a comfort to Shan and myself that Bo had a good friend, and of course the support of Thomas." Frank had formed his own idea of Wei over the years but now saw that his assumptions had been wide of the mark. Wei was slim and steely-eyed, wearing an expensive suit and displaying impeccable manners, and was nothing like what Frank had imagined.

"Yes we had a great time together and I am sure that we can work well as a team now that we have to look after your businesses." Shan was also studying Frank as she and Bo Senior would be needing his help if their drug supply operation ran into any trouble with Chris his replacement. She thought that she saw a young man with more steel in his nature than her son Bo.

"I know that you will enjoy working with Bo and your Mandarin is excellent, although not quite as good as Thomas's. If you ever feel like visiting the real China, Bo's grandfather and I will be happy to take care of you in Shanghai for as long as you want to visit." Frank could see that Shan, who was in her late forties, was elegantly dressed in a black jacket and short skirt that exposed very shapely legs. Still this was his best friend's mother and he shouldn't even be thinking like that about her.

"That's very kind of you, I will visit Shanghai as soon as I have time," he said smiling. Thomas had been puzzled ever since he had heard about the separate division, and the way that the subject was changed whenever it was mentioned. He now decided to test the waters.

"I can see that forming Oxysung Int., will leave the Chinese businesses separate from the free market businesses, but is that the only advantage?" Wei scowled at Shan making sure that Thomas could not see him, and Senior Bo chose to answer.

"Apart from shielding the Chinese businesses from the higher overheads of the worldwide conglomerate, which relies more upon marketing, the main reason is that Shan and I are better able to protect them from the party straightjacket without the distraction of foreign businesses that don't affect China at all." Thomas could recognize a political speech when he heard it, so he just said,

"Yes that sounds very sensible." At the same time Thomas's mind was telling him to get closer to Frank and find out what was really going on. Frank recognized the need to change the subject of

149

the discussion away from the drug-supplying Chinese businesses and asked Thomas,

"Why don't you do what I am going to do, and invest in Oxysung Int., we have funds in hand and an expansion plan, so you should get a good return?" Thomas smiled as he recognized that the whole board had heard of his inheritance.

"Yes I will consider it," replied Thomas, "but first I had better go home and talk to my wife," he concluded to general laughter.

As the board members broke up to go about their business, Bo and Frank returned to Bo's apartment where Emily was waiting for them. Senior Bo followed Wei into his office and murmured,

"I think Thomas is beginning to suspect that drugs are involved in our Chinese business dealings." Wei had already come to the same conclusion.

"Yes Shan has been indiscreet and who knows what else she has let slip. Why don't you have a word with her and find out." Bo had already done that before the meeting and now assured Wei that Shan and Thomas had ended their affair. What the old man didn't mention to his son was that the party at the highest level had recently been taking more interest in the drug dealing. The operational details had always been down to him in his position at the top of the Shanghai security service committee, whilst the Politburo had merely indicated that they wished to weaken the West by any means available. To date Senior Bo had been able to operate unchallenged in the business, but now one Politburo member was asking questions?

The re-united lovers Bo and Emily were only too happy to demonstrate their feelings in front of Frank, who congratulated Emily as this was the first time that he had seen her since Bo revealed their affair.

"But why are you keeping it secret," asked Frank, "I can't think of any reason why you should." Emily smiled at him and agreed.

"We are not going to keep it secret it's just that we don't want any big announcement or engagement for some time. We are still very young and want to stabilize our careers before we get engaged."

"Yes," agreed Bo, "and we start this evening by inviting you Frank to dinner out with Emily's father, and we will just do the same with all family and friends to let them know that we are an item."

The following morning Bo and Frank called on Wei in his office and told him that they were off to Switzerland and the UK. Bo would stay there and in conjunction with their lawyers and bankers would implement the merger details approved by the board. Frank would go on to Spain and then Manchester a few days later and meet up with Min Kuang, the Chinese manager chosen by Wei to control his Chinese companies. Frank would line him up to deal with Chris's drug dealing organization, and that would free Frank from any more illegal activity. Wei gave both young men a bear hug and sent them on their way to the airport. They went to Geneva to complete the expansion plans for Oxysung Int., then Frank flew to Barcelona and called in on his mother and Keith in San Carlos de la Rapita. He had kept them informed of his plan and now needed their signatures on several documents. They were quite happy to be free of any involvement in the business. After mailing the signed documents to the new office in Geneva, Frank went on to Manchester. Min Kuang was already established in a city hotel and Frank took Chris to meet him. Min's English was very good and Frank went over his agreement with Bo until they both agreed that they accepted that it was now an agreement between themselves. Of course this was not a written agreement, but now they were in control of their respective parties to the agreement, and Frank was not to be contacted again for any reason. Finally Frank was free to join Bo in Geneva and play his part in the planning of the expansion of Oxysung Int.

Chapter Fourteen

Politics Capital and the Rule of Law

Thomas Latimer was a thoughtful man, he had progressed by steady application of a keen intelligence and a pleasant personality. He found himself strangely attracted to occasional moments of danger, the opposite of his normal demeanour. His recent trip to China had been one such occasion and when he realised that he possessed knowledge that could put others in danger, he had increased his security. Now safely back in Cheshire and viewing country estates with his wife, he had some time for reflection. He was vaguely aware that his parents had relaxed their moral judgement in order to improve their and his lot. Thomas was OK with that in the way that all politicians tend to adjust their judgements according their Party's manifesto. He had however in his early days as a Manchester Councillor been exposed to the problem of drug addiction, and knew that joining the fight against illegal drugs was a vote winner. Unlike Frank Latimer, (who believed that all dangerous substances should be legalized, taxed, and the tax kept separate from the Treasury's general tax pot for the sole use of warning the young of the dangers, and curing those addicted to dangerous substances.) Thomas was keen to be seen to join the fight against drugs. He decided to try his pitch out on his wife Susan as they sat on the balustrade surrounding the terrace of a country house on its own one hundred acre estate.

"Darling I'm thinking of taking a more active role in the fight against drugs, there is far too much crime committed to provide the funds for sustaining drug habits and it's even spreading into the countryside these days." Susan was used to her husband's failure to concentrate on domestic practicalities and wondered if he had picked up this new concern on his recent trip to China.

"Quite right darling, those druggies are killing civilised people on the roads and shamefully abuse their families. Something should be done about it." Susan paused and failing any response from Thomas she continued,

"That drive from the gate to the house will need some attention, don't you think Thomas?" He managed to drag himself back to Susan's world and replied,

"Yes darling we will have to spend quite a bit to get this place up to our standard." Susan was right, it had been his recent trip to China that had started his new concern. Thomas decided that he would have to resign his directorship in Wei's company first; a politician could not afford any link to drugs no matter how remotely. It would diminish his influence in China, but if he were to oppose their involvement in the drug trade, then his influence would diminish anyway.

The rest of that summer Thomas stayed in Cheshire and assisted his wife in establishing their new home. They bought the country house on its one hundred acres and Susan was in her element decorating the eight bedrooms and six bathrooms. Thomas busied himself with directing the building company hired to bring the house and its drive up to standard. He was delighted that he didn't have to think about the cost of anything, as he could afford almost everything. Not that he would be buying an aeroplane or a boat or anything silly like that. Despite promising himself a really fantastic car, he ended up buying a dull Bentley and suffering the indignity of having to wait for it to be delivered. Of course he treated Susan to some spectacular jewellery, and was rewarded by considerably more passion than they had been used to recently. Her real passion was for antiques and Thomas found that he too thoroughly enjoyed buying rare and beautiful objects for very high prices. They both really enjoyed a day at an up-market auction house, and soon their home was full of fine decorative objects. The other activity that they both enjoyed was gardening, but not in the 'down on your knees with a trowel' kind of gardening. More the 'designing and directing the gardener' kind of gardening, although they would occasional clip off protruding twigs or flower stems with secateurs. With such a pleasant summer behind him, Thomas was ready for a return to action in Strasbourg for the autumn sitting.

Although at home during the summer Thomas hadn't been entirely inactive. His resignation as a director of Oxysung Int., had been accepted and he had been sending messages to other MEPs, trying to establish who was already active in the fight against drugs. With a tingle of pleasure and anticipation he discovered that Fabia was chairing a Brussels committee engaged in co-operating with the Americans on just such a war. Leaving Susan happily finishing off their estate and awaiting the arrival of a baby, Thomas set off in his Bentley down the drive from the manor house to the gatehouse. The drive had already been completely relaid, a task that Thomas was proud to have managed. He then drove to the local airport and travelled by chartered executive jet, along with his PR woman and his security man at his own expense, to Milan. Knowing Fabia's liking for being seen in High Society he collected her from Milan and then flew to Paris for the races at Longchamp Racecourse at the beginning of October. The best hotel, a new outfit, and a perfect dinner, it was as though their affair had never faded away, except that Thomas was now an expectant father, who accepted Fabia's congratulations without any desire to renew intimacy. Over dinner he explained to Fabia his decision to try and stop the trafficking of drugs into Europe from China, and asked her to put him in touch with the Anti-Drug Committee that she was a part of. Fabia said that she would be delighted to help him. On the Sunday the classic race was the Prix de l'Arc de Triomphe and no middle-aged women at the event looked more attractive than Fabia. Also on Sunday they found Paris's huge open air antique market and Fabia was happy to buy objects that she knew she could sell to her long list of clients, who still patronized her antique shop in Milan. Thomas accepted Fabia's expert advice on which objects to buy for Susan, both personal and for their new home.

On Monday they flew on to Brussels and settled down to work, Thomas was introduced by Fabia to the European Union's Anti-Drug Committee members, and he told them that, whilst he had been travelling on behalf of the European Union's International Trade Committee, he had accidentally been informed that the Chinese were deliberately trying to flood Europe with debilitating drugs. He believed that he knew which Chinese company was taking instructions from the Chinese State Security Service to operate large scale drug trafficking into Europe. Thomas then asked the committee if they could advise him as to how he could help to stop this trafficking. The committee advised that he talk to the Americans to see if he could help them catch the Chinese in the act of smuggling. If they could achieve this then the Anti-Drug Committee would have some ammunition to help put pressure on the Chinese government to co-operate in curtailing the trade.

Fabia then introduced Thomas to a trade attaché at the American Embassy and left them to discuss their business. It was evident that the Americans were actively involved in the war on drugs, but they needed a time and a place where they could arrest the traffickers. That would be sufficient for them to act as the information came from a respected elected Member of the European Parliament. Thomas left with the knowledge that he had made a contact who could be informed as soon as he had the required information, and it would be acted on.

It would cost Thomas a lot of money but then he had a lot of money. He knew that Shan was looking for a way of establishing a western bank account. She was already wealthy, but only by way of payoffs from Wei out of his share of the drug profits. She could have divorced him and obtained a handsome alimony payoff, but that would have involved the courts and revealing more than was wise. Her unwritten agreement with Senior Bo and Wei was that they all avoid investigations into their business activities, and anyway any divorce settlement would still have to be made in China's Renminbi currency. Thomas called Shan on her mobile and in a very quick conversation told her to buy a pre-paid phone to be disposed of as soon as she had called him on it and completed a deal that would be to her advantage. He gave her the number of his newly purchased pre-paid mobile and rang off. Shan knew that Thomas had resigned his directorship in Wei's business and of course everyone knew of his good fortune with his inheritance. If Wei was angry with Thomas then he wasn't telling her, so with nothing to lose she decided to buy her pre-paid mobile and called Thomas's pre-paid number. Recognizing her voice Thomas quickly made his pitch after warning her not to mention any names.

"Would you like to have one million dollars in a Swiss bank account?

"What do I have to do for that?"

"Let me know the container number, the vessel name and its ETA in a European port for one of your packages. You know the kind of shipment that I am talking about. There will be negligible risk to you, your outfit will lose the value of the shipment and some minor functionaries in Europe will be arrested, and you will be one million dollars richer." There was a small pause before Shan replied.

"One million pounds sterling, and have the bank send a statement of my Swiss account showing twenty percent already deposited to Bo in Geneva."

"OK deal. The bank will contact you regarding the opening of your account. I will ensure that the European authorities make the customs search look like a normal spot check so that there can't be any witch hunt at your end, OK?

"Good, we will need two more pre-paid mobiles so that I can give you the transport details. In three weeks' time call me on your new number. Bye for now."

Thomas disposed of his pre-paid mobile and began to worry about Frank and Bo. How far had they managed to distance themselves from what was going to be a messy business? He quickly discovered that the two young men were busy working in Geneva and, as he had business with a Swiss bank to arrange, he flew there and invited them to meet him for dinner. They were happy to oblige the man they laughingly referred to as Uncle Thomas. After going over some of their plans and emphasising the break with China they queried Thomas regarding his resignation as a director of Wei's businesses.

"That's a difficult question to answer as I don't have a hard and fast reason. As an elected politician I have to avoid any association with matters that the public disapprove of. I never came across any clear indication that Wei's businesses were not quite one hundred percent legitimate, but the occasional remark, the occasional embarrassment when I intruded on a conversation that I was not supposed to hear, and I just decided to play it safe. No need for you youngsters to attempt any explanation as to why you are both now emphasizing your connection only with Wei's overseas businesses, we understand each other. We can treat each other as family and enjoy socializing over a good bottle of wine now that is all settled. Which reminds me, I am a country squire now with a pile in the

countryside, and I insist on you both visiting one weekend soon."
Thomas left Geneva with some bank papers and an account number,
satisfied that Frank and Bo would not be anywhere near a certain
drug shipment that was going to get bust at a European port.

After three weeks Thomas contacted Shan on his pre-paid mobile
number and she responded with the container number, vessel name
and ETA. Shan couldn't resist a quick,

"See you in Geneva sometime, dinner on me." Thomas politely
reminded her to get rid of her mobile and said goodbye. He then
contacted the American trade attaché and passed on the information
that he had just received from Shan. He was tempted to go and
observe the bust from a discreet distance, but knew that this was just
a childish impulse that he must not give in to. Another impulse
almost overcame him that he should let Fabia know about the
progress that he had made, but there was no point in approaching her
until he had some hard evidence that she could take to her Brussels
committee. Only then would they be able to put pressure on the
Chinese government to block this trade.

Instead Thomas went home for the weekend to see how his
country estate was progressing. He found Susan in a state of high
excitement as she was preparing for her first weekend visitors,
mainly family members who were coming to check on her choice of
furnishings and decorations. Thomas, with great foresight, had
bought several beautiful antiques at the Paris market on his recent trip
with Fabia. In fact Fabia had chosen the pieces for him, knowing full
well that a pregnant wife should be spoilt with fine expensive
presents. Susan had found a married couple to occupy the gatehouse,
and on a suitable salary the wife would take care of the indoors and
the husband the outdoors. Of course in these modern times there was
no chance of filling a large country house with servants, but with the
aid of service companies and occasional cash payments to some of
the women from the nearby village, one could still entertain with a
certain style. Susan's family were suitably impressed as she was
known to be a woman with good taste. Thomas fell in with the spirit
of being happy with home and family as he realized how fortunate he
was, but after making love to his wife that Saturday night he still lay
back with a slight niggling worry. Once this current business was out

of the way perhaps he should stop travelling so much. No more dallying with mistresses and he would not stand as a MEP again. Even if his standing in Europe and China was slightly damaged, which he considered to be the worst possible outcome, his standing in the UK was very high and he should be able to mature comfortably at home.

Giuseppe Montaldo the senior customs officer in the port of Naples was surprised to receive a visit by an official from the Rome ministry in charge of revenue and taxation. He explained to Giuseppe that Rome had decided on a series of spot checks to ensure that local customs offices were adhering to the procedures for passing cargos through customs checks before releasing them to the transports. This did not particularly upset Giuseppe as he was familiar with the procedures and he showed his visitor the details of the vessels being unloaded that day. The official from Rome followed Giuseppe's customs officers as they occasionally opened and searched a container, whilst checking through their work papers until he located the freighter from China with the container number that the Americans had supplied him with. He then indicated that they should open that container, and when they did so, their drug sniffer dog became excited and quickly discovered Shan's heroin package. They didn't want the Chinese freighter's crew involved, as they could not be held responsible for all the contents of all the containers, and unless their fingerprints were on the heroin package, which was unlikely, there was no chance of convicting them.

Instead the Rome official suggested that they leave the package in the container and he would arrange for it to be tracked to the dealer who was expecting it. They replaced the package in the carton of clothing addressed to a Milan firm, where they had found it. Once clear of the port the truck with the container containing the heroin package headed north tracked by the Rome official's team and their American counterparts. As soon as the truck was unloaded the customs officials moved in and the sniffer dog led them to the package containing the heroin, which had been secreted in an office well away from the firm's warehouse. An individual from that office was arrested but the law officers knew that he was only a lowly lieutenant, and unlikely to reveal whom he intended to pass the heroin on to.

Giuseppe Montaldo was not surprised the next morning when the newspapers and TV channels across Europe broadcast the news of the Naples custom officers' success in finding 100 kilos of Heroin, worth between six and eight million Euros in northern Europe, during a routine check of a cargo unloaded in Naples off a freighter from China. The Americans were happy to let the Naples customs officers have all the glory as, in order to protect their source, they did not want any suggestion that they had been tipped off. Copies of the evidence were presented to the freighter's captain to ensure that news of the find got back to China, but he was allowed to continue his voyage.

Fabia's committee had their hard evidence and called in the Chinese Ambassador to the European Union. To their surprise the Ambassador expressed his government's determination to fight this evil trade and promised them action in the very near future. When Fabia reported this outcome to Thomas she put it down to China's membership of the World Trade Organization which had brought maturity to their dealings with the rest of the world over the past decade. Only two days later the Chinese announced the arrest of Bo Sung a senior official in the State Security Service on charges of corruption and drug dealing.

In Shanghai the eighty year old Bo was confined to Party accommodation and was not fearful for his physical wellbeing. Reflecting on an eventful life he realized that he had never fully accepted communism as a faith, it was just that events had swept him along. He would rather have given his faith up to the religion that the kind Methodist missionary had demonstrated to him as a child, and yet that had been only a very short period of his life. Once he had had his revenge on Ling Sung, the boss of the Shanghai drug syndicate who had killed his parents, he had come to understand the power of the Communist Party, although he appreciated the vulnerability of any individual who stood in the way of the good of the party. With his good war record and climb up the hierarchy of the State Security Service he had found himself in a position to run the Shanghai drug trade himself. The Party accepted the majority of the profits whilst it suited the Politburo's declared plans, without specifically directing Bo to take the actions that he did. In the early days when an entirely new system of government was being forced upon a puzzled populace, chaos reigned in many areas of administration. He had always given Wei and Shan the impression that their activities were sanctioned at the highest levels of government, and who could prove that they were or weren't? Now it was quite natural for the Party to believe that Bo had acted on his own for his own financial gain, simply because it suited their current policy. Bo knew that the trial was a formality and the result would be the death penalty, which could be suspended in certain circumstances. That was Bo's main worry, what would they want from him in order to suspend his death sentence. He doubted that his age and war record would be sufficient and they would probably want him to testify against some other corrupt official to give credibility to the recent push to tackle corruption. Recent popular unrest was driving the Politburo to show that they were taking action. Bo's worry was for his son Wei. He had encouraged Wei to accept Frank Latimer's merger proposal because it isolated the drug business as solely Chinese and run from China, and kept Wei, Bo Junior, and Frank working in overseas locations and on legitimate businesses. He had no option but to await his first interrogation and find out what would be required of him.

Although her arrest had not yet been ordered, Shan Sung was in hiding and trying not to panic following the arrest of Bo Senior. It was she who had taken Bo's authority into the drug dealing gangsters' dens and collected the rake-off for Bo, who then passed most of it on to the Party. Despite Bo indicating otherwise, Shan had come to realize that there was no written authorization for their activity, but then the Party could always change the perception of any situation to suit its purpose. The higher one rose under communism the more precarious one's grip on the ladder became, and like many others in the same situation, Shan had looked for a bargaining chip. In the early years of her marriage Wei had been more forthcoming regarding his family history, and the need to eliminate Florence Tang had been revealed to her. Florence had been infected with Hepatitis B by Wei and her treatment had been delayed before she was returned to Hong Kong to die. Emily Tang had searched for Florence's medical records in China and had found nothing but that was because Shan had been there first. Shan had documentary proof that Florence Tang had been detained overlong without proper treatment on Wei's orders. Now she needed Wei's help to leave China and be united with the million pounds that Thomas had deposited in her Swiss bank account.

It was a situation that Shan had always planned for. All it needed was for Wei to issue instructions to various branch managers within his Shanghai businesses, to pick up and transport a woman identified by a certain piece of clothing from a certain location to another location. The idea being that managers and drivers would not be aware that the woman being transported was a wanted person, and would not have to know her name. Shan bought a pre-paid mobile and called Wei's regular mobile as she was unsure of his exact location. She gave her location for the transport pick up as the address of a lodging house and the clothing as a black and yellow jacket, but she had in fact rented a room in the same street so as to see if she was being betrayed. Wei said that the driver would have instructions regarding her destination and the van should arrive within a couple of hours. Wei knew what he had to do. He too had belatedly decided to remove the hospital records regarding Florence Tang, only to discover that they had already been removed. He was in no doubt who had them and now decided that he would be safer if Shan did not fall into the hands of the Shanghai Security Service. Within two hours Shan was in the back of a truck, hidden in a space behind and under packing cases, and delivered to one of Wei's freighters alongside the quay in Shanghai harbour. The captain of the vessel explained that she must remain in a storage bay deep inside the vessel until they were out of Chinese waters, when she could move into a passenger cabin. Shan was not surprised when the captain insisted on searching her bag and body, but pretended to be outraged. She knew what it was that Wei had instructed the captain to take from her, but her documents from the Shanghai hospital regarding Florence Tang's treatment were already in the mail to Thomas Latimer in England. Now she was just like one of the packets of heroin that Wei regularly smuggled into Europe and with a bit of luck she would clear Naples harbour without being detected. Even if stopped she had plenty of US dollars, authentic Chinese travel documentation, and her son and a small fortune awaiting her in

Switzerland. With a long voyage ahead of her Shan had no option but to borrow the seamens' reading material and settle down to a patient wait.

Wei Sung was in touch with the captain of the vessel carrying his wife to Naples, and was annoyed that the documents referring to Florence Tang's time in the Shanghai hospital were not in her possession. He was slightly mollified by the fact that the captain had successfully planted a tracking device in her luggage and a bugging device in her mobile phone, as he had been instructed before the ship sailed.

Wei's next concern was Bo Senior whom he knew would be required to implicate somebody else in order to ease his own punishment. Wei feared that he would be the required sacrifice so he was pleased to learn from Bo's legal representative that in fact his father was in the midst of a titanic struggle between two Politburo members. The senior Politburo member had quietly accumulated a large personal fortune, whilst the more recently elected Politburo member from Shanghai had accumulated a huge personal fortune that he and his family made little effort to disguise. With a well published drive to prosecute corrupt party officials in progress in order to placate public unrest, the senior Politburo member was keen for Bo to give evidence against the more flamboyant member from Shanghai who had a growing power base in that city. Unfortunately they also wanted Shan back dead or alive. The authorities had no knowledge of and were not interested in the Florence Tang affair, as they had too many problems to waste time just embarrassing a declining colonial power. The sheer scale of their task, which entailed running a giant agrarian society and a vast bureaucracy, is what preoccupies the modern communist party running a market economy. They wanted Shan because she had been having an affair with the Shanghai Politburo member and would be another good example of how he used his wealth to corrupt lower ranked officials, and build up his power base through members of the State Security Service.

Wei had hoped to avoid this situation but it was clear that Shan's death would be the best outcome for himself. Dead she would not be able to implicate him in Florence's death as she would be able to do if she still had access to the documents from the Shanghai hospital.

Although the authorities were not interested in this matter, Bo Junior would certainly be very upset if he heard about it. Dead she would not be able to divert attention to him when giving evidence at the trial of the Politburo member from Shanghai. Death by a drug overdose would be evidence that Shan had been living on the profits of corruption. Evidence that the Politburo member from Shanghai was responsible for her death would help Bo Senior whose fate was in the hands of the older Politburo member. Wei convinced himself that Shan must die without even resorting to the excuse that she was an unfaithful wife, which deep down, and no matter what prior agreements have been made between husband and wife, most men resent.

Bo Junior had always kept in regular touch with both his parents especially during his time at boarding school in England. He still made a point of calling one or the other each week and disturbed at not being able to contact his mother he called his father. Wei broke the news of his grandfather's arrest and his mother's subsequent disappearance, but did not reveal that he knew where Shan was. Bo was distraught and wanted to fly straight to Shanghai to look for and to save his mother. Wei worked very hard to dissuade him, saying that the authorities knew that their Chinese business division was involved in drug dealing and that they too would be arrested if they set foot in China, and his mother certainly wouldn't want that. In the meantime Wei would start handing out bribes to find out what had happened to Shan. Bo was very anxious and could not bring himself to continue working. He phoned Emily to share his anxiety and asked her to find out all that she could about the political tensions in China and then fly over to spend the weekend with him in Geneva.

Wei had already given his instructions to the captain of the freighter that Shan was travelling on. Shan had occasionally used heroin in the past without becoming addicted and was happy to relieve her boredom when the captain suggested that they both partake of a small portion of the current package to be smuggled ashore at Naples. In fact the whole one hundred gram package was to be payment, half for the freighter's captain and crew, and half for the Sicilian Mafia carrying out Wei's instructions. As the freighter approached Naples harbour with Shan sleeping off a hit, the captain was able to inject her with the first part of what would be a massive overdose that would stop her heart. Wei had been in touch with the Sicilian Mafia and on the regular overnight Italian ferry from Catania in Sicily to Naples on the Italian mainland, was a foot-soldier member of the Sicilian Mafia with his Fiat car. The ferry docked at Naples in the early morning of the day after Wei's freighter had arrived. The foot-soldier driver was familiar with the Naples docks layout and was able to leave the single file of cars disembarking from the ferry and heading for the exit barrier at the main harbour gate. He diverted to Wei's freighter, hidden behind the onshore stacks of containers in the container port, where the unconscious Shan was bundled into the back seat by the captain, the one propping up the other. Whilst the traffic from what was an internal Italian ferry, filed out of the main harbour gate under the uninterested eye of a single duty harbour official, the car with the unconscious Shan in drove the length of the docks to the southern gate that was used by staff and workers. It was rarely manned and nobody stopped them. Once out of the docks it is a short drive onto the Autostrada where they headed north to Rome. The final fatal injection of heroin was given to Shan, and by the time they reached the rendezvous in a derelict suburb of Rome, she was dead. They were met by a car hired in Rome that morning by another foot-soldier of the Sicilian Mafia. They placed Shan's body in the driving seat of the Rome hire car before the Captain and the two drivers returned to Naples in the Catania car. The captain presented the foot-soldiers with their share of the heroin and returned to his ship whilst the two Sicilian foot-soldiers took their car back to Catania on the next ferry. Shan's body with her luggage in the boot was soon discovered by the Rome police, and the Chinese embassy in Rome was informed as there was plenty of documentation to establish her identity. After the usual Italian formalities were completed the Chinese embassy arranged for Shan's body to be quickly returned to Peking.

The Rome police had alerted the press to the discovery of a prominent Chinese official's body in Rome, and that she died from a heroin overdose. Bo Junior discovered that his mother was dead from the press reports in the newspapers, just before he was due to go and pick up Emily at the Geneva airport. Emily had not been able to discover Shan's whereabouts and was not looking forward to telling Bo about the lack of news about his mother. It hardly mattered for it

164

was Frank who met her and explained what had happened to Shan, and its devastating effect on Bo.

Thomas Latimer was happily taking care of his country house and his many business and political interests in Cheshire, when he received a package that contained another package and a letter from Shan. In the brief letter Shan asked Thomas to take care of the enclosed package with her name on it, and forward it unopened when she contacted him and advised him of the address where she wished to receive the package. Thomas did not have a problem with that until he heard the news about Shan's death in Rome. He read the report of the discovery of Shan's body in the Times and was very shocked and sad that this woman who had been his lover, should have succumbed to a heroin overdose. He had to conceal his emotions from Susan to prevent any embarrassing questions from her as to why this woman's death affected him so much. In fact he quickly recovered his composure as he did not believe the report. He knew of Shan's occasional use of drugs but did not believe that the danger that she faced once her father-in-law had been arrested, was enough to drive her to take her own life with a deliberate overdose. It was only a short while since Thomas had broken up with her and he was sure that she would fight tooth and nail to survive to enjoy the one million pounds he had deposited in her Swiss bank account, such was her reactive adrenaline-driven personality. If it wasn't suicide, what else could it be? Thomas was essentially a rational person and the only other explanation was accident or murder. He paused to consider his feelings as a more cerebral exercise. In fact just thinking about her brought back pleasant memories of her beauty and desirability which raised him out of his feelings of sadness but left him feeling puzzled. So he quickly arrived at the conclusion that he had to do something with her package. Either just send it on to Wei or Bo, or open it? Clearly she hadn't sent it to them, so maybe she didn't want them to see the contents. Maybe she had recorded something about her affair with Thomas, something that he wouldn't want Wei or Bo to know about. Thomas came to the conclusion that he had to open the package. Inside was a note from Shan to Thomas.

"In the event that you learn of my death I believe that you will decide to open my package. The enclosed documents are circumstantial evidence that Wei Sung had Florence Tang (Emily's mother) killed in 1996. One of his reasons was that his father had an affair with Florence and nobody is sure who Emily's natural father is, Bo Senior or Li Tang. With the return of Hong Kong to China she would become a danger because she knew too much about our family, and might be questioned by other communist officials. My husband Wei assumes that I have these documents because he couldn't find them in the hospital, but now that I have to leave China, I believe that he will want me dead so that I can't speak out against him, especially to Bo our son. If you are reading this then I am probably dead but I want you to inform Bo so that he will know just what a monster his father is. Thank you Thomas."

Thomas reflected that Shan had given him an unpleasant task, even on the telephone and worse still face to face. He could of course give the documents to Wei and leave Bo in happy ignorance, but then Wei might decide to get rid of him so that nobody would know his secret. No, that was unlikely, but he must remember to put a note with his will to the effect that, should he have died unexpectedly, Wei Sung had a reason to have him killed. All these thoughts about Wei brought Thomas to the conclusion that Wei had arranged Shan's death. Thomas didn't believe that a self-administered heroin overdose was the cause of Shan's death, not when Shan had reached freedom and had a million pounds and a devoted son waiting for her only a few hours' drive away. Who else could have killed Shan? Possibly the Chinese State Security Service, but wouldn't they want her back alive to be prosecuted as a corrupt official for the satisfaction of the people? Thomas took a flight to Geneva to tell Bo Junior these secrets face to face.

Wei Sung was in London. His time in Hong Kong and some bribes had enabled him to spend up to three months of each year in the UK. He was strongly attached to his father and was doing everything that he could to get his certain death sentence suspended. He was also negotiating to exchange his Chinese interests for freedom for himself and his son Bo. In effect the drug supply business had already continued without Senior Bo's and his own involvement, but his Chinese mobile phone, shipping and freight interests still had value. The senior Politburo member was now firmly in control with his main rival arrested and facing trial, and was agreeable to adding Wei's assets to his own extensive commercial interests held by himself and his family. The latest communication from his father indicated that the trial would take place in the spring of 2012 and by the summer his death sentence would be suspended.

Wei really felt for his father as he knew that humiliation would be publically heaped on his head, after which he would be allowed to live quietly in reasonable comfort but in isolation until his natural death in a few years' time. Wei also knew that his father had never quite accepted the communist manifesto with heartfelt fervour, but would nevertheless be depressed by the feeling that his life of struggle, battle and hard work had ended in humiliation. Perhaps he would find some comfort in the teachings that the Methodist missionary had imparted in the short time that she had brought him and his brother back to full health. The worst of the situation was that Wei would never see his father again but wanted to let him know how he felt, and somehow provide for him in his confinement. Wei still had contacts in China and plenty of wealth outside to solve these problems, and he was able to send money and messages to his father in his final years. Nobody is all monster, able to kill those whose existence threatened his own and accept without conscience the immoral mores of the culture that he found himself in, but Wei was in all other aspects of life able to feel, enjoy and suffer in the same way as everyone else.

Frank Latimer was aware of Bo's devotion to his parents and that he made no judgement on them, nor gave any favour to either one of them, for living separate lives. This filial devotion was so strong that Frank knew that the tragedy of his mother's death would really tear Bo apart. Frank had made little progress to relieve Bo's grief before he went to the airport to pick up Emily. That gave them a chance to discuss how they could fully sympathise with and support Bo, who had passed from grief into anger at what had happened to his mother. None of them believed that Shan had taken a drug overdose, and assumed that it had been forced upon her. Emily had, in her capacity as a journalist, picked up the bare bones of the rivalry between the highly placed member of the Politburo and his younger challenger who was now widely believed to be under arrest and charged with corruption. Bo added into the mix what his father had told him about Senior Bo being persuaded to be a prosecution witness in the trial of the lower placed member of the Politburo, and they came to the conclusion that Shan was wanted for the same reason. But why kill her? Surely a live witness would have more effect, and how did she come to be in Rome? At this point Bo broke down again, the thought that his mother had been so close and within mobile range without being able to contact him, was too much to bear.

Emily took the opportunity to simply hold Bo close and murmur her love and devotion and pledge her total commitment to helping him through his time of grief.

Emily herself was powerfully affected by the evidence that the one China two systems imposed by Mrs Thatcher for fifty years from 1997, was looking very fragile. A compulsory curriculum of moral and national education, written by China's Communist party had just been imposed on Hong Kong. It was being vigorously opposed but was another example of the restriction of Hong Kong's remaining freedoms. Hong Kong is still a special administrative region of China but Peking is already insisting that it has the right to appoint Hong Kong's next political leader in 2017, instead of having an election with only residents allowed to stand. As a Hong Kong resident Emily feared that she would not be able to live under a one China with Peking communist political system in full control of Hong Kong, and that it might come before the fifty years are up. She, unlike Bo, felt that she was English, and there was little doubt that she could convert to full UK citizenship. Her father too had a good record as a civil servant who had resisted a full communist takeover, and would also stand a good chance of becoming British.

Bo was comforted by his best friend's presence. He had always allowed Frank to lead since they had first met as room-mates at boarding school when they were eleven. Frank had been heavier set although not as fleet of foot as Bo, and whilst he came from Spain English was his mother tongue, whilst Bo was still acquiring the full fluency of the language and understanding of English culture. It had seemed natural to benefit from Frank's leadership then, and in his current weakened emotional state he was glad of Frank's sympathy and support. As soon as he saw the state of emotional collapse that his friend was in, Frank knew that he had to take some action.

"If only you could go to your mother's funeral that would be of some relief for you Bo. The best thing to do is collect as many facts as we can. We need to know when your mother's body will be released for burial, and if she can be cremated. We need to know if your grandfather will be allowed to attend the crematorium, and whether or not your father would be able to bring her ashes to the West for a service that we could all attend." Emily thought that her body would not be released until after Bo's grandfather's trial, but agreed that they needed to get more information, and persuaded Bo to phone Wei and see if he could find the answers to these questions. Frank said that he would call Thomas Latimer and see if he was in a position to make another trip to China and sniff out some answers.

Frank didn't have to call Thomas because *he* called Frank first. He was due to fly into Geneva in two hours and would Frank alone pick him up at the airport as he had something important to discuss with him. Frank realized that Thomas probably didn't want to say anything about important matters on the phone, so after he had noted down Thomas's flight number and ETA, they quickly terminated the conversation. Both Frank and Bo had long since accepted Thomas as part of their lives and despite noting a certain detached manner in him, they respected him. Whilst Bo was busy talking to his father on the telephone, Frank told Emily that he was off to pick up Thomas at the airport, so they would soon be able to get his opinion regarding their search for facts regarding Shan's fate. After greeting Frank Thomas took him aside to a row of unoccupied seats and quickly sat him down. Speaking calmly and quietly Thomas flatly told him that he had circumstantial documentary evidence that Wei had arranged the death of Emily's mother, and that he suspected that Wei had organized the death of his own wife Shan. Thomas continued,

"I know that Bo is already very upset by the nature of Shan's death and I hate to add to his misery, but I do feel that I should tell him face to face and then offer what comfort and help that I can. What do you think Frank?" Having just left Bo in a state of depression Frank was appalled by the implications of Thomas's statement. He knew however that Thomas was an intelligent, experienced, and well-informed person whom it is difficult to doubt. Nevertheless he found himself saying,

169

"How sure are you about this? Emily is with Bo right now, you are going to cause major distress on top of the grief they already have."

"I am sure as you will be when you read the doccuments. I would like to put this straight to all three of you and then answer your questions. I wouldn't think of trying to hide something as terrible and important as this from all of you, and now that I have told you the facts, you too couldn't possibly not tell your friends," Thomas replied.

"You're right about that," said Frank, "let's go and get it over with." They drove in silence to Bo's apartment and after subdued greetings Emily could see that something was wrong, by their demeanour. Thomas quickly sat down in an armchair and extracted Shan's package from his jacket pocket before addressing the three friends more calmly than he felt.

"About a month ago I received this package in the mail at my home in Cheshire. It contained a note to me from Shan and another sealed package. The note asked me to take care of the enclosed package with her name on it and forward it unopened once she contacted me and advised the address that she wished to receive the package at." Thomas passed the note around and paused whilst they all quickly read it before he continued.

"I was not unduly surprised by the receipt of this package as I have been close to Shan in recent years as you all probably guessed, and I knew that she was preparing to leave China to be closer to Bo. In fact I helped her set up a bank account here in Geneva and arranged for a swap of funds so that she could live independently outside China." Bo interrupted to say that she hadn't mentioned any of this to him, and Thomas decided not to complicate matters by mentioning Shan's help with the drug bust.

"No, I am sure that she was anxious to keep it a secret until she was securely out of China, you know how paranoid everyone living under a communist system has to be. However, when I saw the dreadful news of Shan's death, and you have all my sympathy because I know how much you are grieving Bo, I not only felt grief for her myself, but I had to face the problem of her package. As I saw it I had three options. To send the package to Wei, or to Bo, or to open it myself. Shan had told me some things that she swore me to secrecy about and it was because of what I knew from her that I decided to open the package. Inside was documentation that was circumstantial evidence that Emily's mother Florence's death was not entirely natural, and that Wei Sung had a hand in arranging it. I am sorry to say this Emily it must be a great shock to you." Thomas paused and handed the documents to Frank who was nearest to him. The silence was unnatural and only punctuated by Emily's uneven breathing. Her heart was beating faster and forcing her blood pressure to rise, and her thoughts went back to her own investigations about her mother's past. The Hong Kong hospital records of her mother's treatment for Hepatitis B had included the opinion that if she had been returned from Shanghai sooner in the infection cycle she would have stood a better chance of surviving. Now she turned to Bo and Frank who had been busily reading the documents provided by Shan via Thomas. Frank could see the look of despair on Bo's face and quickly decided that he had better be the one to speak.

"These documents do appear to be Shanghai hospital records that show that your mother was there for several weeks and there seems to have been little treatment given. We would need to let some doctors have a look at them before we could say for certain that her treatment was criminally deficient, but there is also a document that says that no treatment should be given to this patient and it is signed by Wei Sung on behalf of the State Security Service." Frank then turned to Thomas and asked,

"When you said just now that Shan had sworn you to secrecy regarding certain things, was it just this about Florence's treatment or was there anything else?" Thomas was pleased to share everything that he knew as he believed that once the three friends knew everything it was unlikely that any of it would get back to his wife and his life in Cheshire.

"That's why I opened the package because Shan had told me some time ago that she was sure that Wei had murdered Florence. She told me that Bo's grandfather had told her all about Florence being an MI6 agent who had been caught in the act of trying to help another MI6 agent, who was a Chinese citizen, to escape to the west. Senior Bo had laid the trap to catch whoever came to help and was surprised when it turned out to be Florence. He knew Florence was the daughter of the Methodist missionary who had saved his life when he was a child and he wanted to save her from imprisonment in China. As he had to protect his own position he decided to turn Florence into a double agent and then use her for simple assignments that she could complete without any further danger to herself. It worked out OK, but as time went by Bo Senior started an affair with Florence as she made many trips to Shanghai. When Florence became pregnant she assured Bo that her husband was the father of the baby, but he wondered about this because Florence and Li had been married for a long time without getting pregnant. It could be that Bo Junior and Emily are related. With the approach of the return of Hong Kong to China it was Wei who decided that Florence might become a threat to his family, and it was Wei who engineered her death to keep her quiet. Shan also told me that she had recovered the documents from the Shanghai hospital as insurance against Wei deciding that she knew too much. That was a mistake, because Wei also belatedly went to remove the same documents and when he found that they had been removed, Shan thought that he suspected her, and that he was planning to kill her. She felt that even if she didn't have the documents Wei would be happier if she was dead and unable to reveal his secret, especially to Bo." Bo by this time was incapable of rational thought and merely groaned, and Emily was in tears, so it was Frank who responded once again.

"So what you have come to tell us, and what you believe, is that Bo's father arranged for both Emily's and Bo's mothers to be murdered, right." After Thomas had responded in the affirmative, Frank continued, "We three have already discussed our disbelief that Shan would take a heroin overdose, how do you see that Thomas?"

"I fully agree, I know Shan had occasionally used heroin but she preferred other drugs and used none of them to excess. The last time that I spoke to her face to face she was worried about Wei wanting to silence her." Frank was anxious to get all the information that he could from Thomas, in the hope that he could think of some course of action that would ease Bo's grief, so he pressed Thomas again. "How did Shan get to Rome and what will happen to her body now?

"I have no more hard facts," replied Thomas, "I can only assume that when Shan heard of her father-in-law's arrest she decided to leave China. Perhaps she didn't want to risk the airports and used cash to get over a land border. There are several weeks between

Senior Bo's arrest and Shan's body being found in Rome so maybe she went into eastern Russia, and then by truck and train to an airport and on to Rome!" Bo was jerked out of his lethargy by this weak assumption.

"Why didn't she fly to Geneva to be with me, why would she go to Rome? It doesn't make sense. How did Wei track her, if he arranged her death how did he know when she would be in Rome? No, if she was desperate to get out of China she may have asked Wei to help her, thinking that the package that she had posted to you Thomas, was sufficient insurance to keep her alive. He could easily have sent her with the next heroin shipment in exchange for these documents, and the time gap fits with a voyage to Naples. When he found out that she wasn't carrying the documents, that's when he decided to kill her. It would be no use our trying to find the actual killers, they are hired foot-soldiers or working for the State Security Service organization. Maybe in time I could pin it down to a certain vessel captain but it is clear to me that I must tackle my father." With that Bo retreated to his bedroom. Frank got ready to take Thomas back to the airport but they were quickly joined by a tearful Emily. She explained that she couldn't bear to be with Bo anymore, what if his father was her half-brother? Despite their conciliatory words she insisted on going to the airport with them and taking the first flight to Hong Kong to talk to her father. Frank was left to take care of Bo.

Emily was as distraught as Bo and her feelings almost incapacitated her when she decided to go and question her father. She knew that she could not have stayed with Bo at that moment, as she could not control her feelings or express them. Once a woman decides that one particular man is the only one she can live with, have children with, and be touched intimately by, then the possibility of not achieving those things is a fate worse than death and must be postponed at all costs. Emily had been only ten years old when her mother died and she had never been able to fill the emotional hole in her life since. Her father had been forty when she was born and was now in his mid-sixties, and although they had become good friends living together for the last five years, he was emotionally restrained with her. Now she must go home and tell him all that had happened and see if her father could add anything that would give her the strength to fight for what she must have, a family with Bo.

Emily had left Bo's apartment without any luggage but that was no problem for a multi-millionaire with her mobile and shoulder bag. In a chartered plane she arrived in Hong Kong fresh from sleeping in a bed on the overnight flight. Showered and fed, she gained a measure of control that masking her emotional turmoil. At their old apartment her retired father greeted her, clearly relieved to see her looking fresh and well groomed. Emily quickly explained that the documents that Thomas had shown them in Geneva, referred to her mother's treatment in the Shanghai hospital, and did provide circumstantial evidence that Bo's father had been intent on ending her life. She explained how these documents had been sent to Thomas by Shan and how, once he heard of Shan's death, he had decided to take them to the three friends in Geneva. Whilst describing the effect of this revelation upon the three of them her own emotional misery finally broke through and she had to break off whilst her father comforted her. Eventually she gasped out,

"Shan told Thomas that Bo's grandfather had caught mother working as an MI6 spy in China and turned her into a double agent, and that this had led to an affair between them some years later." After extracting more detail regarding his wife connection to the Sung family, Emily's father bleakly confirmed that he knew nothing about Florence's connection with MI6, nor anything about an affair. It was his turn to be distressed by the knowledge that his wife had kept such big secrets from him. Emily tried to re-assure him by suggesting that she probably kept it secret to protect them, her husband and child.

"Oh Daddy, we mustn't let this affect our relationship, I will always love you as my father because that is exactly what you have always been to me." Her father quickly realized that this news was so distressing to his daughter, that no matter how he felt, he needed to be positive and practical, and replied,

"Yes, you are right, it's much more important that you realize that Bo had nothing to do with the tragedies of the previous generation's actions. Thinking about it, it must have been MI6 that guaranteed your school fees in England in the event that anything happened to her whilst she was on an operation for them. They did it through her employer, the newspaper, so that I wouldn't know that she had been with MI6. I did think at the time that it was a very generous and unusual condition of employment, but I was just glad to accept it because your mother had made me promise to send you to English boarding school if anything happened to her, as she knew that I would be very busy with the return of Hong Kong to China. Anyway, the fact that they paid up for the school fees, confirms that they didn't know that she had agreed to be a double agent. I don't care about that, what is important is that we know the truth and learn to live with it. I could approach contacts that I know used to be in MI6 with those documents, but what good would it do? They would want to know why the Sung family wanted your mother dead, and we don't want that do we? You and I are going to move to the UK, we both still want and need that don't we?" Your mother and I had just about given up hoping for a baby when she announced that she was pregnant with you. I didn't question it, I was just happy that fortune had smiled on us, but I can understand why the Sung family think that Bo Senior is your father. So we must sort that out by having our DNAs compared. If I am your natural father that's fine, if not then we will assume that Florence deliberately got pregnant by Bo Senior to make us three a proper loving family. We were drifting apart a little at that time and your arrival was just what we needed. What do you think, it could be a rough ride emotionally, but it could give us closure? Emily agreed, but then darkened the mood again by explaining why Thomas, Frank and Bo believed that Bo's father had killed his own wife, Bo's mother, and how this had filled Bo with despair.

"I still feel the same about Bo but we need to confine these horrors into some form of acceptable memory before we can be together again happily. I will keep on sending messages to him until he feels that he can talk to me, and I will find out all the facts that I can before we leave Hong Kong, starting with the name of the vessel that took Shan to Naples and the captain's name. I have plenty of money to help loosen tongues."

Bo's mind was in complete turmoil, it is not possible to rationalize the thought of your father killing your mother. Until now he had felt only love and respect for both of his parents but now he hated his father and wished him dead, and after that there would be no reason for his life to continue. Even his feelings for Emily were completely blocked off by the knowledge that his father had killed her mother, and that fact too could only be addressed by his own death. Rejecting all Frank's offers of assistance Bo took a flight to London where Wei was still living in a property that he had bought in Knightsbridge. Bo had a key from previous visits and his mind was still in sufficient turmoil to make any hard and fast decisions impossible, or even to decide what he was going to say or do to his father. He entered the building's ground floor to be greeted by silence, a silence that he had no mind to break. Without conscious thought Bo saw nobody in the ground floor rooms and collected a knife from the kitchen. He wasn't trying to move silently and ascended two more floors before he found his father's blood-covered dead body in the master bedroom. The shock was too much for his mind to bear and he fell into an armchair unable to see or think. Recovering his senses he was unsure of what had happened, had he killed his father? Moving closer to the bed on which the body was slumped he established that there was no sign of breathing. The quantity of dried spilt blood from a slit throat that had almost decapitated Wei, suggested that he had been dead for some time. As further re-assurance Bo took out the knife that he had collected from the kitchen and was pleased to see that it was not blood stained. He returned the knife to the kitchen and sat down to think. Should he now kill himself? No, somebody else had created the only situation that he could live with. His hatred for his father had ebbed away from the moment that he viewed his mutilated throat. He could now bury him and try to expunge all Wei's actions from his own memory, whilst mourning his mother. If only he could get her body or ashes out of China and bury her, then he could start thinking about his own life again.

Rousing himself wasn't easy but he needed to make some decisions. Should he just leave and let the staff find Wei's body? Where were they anyway? He made a quick search of the rest of the four storied building and found no sign of life. Wei must have deliberately given them all time off, maybe he had wanted to meet his murderer in secret? Bo realized that he could walk away, but maybe he would be noticed in the street and remembered. Wei had security cameras covering the door, but a quick check showed that the murderer had already thought of that and removed the disc. No record of Bo arriving or departing, but what was the point of leaving and pretending that he had not been there? He had visited the house before so any sign of him having been there could be explained away, but what if he had left a trace when he approached the body. If he was found out he would certainly immediately become the prime suspect. Not worth chancing, better to call the police and let them start hunting for the murderer immediately. Bo dialled 999. The uniformed officers arrived first and after viewing the body they set up a crime scene using police tape at the front and rear doors. Next to arrive was Wei's housekeeper who confirmed that she had been surprised and pleased when Wei had given her the day off until dinner time. She confirmed that she had left Wei alone and that he had not mentioned any expected visitors. The uniformed policemen confirmed that both the victim and Bo were Chinese Hong Kong Resident citizens and that they were father and son. With the arrival of the CID officers Bo was required to give more details regarding his life and family. He decided that the subject of his mother would probably come up if only in an enquiry as to where she was, and when was he going to inform her, so he gave them the details of her body having been found in Rome and then returned to Peking. As for himself he was running the family business from Geneva. He made no mention of Frank, Emily or his grandfather. They took his fingerprints and a DNA swab and explained that, when they had completed their forensic examination of the crime scene, unless they found another suspect, then they would probably consider him a possible suspect and dig into his background for a motive. However, he had done the right thing to contact them as soon as he discovered the body, and they thanked him for his co-operation. They recommended that he contact the Chinese embassy and take their advice regarding legal representation, but he should not leave country without contacting the police to recover his passport, which they would keep for the time being.

Having come straight from the airport Bo now made a hotel booking and having informed the police of its whereabouts he checked in. Bo was getting very fatigued but managed two quick telephone calls, the first to advise Frank of what had happened and to ask him to pass on the news of Wei's death to the other board members and to senior managers in their business organization, and the second to the Chinese embassy to advise them of his presence in London and of his father's murder, and to make an appointment to discuss these matters tomorrow. With that he collapsed into bed and slept for a long time.

Frank decided to pass the news of Wei's death on to Emily and found her more cheerful on the telephone than he had expected. They agreed that Bo's complete recovery hung on being able to bury his mother in England and, to a lesser extent, on his grandfather's death sentence being suspended. With four hundred million pounds between them, they should be able to achieve all this, and arrange UK citizenship for Bo, Emily and her father. Frank still had access to the records of Wei's Chinese businesses and took over negotiations via Wei's Shanghai legal representatives, for their transfer to the senior Politburo member and his family, as had already been agreed by Wei. In the meantime he would have an employee scour the Chinese mobile phone company's records, between the time of Bo Senior's arrest and Wei's body being discovered in London, for the origin of any calls made or received by Wei. Frank also e-mailed to Emily a list of vessels and their crew's names, that were owned by Wei's Chinese shipping company, and that had left Chinese ports bound for Mediterranean ports soon after Bo Senior's arrest.

Emily, also hiding behind Hong Kong legal representatives and their investigators, put the word out that cost was not a concern regarding information about the Sung family and their activities. The vessel that Shan travelled on to Naples was back in Shanghai and investigators soon found more than one crew member who confirmed that a woman had been on board for their last trip to Naples, and they recognized her from the photograph shown. The captain refused all bribes (he had already cashed in on his share of the 100 grams of heroin that Wei had given him for the job of killing Shan) and denied that there had been any woman aboard, which allowed the conclusion that he had been involved in Shan's murder. The phone records showed several contacts between Wei and the vessel whilst in Shanghai harbour and at sea, and Frank and Emily were no longer in any doubt that Bo's assumptions, made after Thomas had told them all that he knew, were correct. That was not enough for the Italian police to arrest the captain if he was ever foolish enough to return to

Italy, and certainly not enough for extradition. The rental car that Shan's body had been found in had been picked up that same day and had Shan's details on the hire form, but the handwriting was clearly not hers. That suggested another vehicle to take her from Naples docks to the Rome suburb. Investigators eventually turned up a witness who had seen the suspicious transfer of a bundle from one car to another. He gave the make of car, from which the bundle was taken, as a Fiat, but could not remember the number plate detail. There was some CCTV in Naples harbour and on the morning after the arrival of Wei's vessel a car was spotted leaving the line of cars exiting the Catania ferry and heading towards the container docks with its number plate visible. Autostrada toll records showed this vehicle traveling to Rome and back on the same day that Shan's body was discovered, and the ferry company records showed that it had completed the round trip to Catania in Sicily. The number plates on the car that was used to transport Shan to Rome were false and no sign of a car with those false plates could be found in Sicily. It was probably in the sea at the foot of one of the many cliffs on Sicily's coastline. This is Mafia country and embarrassments can be made to disappear. Fortunately Mafia foot-soldiers are even more susceptible to bribes than ordinary folk, and the investigators started to uncover Wei's activities in Sicily and his close connection to the Sicilian Mafia.

Bo kept his appointment with the Chinese Embassy in London on the next day after discovering his father's body. It was a tricky interview as the secretary from the political division, whilst he knew of the prominence of the Sung family, he was not privy to the subtleties of their relationship with a senior Politburo member. Bo did his best to hint that this relationship existed but otherwise provided the secretary with a full account of his experiences yesterday, and suggested that this information be passed on to the senior Politburo member in Peking.

Over the next few weeks Frank kept in touch with Bo, trying to keep his spirits up, and one cloud was removed from Bo's mind when the Metropolitan Police called upon Bo to advise him that, unless there were further developments, he was no longer a suspect for the murder of Wei Sung. They admitted that they could see no connection between his mother's death and that of his father, and offered their sympathy for all his losses. They had found no forensic evidence to connect him to his father's dead body, and with Wei's time of death now estimated at several hours before the police arrived, and the checkable fact that Bo had only been in the country for two hours before he called the police, it seemed unlikely that he had been involved.

Soon after Bo being cleared of his father's murder by the police, Frank and Emily arrived in London to explain all that they had discovered about Shan's death. Bo's mind had already accepted that his father had arranged his mother's death, and the unravelling of the sequence of events was in fact a comfort, as it suggested that she had not suffered any indignities or pain as she expired. The investigators that Frank and Emily had used were also awaiting instructions as too whether or not to explore further into Wei's connection to the Sicilian Mafia, in order to see if it would lead to an explanation for Wei's murder. The three friends decided to instruct their investigators to continue their researches into Wei's activities in Italy. Anything that they discovered would not be given to the Metropolitan Police, as it suited their purpose to have the police file marked unresolved with no current leads. Wei's body could then be released for burial.

Emily told Frank that she and her father had taken DNA tests, and that she was definitely Li's daughter. She explained how her feelings had been disturbed by the fact that Bo's father had arranged the death of her mother. She couldn't live with Bo just now without being reminded of that fact every second of every day. She asked Frank to tell Bo that she wasn't Wei's half-sister, and that she still had feelings for him. Bo agreed that it was good news when Frank told him that he was not related to Emily, but he was still distraught by the tragedies that have overwhelmed their families. Bo and Emily remained friends but even that was a strain. They continued to keep in touch, but rarely met.

Throughout the next few months Bo completed the transfer of assets from Wei's Chinese businesses to the family of the Senior Politburo Member in return for Bo Senior's death sentence being commuted to a life in isolation and the return of Shan's body to the UK. Also the acceptance that no objection would be raised against Bo seeking an alternative citizenship, and that China required nothing further of him. Senior Bo was convicted of corruption whilst serving in the State Security Service and given the death sentence, which was quietly commuted to life in solitude some weeks later.

With the arrival of Shan's refrigerated body at Heathrow, and the release of Wei's body from the police mortuary, they were both cremated following a ceremony attended by Bo, Frank and Thomas Latimer. Bo scattered his father's ashes in the local garden of remembrance but took the urn containing his mother's ashes with him until he could find a suitable site for it. Emily was living in the UK and expected her father to join her soon. Li Tang was in the last stages of organizing his UK citizenship, to which his civil services position during the transfer of the sovereignty of Hong Kong from the UK to China, entitled him. Emily already had UK citizenship by right of birth and her English ancestry and Bo had already purchased an African citizenship of convenience to give him a passport whilst he applied for British citizenship.

Chapter Fifteen

Wei Sung's Mistakes

The Chinese communist government changed direction in the mid-eighties with the adoption of a "Socialist Market Economy," and began their world-wide search for raw materials, that has now established their economy as being the second largest in the world. This massively increased economic activity has brought China into competition with the North American, UKANZAC, Western European, Brazilian, Russian and Indian economies, all of which require influence and control over the developing countries. This competition is not just economic but ideological as well. Democracy, Practical Communism, Pure Communism and several Religions, all seek to undermine one another as they try to establish themselves as the main customer at the lowest price in each developing country that must export its raw materials, in order to maintain their corrupt leaders and officials in their luxurious life styles.

Wei was drawn into representing his homeland in this struggle as soon as he was allowed to expand his growing business overseas. His background, and his father's and wife's continuing employment, with the State Security Service, meant that he was expected to report any situation that he should find on his travels overseas, that might be exploited to China's economic advantage. He first established contact with the Camorra when looking for a customer for his heroin shipments to Naples in 2009, and through them found out that he would have to deal with a different Mafia in Sicily. He visited Palermo in Sicily to reconnoitre the port facilities. That was as far as his involvement in the heroin trade would go as all the dangerous activities would be handled by his, the Mafia's and the Camorra's foot-soldiers. From the terrace of the Grand Hotel Villa Igiea Wei could see the Palermo docks laid out before him with the blue mare Mediterranean beyond. The hotel like so many that title themselves as Grand, was based on a one time large villa that had been the home of a prominent Sicilian family. Its floorboards creaked and its furniture was made from the dark wood that was fashionable in previous centuries, but its fittings were luxurious and it served excellent food and wine prepared by a Gold Medal award winning chef. Wei was accompanied by two of his Personal Assistants and a translator. As they enjoyed the evening sunshine a handsome fashionably dressed middle-aged woman approached their table and delivered a written invitation for Wei and his entourage to attend a property exhibition in Siracusa tomorrow. The lady smilingly indicated in English that transport and hotel accommodation would be provided and that she would be in attendance as a guide. Wei indicated that he was interested and that if no urgent business arose in the meantime he would be happy to be picked up at ten in the morning. Wei's interpreter pointed out that the invitation card was in the name of the most prominent legal firm in Sicily.

The next morning's drive across Sicily was a pleasant diversion on a concrete autostrada to Catania that had very little traffic. Their guide explained that the Sicilian Mafia controlled Sicily's concrete production plants and had persuaded local government to purchase their product for use in building autostrada, in lightly populated areas where they were not really needed. On the approach to Catania the active volcano Mount Etna came into view. At over ten thousand feet high and more than one hundred and forty kilometres circumference around its' base, it towered over Catania. It is an active volcano but its many recent eruptions have amounted to no more than steady lava flows that solidify before they reach the main areas of population. Large outcrops of volcanic rock in Catania mark the limits of some of the bigger flows and the citizens often have to sweep up the dusting of ash that descends upon them. Wei's property business was flourishing in America and the UK and he was genuinely interested in expanding into the rest of Europe but was this volcanic belt the best place to start? The property exhibition was held in a grand hotel on the waterfront of the Porto Grande of Siracusa with transport available to some new developments along the coast. The legal firm that had invited Wei installed him in a suite in the same hotel, and arranged lunch in a separate room where they introduced themselves. They represented Libyan interests in Sicily where Muammar Gaddafi had considerable property investments. They had brought another invitation, this time from Gaddafi himself, to visit Tripoli regarding China's interests in raw materials to fuel its market economy. This was just such a lead as Wei had been instructed to look out for.

Wei could see that Siracusa was a quiet backwater that was actually further south than the northernmost tip of Africa in Tunisia, but it was not where he wished to buy property. Despite its good weather and historic connection with Archimedes and Greece, it was not as popular as Spain and the eastern Mediterranean. The next morning he thanked his hosts and flew with his entourage to Rome and made contact with the Chinese embassy. Wei's family history was sufficient to command the attention of both the Ambassador and the First Business Secretary to whom he reported his invitation from Gaddafi, and the possibility of access to raw materials from the African continent. It was decided that the First Secretary and a diplomat from the Chinese embassy in Tripoli would be added to Wei's entourage, thereby providing him constant advice and speedy communication with Peking. The Foreign Office in Peking would be advised so that they could add any input they felt was necessary, but the invitation was to Wei and he would have to be fully briefed and react as he thought fit when one to one with Gaddafi. The Chinese diplomat from Tripoli was flown over to Rome and over the next few days Wei was brought up to speed on Libyan and Mediterranean Arab affairs.

There was unrest in all the countries of North Africa from Tunisia through Libya, Algeria to Egypt in this autumn of 2009. Unemployment, the lack of housing, food price inflation, corruption, restrictions on freedom of speech, lack of educational opportunities and poor living conditions, had all combined to cause strikes, protests and even riots that were brutally suppressed. All these countries with fertile coastal regions where the bulk of their population was concentrated, faded into the Sahara desert in the south, and bands of terrorists were beginning to operate with impunity, terrorising foreigners and hindering oil exploration and production. The euphoria of independence had faded in all these countries and had been replaced by brutal and corrupt dictatorships, removing hope for the ordinary citizen. Not that China was particularly enthusiastic about replacing these situations with democracy, but rather gaining influence by helping to stabilize the situation. The idea being for China to offer infrastructure projects and then capitalize on the gratitude of the ruling clique by gaining control of raw material exports. Little did they know that this unrest would become known in only a couple of years' time as the Arab Spring, and soon after that most of these countries descended into the uncontrollable chaos of warring factions fighting for dominance.

As guests of Gaddafi they were ushered through the airport diplomatic lounge without any formalities and transported by limousine to a state guest house in Tripoli. At a full meeting of both entourages with translators present, compliments and presents were exchanged. Gaddafi made an offer to supply China with oil and anchorage in the event that China needed to station vessels from its growing navy in the Mediterranean and in the event of any other emergency. Both parties knew that Libya didn't have sufficient uncommitted oil production for a regular meaningful supply to mainland China, although that might change in the future. Wei expressed his thanks and assured Gaddafi that he would pass his offer on to Peking. On their return to the guest house and before Wei had time to express his disappointment to his entourage, a messenger arrived to ask Wei if he would agree to an informal talk alone with Muammar.

Without giving his team a chance to comment he turned and walked quickly away with the messenger. Alone together Wei discovered that Gaddafi spoke English almost as well as he did, and the two men were able to question one another until a certain comradeship was established. Eventually Gaddafi mentioned that he knew of some good raw material opportunities, that could be of interest to China's industrial ambitions, and that were available in central Africa. When Wei expressed interest both on behalf of China and himself as managing director of a large business operating outside of China but trusted by Peking, Gaddafi explained the rest of his plan. Libya had been supporting Zimbabwe and its president Mugabe who had managed to hang on to power after a much contested and violent election. Further funds had been made available to Mugabe by a consortium of investment funds in return for the rights to extract Zimbabwe's platinum resources, and with Mugabe's help the investors may welcome China as a buyer. Many other opportunities existed in this area of Africa and Mugabe's backing could be crucial in helping China to gain access to them. Wei confirmed his and China's interest in these matters and their gratitude for Gaddafi's assistance, for which a suitable reciprocation could be expected.

This of course was the crux of the meeting and its undiplomatic informality. Gaddafi indicated that he had selected Wei, a prominent businessman but with strong political connections in China, because he wanted total secrecy. He explained to Wei that the recent unrest all along the Barbary Coast (The collective land of the Berber people now divided into Tunisia, Libya, and Algeria.) was becoming more and more difficult to control, but in the unlikely event that he ever lost power, he of course had a well prepared escape route south across the Sahara desert. He would be able to exist there in a well prepared defensive position using his considerable wealth, but only for a short period of time. The West would turn against him and use all their influence to prevent him gaining political exile with most countries, so he was looking to China to grant him a refuge in China where he and his family could live quietly in comfort. Gaddafi emphasized that no word of this matter could ever be allowed to reach the ears of any citizen of Libya, not even his own family members, or his position would become untenable. He said that he trusted Wei who would be the only one to communicate the Chinese government's response at similar private meetings to this one, which he Gaddafi would engineer whilst Wei was being conducted to central Africa to meet with Mugabe. As an indication of his gratitude he presented Wei with a casket full of jewellery that included a bank draft for five million dollars. Wei had some sympathy with Gaddafi as his own position within his own country, which he wished to escape from, was not dissimilar. As the two men continued to enjoy an excellent wine and tasty antipasti laid out for them, they continued to reveal their personal preferences, habits, and secrets to each other as a way of sealing their mutual pact. They even enjoyed the sexual pleasures provided by Gaddafi's corps of female guards, and parted on the friendliest of terms.

Peking were interested in Wei's diplomacy and provided him with a task force of engineers and managers to investigate new areas of raw materials and precious metals supply in central Africa. This was all above board with Wei authorized to enter joint ventures with local businesses using his own capital. In this way he would have access to the true cost of extraction and be able to ensure that the producing country made only modest profits, before passing ownership on to international and state trading corporations. They would then market the raw materials internationally at much higher prices, willingly paid by competing consumers. In this process there was plenty of room for Wei's business to take a healthy cut which would then be shared with both the local and the Chinese politicians who made the whole process possible.

That just left the matter of Gaddafi's exile in China to be attended to. Of course Wei did not mention this to anyone except his father, Bo Senior. Nobody in the Rome or Tripoli embassies nor on the task force, not even Junior Bo or any of Wei's employees were let into the secret. Wei knew that his father had good access to the Politburo at this time and he managed to start an, "Exchange of Notes," that Gaddafi's government would complete, to the effect that Libya would make fuel and anchorage available to Chinese ships in the Mediterranean should they need it. Once this diplomatic instrument was in place, the Chinese issued an amending protocol to cover Gaddafi's exile in China in the event that he requested it. The original of this single sheet document was taken to Gaddafi by Wei, who then agreed with Muammar the mechanics of implementing this agreement should it ever become necessary. Gaddafi was very pleased with Wei and entertained him with some fine wines and all that a man could require in his tent in the Sahara.

The following day Wei, accompanied by Libya's Foreign Minister and the Head of Libya's Security Service, flew to Harare in Zimbabwe and waited in the Libyan Embassy for their appointment with Mugabe. At eighty-five Mugabe was still in full control of Zimbabwe, thanks to Libyan support, a consortium of venture capitalists, and his Zanu One Party state. Despite his bombastic reputation in the West he was an experienced negotiator and politically astute at least in the politics of Central Africa. At their meeting which included several of Mugabe's ministers who all had multiple business interests, introductions were made and Mugabe's blessing received. Wei was now free to call in his task forces, one provided by the Chinese government, and one made up of his employees from his own business. They proceeded to make individual appointments with the various contacts that he had been given in the mineral rich countries to the north and west of Zimbabwe.

With the task forces busy Wei was free to travel around the capitals of The Democratic Republic of Congo, Uganda, Rwanda, Nigeria, Cameroon, and Burundi. The capitals were well served but Wei ventured further into the rural areas, and he was struck by the failure of these countries to translate their mineral wealth into the infrastructure of roads, railways, airports, schools and hospitals that were necessary for their development. As his task force leaders reported back to him his worst fears were realized as they were required to take local businesses as equal partners, and that those equal partners' prime function was to obtain contracts and permissions by corrupting illegal payments to politicians and bureaucrats. It wasn't a lack of enterprise that held the local people back. He could walk around the local markets and see with his own eyes the extraordinary hard work and ingenuity that the traders and manufacturers put into earning a living. What was missing was equal access to government projects, transport infrastructure to aid expansion, and government-funded education and health to produce a steady supply of skilled workers. He was amazed by the colourful cheerfulness of the people, at least the healthy ones. In one of the countries that he passed through there had been a recent outbreak of the deadly Ebola Virus, fortunately in a remote corner of the country. Upon enquiry it looked as though the government had used the army to isolate the region, leaving the epidemic to fizzle out through lack of contacts. Wei shuddered to think what would happen if an outbreak ever reached a major city. If it did then major quantities of protective suits and plenty of especially outfitted isolation wards would be the only way to persuade health professionals to fight the outbreak. Without the ability to quickly deploy large quantities of equipment and personnel, the virus would be spread around the world by air travel. Problems abounded in Africa but of course the small minority of wealthy Africans were well provided for by plenty of cheap labour, and there was no shortage of luxury facilities to pamper themselves in.

In Kampala Uganda, Wei, whilst enjoying the luxury that his diplomatic status brought him and where it was necessary to be to meet and engage with the dispensers of contracts and power, he became aware that even there he was not far from areas where independent forces challenged the recognised governments and terrorised their populations. The Lord's Resistance Army roamed across Congo, Uganda and Southern Sudan; Boko Haram rampaged across Northern Nigeria and Cameroon; and other Muslim terror groups operated across the Sahel stretching from the Atlantic to the Red Sea, with operations in Algeria, Niger, Chad, and Sudan, and threatening the Southern edge of Gaddafi's Libya. It wasn't just the local people he met and conversed with who made him aware of these problems and dangers, but their agents and facilitators made contact with oblique references to their intent. Their intent was to obtain arms, funds, intelligence, or to negotiate the release of hostages, and they operated in the top class hotels where several made themselves known to Wei.

One such agent was Gamal Haggai, known to all as Haj, the son of a Muslim warlord Abdul Haggai whose experienced battle-hardened troops commanded a swathe of land in Eastern Chad and Southern Sudan. Haj had grown up in Cairo where he attended the American University before going on to take an MBA at Stanford in California. His father made sure that he always stayed in touch with his son, who spent time with his father in The Sahel throughout all of his short life to date. His father had been born in Algeria and fought for independence from the French, but later as a devout Muslim he had lost out to the Nationalists who controlled the country despite a majority in the country who would like the Muslims to take a turn in government. He was a blunt no nonsense fighter with plenty of experience in terrorist attacks. His relationship with his wife had gone from a forceful start to current indifference, but he did his duty to maintain her in Egypt and was passionately attached to his only son. Of course his main ambition was to return to live in Algiers, preferably in triumph. Haj had gone from childhood adoration of his super-hero father who carried a gun and strode around his settlement in fatigues receiving the obvious respect of his men. The occasional temporary substitute mothers were all treated as though they were inferior creatures by his father, and he saw no reason to adopt a different attitude towards them himself. Mother in Cairo was of course on a pedestal for her total commitment to him and more of an influence upon him than his father gave her credit for. She it was who was determined to have her son fully educated and exposed to Western cultures, whilst barely complying with the minimum requirements demanded of a Muslim woman. Haj's father wasn't against him having a good education, he just wished that it would include some military training in the curriculum. An educated son would be very useful to him provided that he was committed to the cause.

As he matured Haj's intellectual capacity was not in doubt and his exposure to different religions, cultures, and attitudes gave him sufficient input to test his powers of reason. He came to understand that Protestant respect for individual rights could not be satisfied by the Muslim religion; and yet the leap to Democracy from the certainties that were taught and that gave so much satisfaction to its adherents; was just too great. Haj's attitude to his father's struggles ranged from admiration for his tenacity to despair at the futility of his efforts. Whilst at Cairo's American University Haj came close to blaming the Americans for all Arab problems, but managed to keep his name clear of any lists of terrorist supporters. In California the mental exercise of the Master of Business Administration course suited his ability for dispassionate reasoning, and he came close to settling for a comfortable life with a major corporation. After a couple of years' experience with a firm of well-known consultants, when he learnt the value of thoughtful negotiation, Haj even considered establishing his own consultancy. He was co-habiting with a blonde blue-eyed lady with her own career priorities, so there was no question of having children. Despite the acceptance that he had earned from his fellow workers, and his darkly handsome appearance that attracted the desire of many American women, Haj could not shrug off his feelings for his roots and culture. Like so many immigrants to Europe and America, who came for the education and jobs that were unobtainable in their countries of origin, Haj looked at Western freedoms and found them hard to accept, despite his success at adapting to Western ways. He left them all behind when he returned to The Sahel to help his father.

Wei noticed the darkly handsome young Arab who never looked in his direction in the bar of the hotel lounge in Kampala, but it was no surprise when he approached his table on one of the rare occasions when he did not have any company.

"Mr Sung may I have a word with you sir?" Haj knew that Wei spoke very good English and addressed him in that language. Wei took a moment to note the smart but fashionable clothing and lack of any expensive watch or jewellery before gesturing to a vacant seat next to him.

"Sir, I must ask for your complete discretion regarding what I have to say to you regarding the fate of some of your fellow citizens. If you feel that you can't give me your word that you will not disclose what I have to say to anyone other than your government's officials, than please say so and I will leave you in peace." Haj noticed how calmly Wei had listened to his initial pitch. Wei was accustomed to being approached by strangers making contact and pitching their business, but he quickly realised that this was different.

"You have my word. If at any time I feel uncomfortable then I will simply stand up and walk away and you should not approach me again."

"Thank you sir. I have been tasked with this approach by the people who have taken three of your citizens' hostage from a mining project in Niger. If your government wishes to negotiate their release they should advise you of their position and I will find and approach you occasionally over the next couple of months, and convey your government's position to the group holding your citizens. The group's price for the release of the hostages is twenty million US dollars and approximately twenty million US dollars' worth of arms, a list of which I will deliver at our next meeting." With that Haj rose and walked calmly out to a waiting vehicle. Wei was not alarmed although news of the hostage taking had eluded him, mainly because it had happened several months ago.

Wei passed on Haj's offer to Peking via the embassy in Rome and received a briefing on the hostage taking in Niger. Uranium has been exported by Niger from the 1950s and is mined close to the town of Arlit, about a thousand kilometres from the capital Niamey. Prospecting a new deposit about two hundred kilometres closer to the Algerian border, under a joint venture agreement between Niger's government and the China National Nuclear Corporation, the three Chinese mining engineers had been an easy target for any of the lawless groups that roamed The Sahel. Protection was available but they had been caught unready by an overwhelming armed group coming out of the Sahara Desert. The three mining engineers had wandered away from their protection and were taken hostage without any struggle or conflict, and without injury. The attackers knew the Sahara well and had vanished without trace some three months ago. Wei's contact was the first indication that the mining engineers were still alive and that a ransom was being demanded for their return. Haj's father had led the force and his group was one of several that China's security agencies had identified as possible perpetrators, but as Haj had not given his name to Wei the connection had not yet been discovered.

Shan Sung was appointed to deal with the hostage matter raised by her husband Wei, simply because as an official of the State Security Service it landed on her desk. China is secretive about its policy regarding hostage negotiations but in practice it is only the USA and the UK who flatly refuse to pay ransom for the release of their citizens. The case of the three Chinese mining engineers in Niger had dropped out from the media's attention and Shan was given the go ahead to negotiate a lower amount for their release. Wei wasn't surprised or disturbed when Shan set up communications with him through the Rome embassy, it was after all her job. They agreed that all he could do was to wait for the handsome young Arab to make contact and then offer one quarter of the cash that he had asked for, in the hope of settling for one third. The arms demand was a different matter. No classified arms could be given away, and it was important to confine any delivery to small arms rather than worry about the value. He was to emphasize the Chinese government's concern that these arms should not be traceable back to China. In effect China would pay a cut out dealer to buy small arms from a known arms trader, who would arrange delivery to the hostage holders. This would be arranged as good faith, but the cash would not be handed over until the three engineers were produced for exchange near to the spot from which they were abducted. With that matter settled Wei resumed his travels around Africa.

Haj was cautious enough to approach Wei obliquely for their second meeting, having his message delivered by courier as to where and when they should meet, and instructing that Wei should come alone and make sure that he was not followed. Shan however was one step ahead of both of them, having sent field agents to keep Wei under observation twenty-four hours a day without his knowledge. She also asked Wei to carry a tracking device which, for his own safety, he could ditch just before he reached the meeting place. The field agents got the photograph of Haj that they wanted which would help identify him. Wei demanded proof that the three Chinese mining engineers were still alive and Haj produced an iPad video showing them holding yesterday's newspaper. To Wei's surprise Haj accepted two million dollars cash for each of the three engineers, and then realized that the main demand was for arms and ammunition when Haj produced an extensive list. Not that it was of great monetary value, probably ten million dollars in total, and was obviously for a fast moving band of terrorists' intent on an attack against a defended position. It included some military vehicles which could be used to transport the rest of the arms and ammunition to a remote part of The Sahel. Wei emphasized the Chinese government's desire for secrecy and that the delivery of the arms would be made in good faith, so that the following day the three engineers could be returned to where they were taken hostage and exchanged for the six million dollars. All they needed was a quick method of communication. Haj produced two pre-paid mobile phones each with the other's number entered but best usable in Egypt. He gave one to Wei and told him to call as soon as the arms were in position to be picked up. With that they parted and Shan's field agents switched to tracking Haj at a safe distance.

With Haj's identity established Shan's agents quickly worked out that his father was Abdul Haggai the leader of a terrorist group in the Sahel, even though Haj didn't go anywhere near him after leaving from his meeting with Wei. Known terrorist groups whether currently active or not, have field agents from various countries checking up on them and their followers, It was rare to be able to insert an asset into a terrorist group's kitchen cabinet, but listening and tracking devices along with the inevitable loose tongues of followers, deserters, and their families and friends often produced an idea of the group's plans. It took a couple of weeks to purchase and assemble Haj's list of vehicles, arms and ammunition and attach some cleverly concealed tracking devices. Wei in Cairo had realized that Haj must also be in Cairo as he had emphasized that their disposable pre-paid mobile phone would only work there. He called Haj and advised him of the day and time that the arms dealer would deliver everything on the list, through Cameroon to a map reference in Chad. Shan's agents kept their distance switching the tracking devices on occasionally but only for short periods to save their batteries. Haj's father was at the handover along with plenty of armed men. All went smoothly and Abdul Haggai then set off to release the mining engineers for cash at a map reference on the Niger/Algeria border. The second exchange was to take place the day after the first one as agreed between Haj and Wei in their Cairo telephone conversation. There was no question of attempting to arrest Abdul Haggai's group at the cash handover as it would have resulted in the death of the three Chinese engineers, and the size of the force needed to capture them would have been easily spotted by the group's outriders, allowing the terrorists to disappear into the vast expanse of the Sahara desert.

As soon as news of the successful return of the three Chinese engineers reached her, Shan advised the Chinese Foreign Office that she had collected considerable evidence that a group of Muslim terrorists were planning an attack on Western oil installations in Algeria, and that her tracking devices could probably pinpoint which one as the terrorists approached. China did not care too much about attacks on Western oil installations, but they did have their own troubles with dissident Muslim groups in China, and they were quite happy to accrue some credit with Muslim Arab nations when they could. China advised the Algerian government of the expected attack and within a few days Shan's agents were able to hand over to the Algerians the mobile phones that were programmed to switch on the tracking device's transponder.

Abdul Haggai, Haj's father, led his men out of the Sahara Desert with the intention of taking lots of hostages and blowing up the plant. Hopefully this would make the Western oil companies unwilling to operate in such a dangerous environment and cause the spread of the Arab Spring to Algeria. Haj's father would then be able to return home in triumph to live under an elected Muslim government in his beloved Algeria. The plant was spread over two hundred acres of flat semi-desert with little in the way of cover for a defensive force. The workers were withdrawn at the last minute and replaced by Algerian Special Forces who threw up barricades with an open field of fire on the approaches to the plant. The main Algerian force with some heavily armoured vehicles remained over the horizon to the north, ready to move in and encircle the plant to block any escape routes. With their newly acquired armoured land-rovers with mounted machine guns, the terrorist group drove at full speed into the plant from the south and then split into three groups. They knew that the plant was normally guarded by a platoon of regular army soldiers who worked in three eight hour shifts, which would mean that there would be about twenty on duty at any one time. Off duty guards were returned to barracks in a town fifteen miles away, so the instruction was to shoot anyone carrying a weapon as and when they passed them on the perimeter of the plant. One group of terrorists was to head for the administration block which included the guard command post. The second group was to head for the workers' accommodation blocks and the third group was to spread out in the working plant. All three groups of terrorists were to engage any guards carrying weapons, confine all Algerian workers in the accommodation block and handcuff all European or American expatriates for taking them as hostages. They would then set explosive charges to destroy as much of the plant as possible, before disappearing into the Sahara before help could arrive. They reckoned that they would have half an hour before the rest of the guard platoon arrived from the closest town, if a message got through to them. The terrorists' group was large enough to deal with them if they did arrive. It would be a good three hours before the main Algerian army could interfere, by which time Abdul Haggai and his men would be long gone. All these plans were made to no avail, as the terrorists were met by a hail of bullets as soon as they entered the plant. Just two of the land-rovers were able to continue at right angles and exit the plant to the east and west with the driver and a couple of passengers still alive, but they were soon captured by the main Algerian force arriving at great speed from the north. Haj's father and a few other survivors of the first attack managed to take cover in various buildings and behind steel and brick structures. Few of them were willing to surrender but their fate was sealed. Abdul Haggai was wounded but found himself in a room with a landline telephone. He called Haj in Cairo and told him that his cause was lost. "We have been betrayed by that Chinese dog, take

care of him my son, don't grieve too much and honour your mother."
Haj did grieve for he loved his father, but first he had a sacred task to
perform to honour him.

Wei was happy to have completed one more successful service
for his country with the rescue of the three Chinese engineers. His
agreement with Gaddafi had not caused China any embarrassment, as
Gaddafi had been assassinated in October 2011 before he was able to
get to the arranged pick-up point in the Sahara. Wei's plan had for
some time been to escape communism and live permanently in the
West with some of his businesses intact. This vague ambition had
sprung from the realisation that his father Bo Senior did not fully
accept the communist philosophy, but had decided to live with it
because his revolutionary army service had given him prestige and
position. Wei's feeling had led to the decision to send his son Bo
Junior to boarding school in England, although he had disguised his
reason to Thomas as being beneficial to growing his Chinese
business interests. Now he felt that he was getting near to decision
time and when Bo Senior was arrested, he knew that he had to make
a move.

What Wei didn't know was that Shan had tracked the arms
shipment, and by passing the tracking device on to the Algerian
government, she had caused Abdul Haggai's death. As soon as the
media reported Algeria's success defending their oil installation and
killing most of the attackers including their leader Abdul Haggai,
Wei realized that Haj would conclude that he had caused his father's
death and would be very upset. How upset he was to discover in the
bedroom of his London house a few months later. In the meantime
Wei was very upset with Shan and it was her deception in this matter,
allied with the possibility that she might inform their son that he had
caused Emily's mother's death, that was the reason that he called in
the Sicilian Mafia to arrange her demise in Rome.

Haj was methodical in pursuit of Wei who now contracted
personal guards and installed alarms and CCTV in his properties.
England was Haj's country of choice as he would receive more
lenient treatment there if caught. Wei's London house was often left
empty and Haj was able to break in without triggering the alarm. He
studied the layout and took an impression of a key to the back door,

before erasing the CCTV evidence of his visit and leaving the camera inoperable. Haj knew that his father would expect him to assassinate Wei by their traditional tribal method of slitting his throat, so he needed to be alone with him to do the job properly. He studied the staff and suppliers' movements to and from the property and had left microphones in several rooms and in the telephone, so he was able to act on one of the very few occasions when Wei was alone in the house. It was just a matter of waiting for the right moment, and when the chance came he was in and out in five minutes, leaving the untraceable knife behind. Haj was on a flight to Turkey using a false name and passport before Bo discovered his father's body.

Frank & Emily had received sufficient information from their investigators to piece this whole complex story together. Wei's own documents and computer files, along with hotel and phone records, a back-hander here and a chat there, had led to the reconstruction of Wei's mistakes. Except that there was no real proof that Haj had wielded the knife, nothing that could be passed on to the British police. When the two detective friends explained all this to Bo it was sufficient evidence for him to accept it as the truth. He was glad that he now knew so much more about his parents' deaths and his pain at their passing was easing. He felt no desire to take revenge on his father's killer, and began to confine thoughts of his Chinese heritage to his sole remaining relative, Grandfather Bo Senior. His mother's parents were dead and China's one child policy had ensured that she had no siblings. He took over his father's responsibility for Bo Senior, arranging through minor bribes the supply of a few pleasures for his palate and a few dollars to enable him to buy more, but Bo had started to look to the future.

The three friends still felt a strong attachment to each other but Emily stayed in England and Frank went back to work in Geneva, whilst Bo travelled the world in search of business, some of it in Africa where Wei had established joint ventures for Oxysung International.

Part IV Money Go Round

Chapter Sixteen
The Investors

Emily Tang had been impressed by The Fallowfield Estate when she collected her inheritance. It had struck her as similar to her boarding school, where she had been very happy once she replaced the loss of her mother with a close group of friends that included Bo and Frank. The Estate Hall resembled the school's assembly hall and administration offices, whilst the sporting facilities exceeded those of the school. The country club members were like older pupils and the staff the younger teachers. Emily decided to book into the Fallowfield hotel and see what her options were. Lady Sarah was very warm and welcoming and Emily signed up as a member of the country club. She bought a luxury saloon car and started taking golf and riding lessons. Soon one of the lodges on the estate came free and she rented it for a month which allowed her to do some clothes shopping whilst she looked for a house to buy. One of the luxury houses built by Tony Latimer on the edge of the estate, close to the one he had built for himself and Lady Sarah, also came up for sale, and Emily bought it just in time for her father to join her from Hong Kong complete with his new citizenship. Emily then found and bought a flat in central London in order to have some independence from her father, but returning to visit him every other weekend.

Emily enjoyed her country weekends with her father and was drawn to the young woman living next door. Becky Latimer was seventeen years old and full of energy and excitement about her future. She had plenty of school friends as she studied for A-levels but there were few young girls her age on The Fallowfield Estate. She was delighted when Emily bought the next door house and intrigued by her family tales, although Emily left out the reasons for the recent violent episodes. The two young women were the product of the public schools education experience and quickly developed an easy and confidential friendship. Emily at twenty-eight years of age, and with actual experience of the crucial decade for women as they come out of puberty, was able to offer advice and guidance by relating her own experiences of just that period of life. Becky was moved by Emily's sadness that her love affair with Bo had been ended recently.

She had been present when Emily received her two hundred million pound inheritance, and told her that she too had an inheritance, from her birth mother Linda, that was worth roughly the same amount. Now it was Emily's turn to listen to Becky's complicated family history and how Linda had an affair with Anthony Latimer who was her business partner and Becky's natural father. As Becky understood it Tony had provided the capital for a business but Linda had created a computer software company and built it up on her own, to the extent that she decided to float the shares on the New York Stock Exchange. It was Emily's turn to be moved by Becky's sadness that her mother had died in the nine eleven collapse of the twin towers in New York, where she was visiting a merchant bank to discuss the float. Becky was in the care of Tony and Lady Sarah, who had come to visit Linda in Houston at that very time, and they simply took over as Mum and Dad for Becky. Tony had made all the legal arrangements for adopting Becky once Linda was officially declared dead as her body was never found. Tony also arranged for floating the company on the stock exchange and Becky was left with a major shareholding which she would gain control of next year when she was eighteen. Both young women wondered what they should do, not only with their future, but with their huge fortunes. Becky thought that maybe she should go to university and study computer science with the idea of helping to run and expand her mother's creation. Both her parents Tony and Linda had been organized methodically minded people and yet Becky had vague notions that she was artistic, maybe she should try architecture as a compromise. Emily was helping her father who was trying to thwart China's efforts to kill democracy in Hong Kong and replace it with a full communist dictatorship. Both women were determined to be useful and both of them were still searching for something to spark them into action. Their now intimate discussions centred upon how they both had suffered from the consequences of terrorist attacks, although Emily's loss of her mother came from a state sponsored attack. What upset them most were news bulletins showing women and children in tented camps due to the Arab Spring that was supposed to liberate them to a better and more prosperous life, but instead had sparked wars and repressions that resulted in poverty. Emily explained to Becky that her friend, and Becky's relative, Thomas Latimer, was already involved in government efforts to help refugees, and that they should talk to him about their desire to be involved. She would also bring in her rich friends Bo and Frank, who had considerable business and organizational skills that she was sure would be needed to get their charitable trust initiative up and going.

Thomas Latimer was, like the two young women on The Fallowfield Estate, wondering what he should do with his inheritance. Life was for him very enjoyable with Susan content with her unlimited shopping budget. He was still active as a senior Liberal Democrat politician and the party had won three seats in the 2010 general election on the southern fringes of Manchester in Withington, Cheadle and Hazel Grove, where his support was welcomed. The Liberal Democrats joined in a coalition government with the Conservatives and thereby gained more power than they had had for more than a century. As an ex-MEP, an active election campaigner, and a generous cash donor for the Liberal Democrats, Thomas could expect some kind of appointment and was not disappointed. He was appointed a special assistant to the Department for International Development and asked to advise on the most effective way of using government donated funds to support the charities looking after the world's growing millions of refugees from war, terrorism and starvation. By 2013 Thomas had gained plenty of experience of the refugee problem and felt that the most effective help depended mainly on the swift delivery of the essentials of life, water and tents followed by as much bulk food and medical and sanitation facilities as could be afforded. Of course the only real solution was to stop the wars and political misjudgements that created the problems, but that was outside Thomas's remit. At the same time he was beginning to appreciate that the funds required for such large scale relief needed to be made available in a timely manner. Many countries' governments made promises that they did not keep and that needed more political persuasion. On the other hand charities received remarkably generous donations from millions of ordinary folk who did not have a lot of spare cash. Some mega rich individuals had formed charitable trusts of their own that gave generously to good causes, and Thomas felt that he might do the same, but it was important to maintain the original capital and feed only the income generated by it to an effectively run charitable trust.

At this time Thomas received an invitation from Lady Sarah to spend a weekend at The Fallowfield Estate to discuss with Becky and Emily their growing interest in his refugee activities and their desire to form a charitable trust. Thomas arrived with his wife Susan, who recognized Lady Sarah as one of her own landed class, and was taken to the stables and kitted out for a ride with Emily and Becky. Susan had recently given birth to a son Christened Horace Damian after his paternal and maternal grandfathers, who had been left in the care of Susan Parents. Before dinner they all sat down in Lady Sarah's lounge and in her presence Thomas outlined the work he had been doing and his plans to make a more effective contribution to help the world's refugees. Both girls liked the idea as it would relieve them of the impossible task of making their own investment decisions. Becky would have to complete university before she could give much of her time, but was now seriously considering a computer science degree so that she could join her mother's company. That would enable her to feed the dividends from her shares into the trust whilst striving to increase the company's profitability. Thomas assured the girls and Lady Sarah that a board of directors would be tasked with investment decisions that would maintain the trust's capital value using the best professional advice. He would also be approaching Frank and Bo as soon as he could track them down, to join in the good work and hoped that the trust would total one and a half billion pounds. Emily felt a frisson of emotion at the mention of Bo's name, as it implied that they would at least meet occasionally if he too joined the board. On the way home Susan said that she thought that there could be an MBE at least for Thomas, if his good work was noticed.

Bo knew that Wei had negotiated some raw material joint ventures on his African travels, as he was responsible for recording and vetting them back in Geneva. Joint ventures were entered into so that the business risk was shared with other companies and/or one of the Chinese government's nationalized industries. He was now in Lagos to meet a school friend whose father was the dictator of a landlocked country behind those that bordered the Atlantic Ocean's Gulf of Guinea. Wei had put together a consortium of interested parties that included Oxysung International and the Chinese mining national industry. Bo's school friend came from a country with a substantial iron ore deposit that had already been tested and was known to be of considerable commercial value at the point of extraction. The problem was that it would need a new railway line that had to pass through another country, to reach a port large enough to handle bulk carrier vessels for the export of the iron ore to be profitable. The involvement of the Chinese government was crucial to this development as private enterprise was reluctant to get involved in such a large infrastructure project in such a volatile area. The Chinese government was interested as there was sufficient iron ore for steady extraction over a long time period, and that was sufficient to justify the construction of the railway. In addition they would be willing to help both countries with roads and education, provided that they gained favourable treatment regarding Chinese citizens establishing commercial interests in all their other industries including farming.

Bo and his school friend Mambu Koroma were enjoying a sundowner on the terrace of the Federal Palace Hotel in Lagos. A strong breeze was blowing up the channel that connected the Gulf of Guinea to the massive Lagos Lagoon, making it pleasantly mild in the late afternoon. It was different on the sea as the wind whipped up white tops on the ridges of the incoming tide, running faster as the sea was forced into the narrowing channel. They watched passively as a twelve man canoe came from Lagos harbour heading towards the open sea and into the tide and wind. In the stern the drummer beat out the timing for the paddlers, who never faltered. It took a superhuman effort and half an hour for the canoe to disappear from their sight and they could only express admiration for the effort of what they assumed were fishermen. On reflection they decided that they were more likely to be smugglers, or maybe they were an armed pirate gang on their way to board and rob one of the ships anchored offshore awaiting permission to dock in the harbour. Mambu expressed this last opinion that brought a cynical laugh out of Bo as he reflected that, if they were pirates they would surely be able to afford an outboard engine.

Bo had visited Mambu recently but before that he had not seen him for a few years. Now he looked prosperous, perhaps too prosperous, for their school's best athletic sprinter was considerably heavier than he had been when they were both at school. They enjoyed some nostalgia as they talked of their school experiences, especially of when they had first explored one another's backgrounds. Neither appreciated their father's importance as Mambu was not impressed by communist officials, and Bo did not count an army officer as somebody of great importance. Much had changed however by the time they met in Lagos and Mambu expressed his condolences to Bo at the loss of his parents. On the other hand Mambu's father was now the President of his country, something that Bo could congratulate his friend on. As the sun began to set, which at this latitude did not take long, the two friends went in to dinner in the air-conditioned hotel restaurant.

Having ordered their meals and before they started on the wine, Bo thanked Mambu for having organized citizenship for him in his country. He had explained his predicament to Mambu on a previous visit to his landlocked country, explaining all his family's misfortunes that had led to his exclusion from China. Bo did not hide his desire to eventually achieve British citizenship and explained to Mambu that it was his long-term aim, but as the murders of his parents had not been solved, there might be objections, especially as nobody had been convicted of Wei's murder. The London police had cleared Bo of that crime but would it help if he told them that he had a suspect in the name of Gamal Haggai? At this point in time he couldn't make his mind up as to whether it would help or hinder his citizenship application. Bo then brought up the matter of Wei's joint venture plan to export iron ore from Mambu's country, and asked his friend to arrange a meeting with his father. Mambu saw no problem with such a meeting and told Bo that his father was anxious to get the Chinese government involved. Jonathan Koroma was a dictator having used the military to remove the last elected government, and was coming under pressure from younger military officers who were anxious to exploit the country's only natural resource, the mountain of iron ore. Mambu admitted that his father had succumbed to a certain amount of corruption, as it was impossible for him to resist. West African society was based on being the loudest with the most and Jonathan had a large family to support. In fact that was another trait of West African society, the family was not limited to blood relatives, but extended to the whole tribe, who looked for small favours from any successful politician, businessman, or even university graduates likely to establish themselves in profitable professions. Mambu believed that Jonathan was genuinely working for the good of the country by licensing the mining and export of iron ore, but that he had a better understanding than the younger army officers, of the need to maintain credibility with international money markets and businesses. To that end he was restricting the tax take to only twenty-five percent of the price of the iron ore at the port of export. The younger officers were pushing for a higher tax and guarantees that the country's income would be spent on infrastructure, schooling and health. Mambu told Bo that they should both fly to the country's capital Boako tomorrow as he had arranged a meeting with his father. Bo assured Mambu that there would be a consultancy fee for him whether or not the meeting was successful.

Flying over the West African rain forest it used to be hard to imagine human activity underneath the forest's green canopy. Mud brown rivers used to be the only highways and red laterite roads were few and far between. What Bo now witnessed was the occasional patch of forest and a patchwork of mainly unmade roads inhabited by ever-increasing populations. In the past few months he had done his preparation, meeting with the political decision makers in the coastal country with a sufficiently large port to load the iron ore for export. They were interested in a railway passing through their country and any other benefits that China might supply, provided of course that the country's treasury received a royalty on every ton of iron ore that entered their country. Certain consultancy fees would ensure the required legislation and local co-operation that such a large project required. China's interest in the project had already been stimulated by Wei, and now that Frank, with some help from Thomas, had put together a consortium of banks and private equity funds to join Oxysung International in the joint venture, the costs would not all fall on China, which enabled them to commit to the project. All now depended upon Mambu's father, who had suggested the project to Wei in the first place, giving the go-ahead.

Mambu was careful in his dealings with his father, he knew the pressures that all dictators face. His father Jonathan was in a good mood and told his son to introduce his school friend Bo straight away. Bo was not overawed in these circumstances and after reminiscing about his and Mambu's misadventures at school he quickly set about assuring Jonathan that he had the finance, the co-operation of the country through which the iron ore would be exported, and China's backing for the whole project. Jonathan assured Bo that he just had to hold a meeting of his cabinet and he would put the document, giving Oxysung International the mineral rights to the area with the proven deposits of iron ore, in Bo's hand. In the meantime he would like to introduce Bo to his family. Jonathan lived in the very large presidential palace and he needed every inch of it. Several wives had produced many children who were all very noisy and colourful. Of course Mambu was the number one son by the number one wife and as such the target of much playful attention from the rest of the tribe. Bo and Mambu were obliged to play kick about football with the sons, many of whom demonstrated considerable ball control. The girls preferred tennis and swimming and many of them were of an age and shape to interest any man as they demonstrated their agility in the skimpiest of outfits. Bo excelled at table tennis whilst the wives directed the many servants to provide a constant stream of food and drink. With the sun setting quickly the whole family spilt into several rooms, each showing a different video film, whilst Bo and Mambu joined Jonathan and some of his advisors for a quiet beer and a discussion of the African news programme that they had just viewed. As Bo prepared to go to bed, Jonathan gave him the documents that he had hoped for, the right to mine the iron ore in his country.

Bo set to work immediately, calling Frank that night to ensure the funds for Oxysung's consortium were in place. Frank confirmed that the consortium was committed to one billion dollars, of which Oxysung International was contributing one hundred million dollars, as soon as the rights for mining the iron ore were in their possession. He advised Bo to press China for twelve and a half percent of the operating company, but settle for ten percent if China committed to nine billion dollars for their ninety percent share. Bo responded by asking Frank to join him in Africa whilst they got this operation off the ground. His next call was to the minister of the country with a port access to the Atlantic Ocean. He told him the good news and said that he was mailing him a copy of the document that Jonathan Koroma had signed, and that would satisfy the terms of the letter of intent that his government had given Bo. The minister sounded pleased and Bo said that he looked forward to seeing him again at the formal meeting that he would arrange for all parties to commit to the project. Wei had started all his African projects using China's Rome embassy as his contact point for dealing with Beijing. Despite his status as a non-resident ex-citizen, he had passed on useful intelligence and received support for commercial ventures beneficial to both Oxysung International and to China. Now Bo took the same route meeting with embassy officials in his Rome hotel, and after several days' negotiation, Beijing agreed to commit nine billion dollars and send representatives to the project signing conference in Jonathan Koroma's capital city Boako.

A month later Bo returned to Geneva to join up with Frank and make sure that the preparations for the conference to launch the mining and export of iron ore project, for which they held the rights, would go as they wished. Consultants had been hired, legal documents prepared, and bank accounts opened. Mambu joined them in Geneva to approve the preparations, accompanied by one of his sisters. Victoria Koroma was, like her brother, educated at an English public school and university, and a successful model in Lagos where she was mainly resident. Her skin colour could be described as milk chocolate and clothes were transformed into a living sheath on her statuesque body. Her smile was warm and friendly and Frank was smitten as soon as he took her hand and returned her smile, declaring himself delighted to meet her. At twenty-eight Frank was himself handsome, fit and confident in the presence of beautiful women, and as soon as he got a chance he invited Victoria to have dinner with him alone. He did not have the average Englishman's attitude to other races, having spent his early years in Spain where he was in a minority regarding nationalities, and then spending his time in England where his closest friends were Asian and African. For Frank meeting Victoria did not for a second cause him to consider her African heritage, and his natural relaxed attitude, along with his blue eyes and fair hair was immediately attractive to Victoria. For their second date he took her into the mountains and produced two pairs of walking boots from the trunk of his car so that they could ramble through the beautiful Swiss countryside. Nothing very steep or difficult, and Frank had some tasty sandwiches and orange juice in his haversack, so that they could rest and enjoy the view in the sunshine. They had their first kiss as they sat side by side and they both enjoyed it. After that Victoria did not want to let go of Frank's hand until they arrived back at his apartment, which was tastefully and expensively furnished. Victoria was impressed by Frank's style and cooking as he prepared a tasty snack. With the sun setting and without turning on any lights they retired to the bedroom and had lusty and satisfying intercourse. The second time that they went to bed they made love and Frank surprised himself by proposing marriage, which Victoria accepted without any hesitation.

Bo, Mambu, Frank and Victoria flew to London and were driven to The Fallowfield Estate for an informal engagement party. Of course Bo had managed to corner his friend on his own and ask him if he was sure that he was doing the right thing. Bo had stamina and was less impulsive than Frank who was a sprinter, and he would never have made such a hasty commitment. However Frank's outpouring of his conviction that he was truly, deeply, for ever in love with Victoria, removed Bo's doubts so that all he could do was go along with Frank, and accept that there was no alternative. Frank's mother and Keith arrived from Spain for their first visit to the source of his inheritance and were duly impressed. Thomas and Susan, Emily and Li, along with Lady Sarah and her relatives made for a whirlwind of introductions for Victoria. With Frank and Victoria sharing a hotel suite everyone could only offer their congratulations and admire the engagement ring with its brilliant diamond, which Frank had purchased in the Geneva airport duty free shop. Frank and Victoria had both committed themselves to the very strong emotion that they had both felt, without knowing anything about each other. All their friends and relatives were holding their breath and hoping it would work out for the best, but the two lovers were discovering new things about each other every day, and each new discovery strengthened their bond. Both Mambu and Victoria had telephoned their parents who had expressed their delight but now wanted them in Boako so that they could have visual confirmation that this was a happy event. With the signing of the iron ore mining and export project agreement due in a few days' time, Bo and Mambu, Frank and Victoria were on their way, and on arrival, Frank was plunged into an even greater whirlwind of introductions and embraces.

The parties to the agreement to mine and export iron ore from Jonathan's landlocked country, by rail to the Atlantic port in the adjacent country, arrived in Boako soon after Bo and Frank. The consultant engineers had completed their survey of the railway line and the iron ore mountain, and all parties had been given copies of the details along with the current budgeted costs. The rights had been awarded by the two countries involved, and China and the private consortium had come to prior agreement regarding their respective share of the costs and returns. After minimum discussion the required legal agreements were signed, that included specified funding payments into the bank's operating account. Oxysung's recommendations regarding the award of the two main contracts: for the mining operation and the construction of the railway, from those companies that had submitted a bid, were accepted with a starting date at the end of the rainy season in a month's time. That completed the business and all delegates were invited to a celebratory dinner by their host Jonathan Koroma in his Presidential Palace.

The senior members of Jonathan's family attended the dinner, making it a lot less formal and Bo was able to talk to the Chinese delegates about matters in Shanghai. Victoria helped her mother direct the servants and made sure that Frank was well served with everything that he wished for. Jonathan stood and tapped his glass for order and thanked the delegates for all that they had done to progress his country to a more prosperous future. Smiling Jonathan then announced the engagement of his oldest daughter Victoria Koroma the fashion model to Mr Frank Latimer, an English businessman, and expressed his and his wife's delight and hopes for the future of the marriage. This was the first that the country's ministers had heard of the proposed union and the dinner became a second engagement party. After congratulations all round, Frank found himself subject to an inquisition by Victoria's brothers and sisters, how rich was he, where did he live, how big was his house, how many brothers and sisters did he have, and where was his father? His answers were greeted by mock expressions of disbelief when he told them that there was only his mother and a couple of cousins, but he assured them that he had enough money to have ten children with Victoria. Surprisingly to Frank, Victoria did not make any expression of horror at the joking mention of ten children. Bo agreed to be best man and the wedding was planned for Boako in six months' time. Frank and Victoria had already decided upon this by themselves in private, they wanted everyone to understand that their commitment, although so sudden, was very real and not because of any accidental pregnancy. Although Victoria's reputation as a model was mainly in Africa and based on Lagos, she had been hired for shows in London, and she and Frank decided to base themselves there. Bo would be visiting the mining project quite frequently and it would be convenient for Victoria to accompany him when he did so, to ensure that the wedding plans were progressing as she wished them to. She was however ambitious to be a business woman in the fashion industry and would look for opportunities in London and Lagos, where Frank could finance her, (provided that she could produce a convincing business plan, he warned her).

Back in his London apartment Bo was trying to motivate himself to start checking through the pile of, documents, contracts, and e-mails piled up in front of him on an occasional table, as he watched the television news. He could never recall how he felt or reacted when the news reader said,

"There has been a military coup in the landlocked country to the south of the Sahel. Gunshots were heard in the capital Boako, and communications were suspended for a time. We will report on the situation as soon as we receive more information." There on the screen was an old picture of the Presidential Palace in Boako, now quite familiar to Bo. He immediately telephoned Frank who had seen the news bulletin and said,

"Victoria is on the telephone now to her consulate, I will let you know as soon as we find out anything. Why don't you try the Chinese embassy and I will try the Foreign Office and we can call back later." Bo agreed and by the next morning they had a good idea of what had happened. Jonathan Koroma had gained power when he was a

Brigadier in the army and now the next generation of dissatisfied officers had lost patience. Jonathan's personal guards had put up some resistance which accounted for the gunshots, but their commander had already been included in the plot and with the country's entire army surrounding the Presidential Palace the police commander and Jonathan realized that resistance was pointless. His family was allowed to go to a property that they owned, but Jonathan was held whilst the new government decided what to do with him.

Jonathan Koroma had decided to award the iron ore mining and export rights to Oxysung International in order to avoid being ousted by a coup. He knew that his country needed more revenues and thought that the agreement with China would ensure a lot more money for the national budget, and provide the stability that the country needed, even if he did divert a small portion of the income to himself, his family and his ministers. Unfortunately the army had convinced themselves that with China entrenched in their country, they would become less influential. The army council publically justified their coup by claiming that the deposed President had given away too large a percentage of the forecast profits to the Chinese and the private consortium. They decided to act straight away before the project operations got underway and the Chinese became entrenched. World reaction was unfavourable, as Jonathan told the coup leaders it would be, when he was first interrogated. The rest of the world wanted stability in this region, and even though Jonathan had taken power in a coup of his own, the mining project was seen as progress with the country getting a reasonable portion of the profits. The new military government claimed that they had an alternative consortium to take over the mining project but confirmation was proving difficult, and they had created exactly the situation that was off-putting to potential investors. Ignoring Jonathan's pleas not to do so, the new military government rescinded Oxysung International's iron ore mining and exporting rights.

Bo felt that he could rectify the situation if only he could get to Boako. Victoria had been told by her London consulate that it was better if she did not try to return home for a while, and that they had been instructed not to issue visas for visitors until further notice. Frank had been told by the Foreign Office that they were not recommending travel to Boako at the moment, and Bo didn't want to talk to his Chinese contacts until he had something positive to report. Bo took his bodyguard and driver and flew to Bomako the capital of Mali, where he hired three vehicles with local drivers, translators and guides. They headed west intending to enter Jonathan's landlocked country through the back door with the aid of cash in envelopes. The government of Mali's curiosity regarding their plans was also satisfied in a similar manner. After many hours driving through the dusty semi-desert featuring thin scrub and the occasional skeletal remains of livestock, Bo called a halt at a small town with a little more vegetation than the surrounding countryside. Water was available and they purchased some bottled French water that is traded world-wide, but the atmosphere in the town was so subdued as to carry almost the feeling that something was about to happen. As they left town it did, suddenly they realized that they were not the only vehicles on the rough track. Surrounded by armed Arabs there was no question of either flight or fight, they were hostages of a terrorist group from the Sahel. Two Europeans and one Asian would fetch a good ransom. They were relieved of their possessions but not treated particularly roughly and the locals that they had hired were abandoned. There followed a long drive to the group's base far to the East. The group's leader, Nasser Kano, spoke English and after he had examined the documents that Bo had been carrying, he understood the massive investments involved in the project that Bo had set out to save. During Bo's interrogation Nasser immediately disabused him of any idea that this matter could be settled by a small cash payment, and asked him to nominate a possible negotiator from Oxysung. Bo gave his mentor's name, Thomas Latimer. It was obvious that Bo could be ransomed for a very large sum. The two Europeans hired by Bo were Swiss, but payment would not come from their governments, rather from corporate insurance and Bo's own private wealth, and their release could be used to establish good faith. Kano started to arrange contact with possible hostage negotiators to represent him in contacts with Thomas Latimer and he had the amount of one hundred million US dollars in mind, but would initially ask for much more.

Frank had tried to persuade Bo not to attempt his risky back door entry to Jonathan's landlocked country and became aware that something was wrong when he managed to contact Mambu Koroma in Boako. Mambu confirmed that Bo had not arrived. In the Sahel the terrorist leader was looking for a negotiator and arranged a meeting with Gamal Haggai. Haj quickly realized that he was dealing with the son of the man whom he had murdered in London, but Bo was not given any hint as to who would be negotiating his release. At the meeting Haj was able to assure his prospective employer that he already knew all about Oxysung International and agreed to make contact regarding Bo's ransom, He assured Nasser that the company and even the individual directors were all sufficiently wealthy to meet the demand for one hundred million dollars. Haj emphasised that it was essential to contact Bo's company quickly and tell them that they must negotiate directly with him and not appoint a professional hostage negotiator. The recent proliferation of ship hijackings by pirates in the Indian Ocean had resulted in the insurance companies turning to a growing band of hostage negotiators. Nasser Kano realized that Haj had the inside track for this job, going by his reaction after reading Bo's captured documents. He did not press Haj for any details as he already knew about his father's life and death, and after a full briefing he sent Haj on his way to make the first contact.

Bo meanwhile was incredibly frustrated, spending his days alone in an airless room with nothing to do, and he began to have irrational fantasies about escaping. The guards silently delivered his unappetizing food and escorted him to the shower and toilet facilities without responding to any attempt at communication. Nasser had decided to keep the Chinese man separate from the Europeans so that they could not plot strategies or plan what to say if one was released before the other. The Chinese government would not wait forever for the stability that such a large scheme in Africa required and Bo's thoughts turned to the hope of rescue. Before Bo had left London, Frank had given him a tracking device and insisted that he take it with him, and he had attached it to his hire vehicle without anyone else in his party knowing about it. Frank pointed out that this was necessary, as his crew might curry favour with any hostile authorities, by telling them about the tracking device. Frank had synced two mobile phones to operate the device, as the battery would go flat if it was left on all the time. Either one of them could switch the tracking device on with their mobile phone. Of course Kano had taken Bo's mobiles from him as soon as he was captured, but Frank could switch the tracking device on for a short period and receive a location pulse via a satellite. Bo began to think about what he could do to protect himself if a rescue force attacked the terrorist's camp. If he could jam the door with wooden splinters from the table leg and use the rest of the table leg to stop the door handle from being pressed down, by crouching behind the rest of the table and his mattress he might avoid being shot just long enough for the rescuers to reach him. As far as Bo was concerned it was better than months sweating in this hole waiting to be ransomed. He had no family to miss him, and began to think more about Emily. The shock of the violent deaths of both of his beloved parents had disturbed his mind more than he cared to admit. He dare not even think about his intensions when he went to his father's London house and took a knife from the kitchen before finding his father already dead. Now he had time to calm his mind and bury some of his worst thoughts and regularise the good memories. As he completed this process he realised that Emily had faced equally distressing emotions and yet had never done anything to add to his misery. The realisation slowly came to him that they still loved one another and would be better able to deal with the past together. Bo was now hoping that Frank would risk the rescue mission, just as Frank's father William had done long ago in the Delamere Forest.

Haj wasn't going to visit the United Kingdom; he knew that people had been asking questions since Wei's murder and, whilst he didn't believe that he had left any evidence behind him, he was not going to risk entering England. Instead he contacted Oxysung International in Geneva. Nasser Kano had forwarded a picture of Bo holding a recent copy of a newspaper and Haj had it delivered to Oxysung's reception desk with a note. The note explained that he was merely a person selected to negotiate the freedom of Bo Sung by the group holding him, and should be referred to as Franco. The note gave a list of numbers for disposable mobile telephones, each of which could be used only once, preferably by Mr Thomas Latimer. It wasn't long before Haj received a call on the first mobile phone from a director of the company asking to speak to Franco, and advising him that Mr Thomas Latimer had the full confidence of the board and was available. Haj simply told the caller to have Mr Thomas Latimer go to Cairo and call him on the second mobile number as soon as he arrived.

Frank meanwhile was on his way to Boako having received a message from Mambu that the Military Junta had agreed to meet him as they now realized the importance of convincing the Chinese that their country's stability could be maintained. Mambu was a colonel in his country's army on attachment to the President's Office, at his father's beck and call in other words. The coup plotters had excluded him from their plans for obvious reasons, and at the time of the coup Mambu was fortunately not at his father's side. He found himself a wanted man for a few days and had to keep on moving around in the bush to avoid capture. As the Military Junta's financial problems escalated after they cancelled Oxysung International's rights to mine iron ore, Jonathan the ex-president under interrogation, began to convince them that he could regain international confidence if they reversed their decision and allowed him to serve them as Finance Minister. The Junta of five high ranking officers would remain in control and ensure the fair distribution of income from the mining project. Jonathan inwardly smiled to himself when he used that phrase, knowing full well that they would extract their cut, before he could make sure that the people enjoyed the benefit of whatever amount he could divert to schooling and medical services. Jonathan finally convinced the Junta that he could only succeed if they could quickly free Bo Sung so that he could persuade China to continue with the mining and export of iron ore project. Word of his father's plan reached Mambu who contacted the Junta and proposed that he lead the army special forces to rescue Bo. It worked and the junta agreed that Mambu could send for Frank Latimer, who was the only person who knew where Bo was being held. When Frank landed he and Mambu set to work on their plan to rescue Bo.

Thomas arrived in Cairo with two bodyguards and Emily, who insisted on accompanying him as she was now emotionally committed to ensuring Bo's survival. Emily didn't at this stage ask herself why she was so upset by him being in danger but if she had paused to rationalize her feelings it would not have been hard to come to the conclusion that she had never ceased to love him. The violent fate of three of their four parents had been a huge shock, enough to disrupt their real feelings for a while, but not enough to destroy them for ever. As soon as they had checked into their hotel

Thomas, who had no knowledge of Haj's involvement with Wei Sung, used the second mobile number to contact Franco, from whom he received detailed instructions on how to reach a certain café in a suburb of Cairo. Thomas knew that the presence of Emily or the bodyguards would probably spook his contact so they dropped him off and parked out of sight of the café. He ordered a coffee and was already drinking it by the time Haj arrived. Haj had been able to watch Thomas's arrival at both his hotel and the café and had a photo of him for recognition purposes. He was not worried by Thomas's companions parked nearby as he had assistants outside to facilitate his own safe departure. Introducing himself as a facilitator for the terrorists who were holding Bo Sung hostage, he assured Thomas that he had been told that the hostage was in good health but rather bored with his confinement. He also stated that the group were well aware of the financial position of Oxysung International and that the ransom would be for two hundred million dollars. Thomas responded by stating that the board of directors had authorized him to offer seventy-five million dollars, but that he and some relatives were in a position to add twenty-five million dollars on condition that Bo's release could be effective within one month. To Thomas's surprise Haj indicated that he knew about the Latimer inheritance and pointed out that the group holding Bo were aware of the military coup and that the whole ten billion dollar mining and export of iron ore contract could only be rescued by Bo's release. A speedy release would also increase the risk to the group hiding in central Africa. In view of these facts Franco did not believe that one hundred million dollars was enough to ensure a speedy release of the hostages. He would however contact them immediately if Thomas raised the offer to one hundred and twenty-five million, with twenty-five million dollars payable in two weeks for the release of the two Swiss citizens as an indication of good faith. Thomas agreed and said that the first payment would be assembled in a reasonably stable country like Spain and then loaded onto an aeroplane and parachuted onto any map reference in Africa that Haj supplied them with. Thomas was to call the next mobile phone number as soon as the money was ready and obtain the map reference for the drop zone. An armed group of a dozen private security personnel in a maximum of four vehicles would be allowed to within two kilometres of the drop zone, which itself would be within one day's drive of a city. They would be shown the two Swiss citizens in good health before they gave instructions for the drop to proceed. They would remain in view until the ransom had been verified as the amount agreed and would then be released into the care of the security personnel. The whole process would be repeated one week later for the release of Bo Sung for one hundred million dollars. Back at his hotel Thomas reassured Emily regarding Bo's health, and they made contact with Geneva to pass on the agreement details to Frank.

Frank, Thomas and Emily had agreed to use their inheritance to finance Bo's rescue, and when they heard the ransom demand and method of payment, they could see that it held no guarantees for Bo's release even after the payment was made, and payment would be quite expensive anyway. Mambu Koroma had been well trained by the British army and had served with their special forces. As soon as the Military Junta asked him to come out of hiding and help reinstate their country's international credibility, Mambu had started to contact some old comrades in arms who now were employed by a security company. Several were on their way to Boako to join the small company of regular soldiers commanded by Mambu in Boako who had also received British military training. Frank's arrival and the knowledge that he knew the exact location of the vehicle that Bo had been travelling in, made the mission feasible. With unlimited funds they had bought the force's motivation, reliable arms, ammunition, equipment, and the hire of air transport big enough to carry the latest armoured fighting vehicles. Frank had not had any military training but had developed a rapport with Mambu who was soon to be his brother-in-law, and they set up an operational headquarters with maps of the region in which Bo was held captive. Without marking the map Frank indicated to Mambu the location of the tracking device that Bo had fitted to his vehicle. The security company that Mambu had already contacted, advised that the strengths of these central African terrorist groups fluctuated wildly, but with such a valuable asset in their midst, few of Nasser Kano's soldiers would be taking leave until the matter was settled. That meant at least two hundred fighters in the camp. Algeria had benefitted from Chinese intelligence supplied to them by Bo's mother Shan, and they now gave permission for Mambu's hired air freighter to land at an airstrip in the south of their country when the situation was explained to them. They were only too happy to have Mambu's forces attack and hopefully destroy a terrorist group that continually threatened their borders.

They all waited until Thomas had completed his bargaining with Franco. When Thomas in Cairo phoned to report progress they all agreed that the rescue mission should go ahead, provided they could insert an advance party of four specialists to get close to the terrorists' camp and identify Bo's position and the location of guards, and the strength of the gang's numbers. Emily's voice was the only dissenting one and she departed for Boako to anxiously await the outcome. Thomas remained in Cairo and contacted the British Embassy with the news that he still had a list of phone numbers for one time disposable mobile telephones held by a negotiator for a terrorist group in the Sahel. Thomas and Bo had accepted Frank and Emily's research into the deaths of Shan and Wei and agreed that Haj was a prime suspect. Now in Cairo Emily had wondered if they were dealing with the same man. Whether this was the case or not Thomas put all that they knew to the embassy anti-terrorist unit, who agreed that this man Haj should go on the list of terrorist suspects and be investigated. Using the next phone number on the list to advise Haj that the ransom was ready and available, if Haj would provide the map reference for the drop, the anti-terrorist officers were able to pinpoint the source of the telephone call recipient and managed to get sight of Haj and follow him to his home address. With this information they were able to build a full profile of Haj, and without being able to pin Wei's murder on him just yet, they had him on the list of suspects to be tracked and arrested if he strayed into Europe.

The four specialists in the advance party were despatched to Southern Algeria with an Armoured Fighting Vehicle (AFV) in which they travelled to within ten kilometres of the terrorists' camp. Three of them covered the last ten kilometres on foot and scraped shallow hollows in which they could remain still and camouflaged in close proximity to the terrorist gang's camp during daylight hours. They were able to retreat to thin vegetation nearby occasionally during the night time when relief was required, and for regular communications via the AFV with Mambu who was already in southern Algeria. Their mission was to observe, although they were lightly armed and had planned their retreat in the event that they were discovered. A radio call would summon the Armoured Fighting

Vehicle so that they could be picked up if they could maintain a fighting retreat for fifteen minutes at the most. Once they had located the hut that Bo and the other detainees were held in and noted the gang's strength at about one hundred and fifty males with arms, their spread out locations allowed them to map the camp in some detail. The vehicle pound almost cut the camp into two halves, with the off duty armed men spending most of their time in the eastern half and the women with the cooking and laundering facilities in the western half. Guards were posted but as with most sentry duty it is very difficult to maintain concentration for two hours at a time, and the advantage is always with the attackers. Satisfied they radioed the information to Mambu and his force who had now moved to their forward position in southern Algeria. With more than adequate funds Frank had used all his organizational skills to ensure the supply of ammunition, weapons, desert uniforms, body armour and supplies of food and water. As soon as they received the radio call from the advance party, regarding details of the terrorist groups' camp, Mambu's force of one hundred elite presidential guards and a dozen security company operatives, set off in their Armoured Fighting Vehicles in a south easterly direction. With night vision and sniper capability along with mortars they were a formidable fighting force. They had about six hundred kilometres to cover, which they managed easily in one day in the especially adapted for semi desert conditions vehicles.

After a rest and preparation period of a few hours, the advance party rendezvoused with Mambu's force and led them to the camp perimeter, a tense journey in the pre-dawn darkness with each man rehearsing his role in the coming battle in his mind. A short mortar barrage was laid down on the eastern end of the camp forcing a violent and disorientating awakening on the terrorists, followed in the first light of dawn by the AFVs overrunning the guards on duty in the western end. The deliberate strategy was to destroy the terrorists' transport whilst keeping any survivors pinned down in the eastern end of the camp. The dozen security company operatives were delivered by AFV to the wooden block that held Bo in the western end of the camp. Bo was busy as soon as he heard the first mortar explosion, blocking the door to his cell and lying on the floor behind whatever furniture he could muster. Surprised, Bo's guards were reluctant to shoot their one hundred million dollar asset and the attackers soon overwhelmed them whilst suffering only one wounded man. Bo responded to a voice advising him that they had been sent by Frank Latimer, and cautiously joined them in an AFV with the two Swiss hostages who had been freed from the adjoining hut. Mambu gave the order to withdraw and as soon as they cleared the western end of the camp, the mortar team laid down a second barrage, as a noisy deterrent to pursuit. A quick pause a few kilometres from the camp to check that everybody, including the advance party, was present, revealed one fatality and two wounded but nobody missing. The medics stabilized the wounded and their return journey to Algeria was uneventful. They left only cartridges behind at the target camp, and loaded everything else onto the chartered air freighter in southern Algeria for the short flight to Boako. As soon as the plane took off Mambu sat down with Bo and after making sure that he was uninjured he brought him up to date with events in Boako since he had been taken hostage. Their return to Boako was deliberately kept quiet as Bo's mission now was to persuade China that the mining project was still viable in a now even more stable country. First though Mambu had to introduce him to the military junta who were keen to impress on Bo that he must deal with them now. Bo satisfied them by shaving an extra one percent off Oxysung International's share of profits and assuring the officers that they would be free to allocate these funds as best benefited the people of their country. The world had barely noticed the gunfight in the Sahel and Jonathan Koroma's appointment as finance minister had restored international confidence.

Despite the secrecy surrounding Bo's return to Boako, Emily was the first person to greet him with a meaningful hug and a kiss on his mouth. She had been anxious ever since hearing the news of his capture. Bo too had thought a lot about Emily during his enforced idleness, and was delighted with her greeting. First things first though, Bo needed to travel on to the Chinese embassy in Rome and persuade them that nothing had changed. After a brief meeting with the Military Junta at which they presented Bo with a document endorsing the rights given to Oxysung International by Jonathan Koroma's government, Bo was on his way to Rome, taking Emily with him. She didn't want to let him out of her sight, and he appreciated the combined financial strength of Thomas, Frank and Emily, whose inherited wealth had saved him without having to wait for the directors of Oxysung International to organise the payment of the ransom demanded. In Rome the Chinese Embassy communicated with Beijing who accepted that the military coup added to the project as their stated intention was to ensure that the workers of the landlocked country in West Africa received a fair share of their own natural resources. Bo nevertheless, and off the record, described the fire fight in the Sahel that had freed him from the clutches of the terrorist group, in colourful detail to his friends and business contacts. All boys love tales of derring do and are happy to repeat them whenever they find an audience. Bo and Frank had reverted to risk taking teenagers as the adrenaline kicked in for the brief period of action. Bo and Emily shared the same hotel suite in Rome and consummated their return to full commitment until Bo's work was successfully completed. They had time to revive their love for one another, which had been interrupted only by the traumatic effect of the revelations regarding their family tragedies. Now they travelled on to London to meet up with Frank and Victoria, where the subject of marriage was raised. A double wedding at The Fallowfield Estate would not only make them happy, but would solve Bo's and Victoria's nationality problems. It was agreed that it should be arranged for next spring.

The guest list included Lady Sarah and her family and friends who had also been engaged professionally to make all the arrangements. Frank's mother and Keith arrived from Spain, and Emily's father Li was already in residence on The Fallowfield Estate. Mambu was to be Frank's best man and was staying at the hotel as were Thomas with his wife Susan and their two year old son. Thomas was to be Bo's best man. Victoria's family was the problem; if they left home they might not be allowed back in the country. Jonathan's action in helping the Military Junta regain international credibility had caused all charges against him to be dropped, but a mutually agreed exile would be the most acceptable arrangement for the future once the iron ore project was completed. As President he had salted away enough capital in Nigeria and London to keep his family in reasonable comfort, but he wanted Mambu to remain in the army of the landlocked country so that he could visit in his old age. Eventually about a dozen of his extended family were selected to attend Victoria's wedding. Cousins once and twice removed and descended from Helen Green and Li Tang were also traced and invited after long explanations of their relation's complicated family. Marriage would greatly ease the applications for British Citizenship of Bo and Victoria, a useful side effect for genuine love matches. Bo and Emily's love had slowly simmered and been harshly tested, was now firmly established as they were meant for each other, with both of them having no significant other affairs. Frank and Victoria's instant attraction had not been diminished in the few months since they had met. Both had previous sexual partners, but the lightness of those affairs had only served to convince them that this would be a real union strong enough to survive the arrival of children.

Two days prior to the wedding Thomas, Frank, Bo, Emily and Becky with Lady Sarah in attendance, met to discuss how best to turn Emily's and Becky's recent discussions, regarding making the best use of their extraordinary inherited wealth, into a practical organization to help the world's refugees who were displaced by war and terrorism. After some discussion this seemed to them to be the greatest horror, to be forced to flee one's home without possessions, job, schooling, or medical facilities. Frank thought it important to divert a relatively small portion of their capital to promote the legalization of all dangerous substances under controlled conditions. His friends already knew of his opinion that a competitive commercial market, as already existed for the supply of the equally dangerous alcohol products, could be established for the supply of drugs. Taxes collected from the sale of all dangerous substances including alcohol should be ring-fenced and spent only on educating the young regarding the dangers of the use of both recreational drugs and alcohol, and on treating and curing those who health is adversely affected by the use of recreational drugs and alcohol. Prohibition wasn't working, as it hadn't for alcohol in America in the nineteen twenties and thirties, and the minimum benefit would be the removal of criminal activity from the supply and purchase of recreational drugs. Bo was the majority shareholder in Oxysung International now that his father was dead and his personal wealth matched that of the three inheritors of Anthony Latimer's estate combined. He now suggested that, as Becky was the majority shareholder in a major American computer software company whose holding was worth three hundred million pounds, she could agree to a friendly takeover of her company in return for shares in Oxysung. Similarly Thomas, Frank, and Emily would invest their spare wealth in Oxysung shares. This would involve a share issue but in the end the five of them would own Oxysung shares worth one and a half billion pounds, and they would each donate the majority of their Oxysung shares to the Trust Fund to be set up. They would each retain sufficient capital and income for their own families' needs as each individual decided. Bo and Frank would continue to run Oxysung International as employees with the sole aim of maximising its dividends to be paid to the Trust Fund, whilst diversifying its spread of interests to guard against the failure of any one particular business interest of the group. Emily and Becky would set up and run the Trust Fund assisted by Thomas and watched over by Lady Sarah, who by now had accumulated considerable business administrative skills. Thomas in his position as special assistant to the Department for International Development would advise Emily and Becky regarding the areas of the world that most needed their trust's help, whilst Frank would ask for funds for his fight to legalise the supply of recreational drugs and Li would ask for funds to support those fighting to retain democratic rule in Hong Kong. All five of them would sit on the board of the Trust Fund to allocate the regular income for the relief of refugees. There was some work to be done to set everything up, but first the weddings had to be enjoyed.

It was a fine English spring day for the double wedding, which meant sunshine and showers. A bit cold for some of Jonathan's family, but he was in no mood to hand over his oldest daughter without plenty of music and exuberant celebration. The military junta had agreed that he would be allowed to return home after spending a long weekend in the UK to attend his daughter's wedding. They now realized that they needed both Jonathan and Oxysung International for the good of their landlocked country, and that tying Oxysung's financial director in marriage to one of their citizens was not a hindrance to their interests. Jonathan was greeted as royalty by Lady Sarah, who was immediately enchanted by Jonathan's exuberance. His practised complimentary attention to whomever he was speaking, allied to a natural charm and a constant stream of interesting gossip and anecdotes resulted in him being feted by all the ladies attending the wedding. The response from the ladies was so encouraging that Jonathan began to contemplate adding a European wife to his already large family, until Victoria noticed and guided him into the company of the gentlemen. Thomas was as relaxed as he had been for a long time and his efforts to form the Trust Fund for the relief of refugees from war and terrorism, had gone a long way to allowing him to put his suspicions regarding Frank's and Bo's activities to rest. Parts of his family had been involved in drug trafficking for a long time and now he had organised restitution and safety for all of them, he hoped. His activities both on behalf of the UK government and the Trust were of considerable interest to Jonathan, whose country was affected, and they agreed to discuss the matter seriously in the near future. Frank's mother was equally inclined to enjoy the ceremony as it awakened her hopes for grandchildren. She didn't know that Victoria was of the same mind, as she hadn't had time to get to know her daughter-in-law yet, she could only see an elegant and fashionable model in a stunning dress, and not the broody young woman that Victoria actually was. Frank had already assured his mother that he would arrange for her to travel more in order for her to enjoy a closer relationship with Victoria and him. He was also planning a home in the UK for her so that she could break her connection with what had been a drug gangs' retreat in Spain. Keith could organise the handover of the Spanish Hacienda to his successor and then join Margaret on her travels from their UK base. Emily's father Li was probably the guest with least to celebrate as he was a widower with no other children and faced the loneliest future. At least Emily was marrying a Chinese man and he was beginning to like Bo, whose family history was entwined with his own. Li was beginning to understand that Bo's grandfather had never fully accepted the communist doctrine, but had used it to stabilize his own life after a rocky start, and then push his son and grandson towards freedom in the West. Some of the money from the Trust's dividends was to be allocated to Li's attempts to support democracy in Hong Kong and that would keep him busy for the rest of his life. Bo was happy enough on this day of his wedding, except for a twinge of regret that his grandfather was not present. Bribes could bring a few comforts for Bo Senior but there was no chance of freeing him from the Chinese communist party's clutches. Becky was to be Emily's only bridesmaid and she was happy and excited because Emily was pleased to share her feelings and experiences that were invaluable to the teenager. With the cost of the weddings of no consequence the day was one long visual celebration that was recorded on dozens of mobile phones and digital cameras, with the final shots recording the departure on separate and secret honeymoons of the happy couples.

As the guests returned to their normal lives, full of tales as to how they had all come together on a spring day in 2015, who amongst them could tell what the future held for this diverse family? For the moment though they were in as good a position as they had ever been. In Cairo Gamal Haggai was not celebrating. He was aware of the dual wedding but his personal fortunes were at an all-time low. His beloved mother had recently passed away and although he had avenged his father's death, the thought of his betrayal still caused Haj considerable angst. Now Bo, the son of his father's betrayer, and his friends had deceived him. There would not be any payment for his work as an intermediary regarding the release of Bo who had been held captive by a terrorist group, and even worse, his reputation as a negotiator had been damaged. Fortunately for Haj the world had never had so much terrorist activity. The Arab spring had resulted in large areas of land under the lawless control of armed groups, who were pitting themselves against the dictatorships that were still in control of the rest of the countries created by European colonialism in the Middle East. Somewhere in this turmoil there was surely a place for Haj to prosper and help bring terrorism to Europe and America.

Characters in The Billion Pound Question. (Not Whole Blood Relatives of Anthony Latimer-AL):

Lady Sarah:	Non civil partner of Anthony Latimer as detailed in The Lucky Banker novel.
Mary:	Aberdeen based friend of Lady Sarah, as detailed in The Lucky Banker novel.
Marit/Fabia/Barbara:	Mothers of ALs illegitimate children, as detailed in The Lucky Banker novel.
Per/Gina/Becky/Harry:	ALs illegitimate children, as detailed in The Lucky Banker.
Pamela:	ALs race horse trainer, as detailed in The Lucky Banker.
Fiona/Nicole/June:	ALs Personal Assistants promoted as managers, as detailed in The Lucky Banker
Coldstone & Logie:	Law firm Sandyhill town, acted for AL in purchase of Fallowfield Estate December 1998.
Peter Coldstone:	Senior partner law firm Coldstone & Logie.
Fergus Logie:	Junior partner law firm C & L. Married with 2 young daughters.
Fortune & Fulbright:	London Law firm, acted for AL and recommended C&L to AL as their representative in Sandyhill.
Jill Latimer:	Married David Latimer, older nurse.
Jennifer Latimer:	Married Brian Latimer, was his work assistant, became his business partner.
Margaret Latimer:	Married William Latimer
Keith:	Took over Manchester drug gang when William Latimer murdered, became non–civil partner of Margaret Latimer

Susan Latimer:	Married Thomas Latimer aged thirty. Tall elegant interior designer, daughter of minor aristocracy.
Mr Benson:	Joan Richard's fellow passenger on voyage to China 1936. Real name John Lane working as British spy in China.
John Lane:	Married Joan Richards.

Chinese names have been presented in the English format of given name first and family name second.

Bo & Wei (Senior) Sung:	Orphaned starving children aged approximately 5 and 3 when helped by missionary Joan Richards in 1936
Jing Sung:	Shanghai crime boss.
Wei (Junior) Sung:	Son of Bo (Senior) born 1960
Shan Sung:	Married Wei's (Junior) 1983.
Bo (Junior) Sung:	Born 1985 son of Wei (Junior)
Min Kuang	Manager of drug business for Wei
Delamerenet plc. OxysungInternational.	Frank Latimer's legitimate business. Wei Sung's legitimate non-Chinese businesses.
Giuseppe Montaldo:	Naples senior port customs officer.
Abdul Haggai:	Algerian terrorist group leader.
Gamal Haggai:	Abdul's son known to all as Haj.
Mambu Koroma:	School friend of Bo, son of African dictator.
Jonathan Koroma:	Mambu's father. President of West African country.
Victoria Koroma:	Mambu's sister, Jonathan's daughter.

Nasser Kano: Terrorist gang leader.

Characters from The Lucky Banker:

Anthony Latimer (AL): Is The Lucky Banker.

AL's PAs:	Fiona, Nicole, June. Promoted Managers of various aspects of the Fallowfield Estate.
AL's Women: Per.	Marit:	Met Stavanger Norway Summer 72 mother of Per.
	Mary:	Met Aberdeen summer 75, former business partner.
	Melba:	Met Mar 77 Houston Texas, former business partner.
	Fabia:	Met Autumn 82, Milan Italy, mother of Fabia and former business partner.
	Linda:	Met 93 Houston USA, mother of Becky and former business partner.
AL's Kids:	Per:	Son Marit born Apr 74.
	Gina:	Daughter Fabia born Jun 85.
	Becky:	Daughter Linda born Sep 96.
	Harry:	Son Barbara born Jan 01 Fallowfield Estate England.

Sir John Wallden: Norwood Estate owner, wife Sarah, Daughter Pamela

UK Intestate Law from 1st February 2009:

The Billion Pound Question:

Without any living spouse, civil partner, children, parents, brothers, sisters, or grandparents, **Anthony Latimer's** estate is divided equally between living whole blood Aunts and Uncles or their descendants? Research produced the following **Family Tree: Showing Anthony Latimer's** relatives and beneficiaries.

Grandparents

Horace Latimer	Brenda Oliver	George Richards	Helen Green
Paternal Grandfather	Paternal Grandmother	Maternal Grandfather	Maternal Grandmother
Born 1897	Born 1900	Born 1887	Born 1890
Married——1918——Married		Married——1912——Married	
Deceased 1976	Deceased 1929	Deceased 1946	Deceased 1957

Aunts and Uncles

Brian Latimer	Jennifer	David Latimer	Jill	Warren Latimer	Anne Richards	Joan Richards	John Lane
Uncle	Aunty	Uncle	Aunty	Father	Mother	Aunty	Uncle
Born 1929	Born 1932(A)	Born 1928	Born 1923(A)	Born 15th Aug.1918	Born 10th Aug.1922	Born 1915	Born 1910(A)
Married——1960——Married	Married	Married——1946——Married	Married	Married——June 1947——Married	Married	Married——1945——Married	Married
Deceased 1996	Not Whole Blood	Deceased 1985	Not Whole Blood	Deceased Oct.1969	Deceased Oct.1969	Deceased 1967	Not Whole Blood

Cousins

Thomas Latimer	Susan	William Latimer	Margaret	Anthony Latimer	Florence Lane	Li Tang
Cousin	Cousin's Wife	Cousin	Cousin's Wife	Principle	Cousin	Cousin's Husband
Born 1961	Born 1965	Born 1946	Born ???	Born 5th Jan.1949	Born 1946	Born 1942(A)
Married——1995——Married	Married	Married——1978——Married	Married	Never Married	Married——1974——Married	Married
A.L.Beneficiary	Not Whole Blood	Deceased 1985	Not Whole Blood	Deceased 27th Dec. 2011	Deceased 1996	Not Whole Blood
Aged 50						

1st Cousins Once Removed / Children

Frank Latimer	Per	Gina	Becky	Harry	Lady Sarah	Emily Tang
1st Cousin Once Removed	Son	Daughter	Daughter	Son	Partner	1st Cousin Once Removed
Born 1985	Born Apl.74	Born Jun.85	Born Sep.96	Born Jan.01	Born 58	Born 1985
A.L.Beneficiary	Aged 37	Aged 26	Aged 15	Aged 9	Aged 53	A.L.Beneficiary
Aged 26						Aged 26

A.L.'s four children Illegitimate so not beneficiaries. Not Civil-Partner A.L. didn't marry/enter civil partnership with 4 mothers -Partner

Yet another Poem about Scottish Heather

Late summer every year the purple flower
Colours the Aberdeenshire hills above the tree line.
West up the Dee valley past Glen Tanner's gate tower
Morven is seen to be no exception in the sunshine.

A Ben that stands on privately owned land
And fails to be a Munro by one hundred and thirty nine,
Of the required three thousand feet. With stone butts to hand
That give the game hunters protection and a free fire line

Standing on Morven's summit many years ago
Looking down into the cockpit of a jet fighter,
I could see the pilot oblivious to my ego,
Concentrating on instruments to make turns tighter.

All his attention was on keeping his volatile craft stable,
Whilst practising his low level attacks under the radar's reach.
To notice the beauty of the heather in passing he was unable,
Just another hunter training for Desert Storm, Shock and Awe, each.

To preserve our Northern European peace, we may
Advertise our democratic freedoms by internet boards,
As we use our jet fighters to keep at bay
The fast breeding Southern hoards.

Populations no longer held in check by disease at home,
And unable to throw off corrupt ruling mafias, they
Pray for the freedoms they can see on their mobile phone,
And begin civil wars that cannot be resolved for many a day.

Now the displaced and hungry refugees head north
Seeking the freedom to work In Europe,
Knowing that worse disruptions had come forth
During the previous century when Europe learned to cope.

They arrive where prosperity and contraception
Has created the need for Guest Workers ready to labour.
Will the Refugees settle in Europe where belief in God is an
exception?
Where the human rights of individual freedom; is to savour.

Or will they seek revenge on those whose bombs
Destroyed their ancient cultures, leaving survivors to cope
Without homes, food, and with the dead buried in rubble tombs.
Will integration happen or will terrorism be their only hope?